— A —
BURNING
HILLSIDE

— A —
BURNING
HILLSIDE

Conrad G. Horchos

Apprentice
House Press
Loyola University Maryland

First Edition

Casebound ISBN: 978-1-62720-569-6
Paperback: 978-1-62720-570-2
Ebook: 978-1-62720-571-9

Library of Congress Control Number: 2025932934

Cover & Internal Design by J.P. Stromberg
Editorial Development by Adriana Leszczynski
Promotional Development by Maggie O'Donnell

Published by Apprentice House Press

Apprentice
House Press
Loyola University Maryland

Loyola University Maryland
4501 N. Charles Street, Baltimore, MD 21210
410.617.5265
www.ApprenticeHouse.com
info@ApprenticeHouse.com

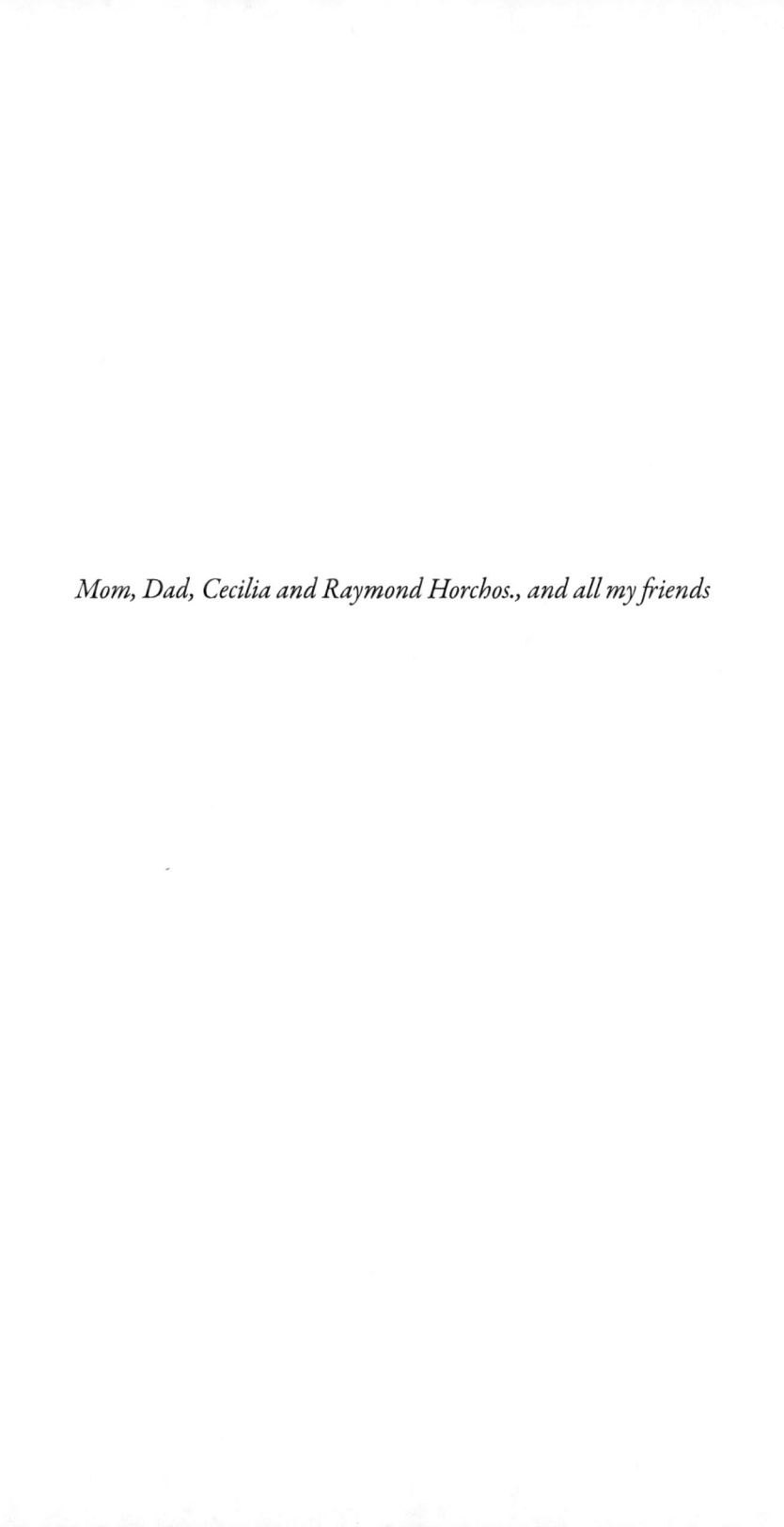

Mom, Dad, Cecilia and Raymond Horchos., and all my friends

Preface

This book was born in the spring of 2020 during the Covid-19 Pandemic, and with little to do and few places to go I needed to occupy my mind and my time. In March of 2020 I busied myself with movies by Jean-Luc Godard, the music of Django Reinhardt and Francisco Tarrega, and the books of Ernest Hemingway. These were the sources of inspiration for the conception and creation of this novel. It was fun at times, boring and aggravating at others. I worked quickly some days and very slowly most. I might have spent a whole day sitting down at my laptop to write and for the month after I did not touch it. This was a long journey and notwithstanding three rounds of reading and editing on my own was completed in December of 2023. A labor of love and an exploration into the questions of what we do and why.

Chapter I

It was dry and still quite warm, but the sun was just about to set. After that, the heat would dull. Occasionally a cool breeze would run through daylight air like a stream, nevertheless it would come or go as it wished. The trees were sparse here. Those that survived spun out tendrils that twisted thick on themselves, and dried like minerals, standing alone or with a few friends in the baking sun over centuries. The bushes and low weaves of grasses still felt lush and green, filling patches beneath and between those trees. Sometimes greener, sometimes a drier gold color from the day.

A splinter of flat rock that pierced the slope of the fielded countryside making an overhang, our camp. Cave would be generous. It was a cold outcropping when we found it. Now the roaring fire brought a simple and pleasurable sense of homeliness and comfort to the campsite. Emirhan had cooked some of the wild goat we had caught in the fields after moving north from Ankara; you could barely taste the meat with all the spices, although it was still delicious.

"What is this?" Pierre examined his piece of goat as if he were judging it. He carefully selected and sliced pieces of his portion with hand and knife.

"Is the spice, you like the spices, yes?" Emir said, sounding almost confused.

"This is not how you cook the goat. You cannot taste the

meat." He responded condescendingly while furrowing his dark Mediterranean eyebrows.

"Oh, jaw up and eat. Who knows the next time we will find this much food at once." Charles looked over as he adjusted his thin-rimmed round glasses. He was a tall Englishman and had a thick beard and hair all combed straight back, all of which was gray. "IT is rather tasty I might say. Reminiscent of some dishes I had years ago." He ate well.

"Maybe it will taste better with cognac," a smile sprawled out halfway across Pierre's face. He raised up a glass bottle shaped like a large egg that bottlenecked at the top. He bit down on the cork and yanked it off with his teeth. His head bobbled, and the cognac sloshed inside the bottle. It appeared that it required more effort than he had anticipated. He tipped it in his hand, pouring some out into a slightly blackened metal cup. He then handed the bottle to the left, passing it off to Charles, who was staring deeply into the flames.

"What's the problem mon copain, missing your wife again?" Pierre asked rhetorically.

"At least I have a wife and kids to think of, you *biscuit*." He quipped back while also sipping from the bottle.

Pierre laughed it off, saying, "I don't like to be tied down; it takes away the adventure ami." He snapped, popped, and tossed some twigs in the hotter places of the fire to watch it catch and get bright again.

"No adventure? I have four." Emir said, laughing while he spoke.

"Wives or kids?" I asked with a grimace.

"Both!" Emir smiled and glanced over at Charles. "This is kind-of a joke."

"Have some, won't you?" Charles said, offering up the bottle.

"No, no, no!" Emir retorted quickly, "I never drink. You must know this."

"I shall take your place then!" Pierre intervened; he was clearly looking for an excuse to drink more.

Emir reached near the fire to hand me the last piece of goat, and mocked Pierre. "I would not want to waste the last piece on Pierre so you can take his place. May you enjoy it."

"You Arabs do not get it. The best food is simple food, with few ingredients." Pierre gestured his hands as he spoke. "This way, each flavor is stronger. You must always taste the principal component."

"I am Armenian, you dimwitted Spaniard." He said, teasingly waiting for a response.

"I am not a Spaniard; I am a proud Frenchman," Pierre declared, taking more offense than Emir had.

"Ah, I see. Now I understand, eh." Emir gave Pierre a friendly but floozy smile, but simply did not want to talk.

"You are a bit young to have so many children... no?" Pierre asked inquisitively.

Emir smiled, "I'm a little over thirty, not so young as you may think."

Pierre was a little surprised. "I'm twenty-five and you look ages younger than me."

"There is something to the spices I think, there is more to them than flavor you know." Emir pointed out.

"Perhaps, I would not pick this fight now." Pierre shook a little and became quieter.

By this point, it was dark out, and the air was cold now and still dry. I had felt the wind picking up a modest amount, but not too much. The fire had kept the overhang warm. It was not long before everyone else fell asleep, then I walked out from under the overhang. I could see the glowing gray and white crescent of the

3

unusually bright moon that sat beside the thousands of stars, all suspended in the sky. The moon had caught my attention the most. The view offered a temporary peace, then accompanied by the gentle flow of cool mountain air. There were interspersed patches of woodland in Anatolia's Highlands, but shrubs and small bushes were more common.

The absence of many trees made the land feel expansive and grand, as you could clearly see all the rolling mountains in the distance. However, the 'clans' of old and firm trees that sat out in their bunches reminded me of animal herds. It did not take long until I was re-grounded and made my way back to the respite of the overhang camp. I stared into the fire and watched the flames dance until I drifted off.

The following day we packed up again and covered our tracks. We spread the coal and ashes, picking up all our belongings and scraps. It was still early morning, yet I could tell as the sun rose it would be hotter than usual.

Before deployment when we were on the north coast of the Black Sea, Captain Hughes provided the smallest vehicle available so as to not "attract attention" from any planes or enemy scouts, but we knew it was simply cheaper this way. Shortly before the sun rose entirely, we started off in the auto car. There was room enough for the four of us along with our bags, and that was all. Charles was in the passenger seat, and Pierre was the driver. Both Emir and I sat in the back. There was no roof, only a simple glass shield in the front, but how it drove on the rocky and dusty road woke me up more than a cup of coffee.

Charles the Colonel, ranking highest among us, as always, opened his logbook and debriefed. "We are headed west and are supposed to meet an ally scout group in the mountains above Devrek."

"What must we do there?" asked Pierre with a slight distaste and bore with his words.

Charles responded, "A supply of tools is leaving Devrek to Constantinople for the Ottomans, and we are to intercept it."

"Better not be any more Frenchmen in their scout group," Emir commented just loud enough for Pierre to hear.

Pierre snapped back jokingly. "If they are anything like you, I shall crash this car immediately."

The banter continued as the sun rose. The sky was blue, and as I expected, hot. We were heading out of the mountains, so it only got warmer as the day went on. There were scattered arrangements of trees, and it was a nice change of scenery. Charles was keeping his eyes out for anyone who might spot us or alert the Ottomans. He constantly reminded us to do the same, but as far as one could tell we were in the clear.

"What are you looking for? There is no one out here." Emir stated. "We are in a middle of nowhere."

"The middle of nowhere, I think it is what you mean, mon copain." Pierre said, excitedly anxious to correct Emir.

"This is what I said, correct?" He looked over to me to affirm.

I shook my head and smiled. "As much as I hate to give this one to Pierre, sorry, he was right this time."

"No goat for anyone but Charles now. All you are wrong." He threatened without any degree of sincere seriousness.

"Then I will cook our next goat. It should be magnificent compared to yours." Pierre championed.

"You can have your cook-off later. Let us worry about our mission, men. Keep your eyes out." Charles attempted to regain our focus.

"I will worry about the mission..." Pierre countered, "You can worry about your wife and kids, not you, Emir. You would have a heart attack."

"I'm sure you might do a fine job of that." Charles smirked.

"You will have a heart attack first Pierre; I see how much you smoke and drink." Emir insisted.

"I simply do what I feel mon copain; that is how to live the life."

"There is more than this. You know that." Emir countered.

"The spirit is willing, but the flesh is weak." Charles rebutted as he lit a cigar.

"Yours too?" I joked.

"We all have our Achilles heel; chap. Mine is all the way from Cuba." Charles jested as he lifted a cigar to his thick gray beard. He pulled out a small box of matches from his breast pocket, and with defined precision, he lit the match. The match made its way to his cigar and quickly stirred a fragrant smoke.

"Mine was from Milan," Pierre teased. "She had it out for me from the start." We paused, and things went quiet for a moment.

We were no longer in the mountains but in the hills now. Mostly pine and spruce are divided by large swaths of bushland and field. So, there was cover if needed, but it was certainly not a woods or forest. Charles lit a cigar and held it in his mouth while he read and wrote in his logbook. Pierre reached into his pocket with one hand on the wheel and pulled out a pack of cigarettes. He teased a single out with his one free hand; and before he could stick it in between his lips, Charles reached over and put his left hand over the end of Pierre's cigarette.

"Put down that trash, young chap; have a cigar, one of mine, on the house it is." Charles pulled a small box out from under his seat and lit Pierre's cigar with the soft glowing cherry of his. He gently kissed the two ends and then handed it over to Pierre, who still had one hand on the wheel and the other on the dirt road.

"Merci, it is a pleasure to share such a delight with you." Pierre smiled as he released a large cloud that quickly dissipated into thin air behind the loud auto car. Pierre took a hard right turn, then the trees became sparse. It was a field of golden wheat and other grains. The road led past a small cottage that was made of gray cobblestone and had no glass in its windows and a roof of soft orange clay tiles.

"This ought to be it. All the directions tell me we have arrived, men." Charles took one last draw and tossed the cigar onto the dirt road.

"Where are the men?" I opened the car door and looked around, searching for a sign of anyone.

"They are probably inside or down on the other side of the hill." Emir looked as confused as I.

"I pray they have food." Pierre walked about as if he were in a park, lacking the discretion of a soldier or any degree of worry in a situation such as this.

Charles looked over to Pierre quickly. "I hope they are good company. Or at least the company we are expecting." He let out a silent grin, it was a routine to him at this age and to lubricate it with a jest was nothing unusual.

Charles paced around the corners of the house, then stepped up to the door once he had found it. He pulled a small pistol out of his back pocket which had a holster fastened inside it. Sturdy and quiet, in a mechanical and tactile fashion as a man like him would have done dozens of times before. The pistol was in his right hand, and he held it forward, pointing its tip level at the wooden door.

He felt his hand up against the door on its fixed wooden planks with his left hand. It was closed. Scanning up and down, and examining it, he then grabbed the brass doorknob and paused a moment. Turned it clockwise, then pulled it towards himself. He hid the pistol behind him aimed down along the base of his back. He breathed, not entirely knowing what to expect. He eased it open and peered in by tilting his head.

There were four men sitting there playing cards, and they all stopped to look at Charles like deer all glancing over at the same thing in a swift alertness.

"Italians." Charles hung his head into his perched and angled arm of impeccable form. He sighed with a hint of disappointment but wholly overwhelming relief and ushered us inward. "The coast is clear!"

Some of the men stood up and shook hands with Charles, as well as each of us; still, others continued in their card games and chatter. It was almost sunset by now, so I was happy to have arrived.

Pierre and I stepped out, walked around the cottage some more, and went to the backside. There was a small fire, and five to ten men were sitting around talking and smoking. Some of them looked over and stared or said something cordial but quick in whatever language they knew (usually Italian). Others simply did not care. Pierre and I sat down on a flat boulder a few paces from the fire and began talking.

"I don't like you Americans, but the Italians I hate more." He pushed his slicked black hair aside and took his backpack, lifting it close to him on his lap.

"Thank you, I suppose." I wasn't sure how to respond appropriately. I think he saw it as a compliment in some form.

"I suppose Charles may miss his wife, but I miss my true love." Pierre looked over into the warm glowing fire.

"Who would that be?" I said with vague curiosity.

"France! Mon copain, France. The eternal lights all the way to the warm Mediterranean coast. The delicious food and the delicious women." He moved his attention back to me and sighed.

I gazed around at the Italians chatting and jesting with one another. I peered through them, and eventually, my eyes settled on the landscape that was set deep behind them. I saw the mountains and plateaus that were broken by ridge lines and splotches of woodland. "I've never been to France, but Anatolia sure is beautiful."

Pierre caressed his black mustache for a moment and responded. "Many places are beautiful mon copain, but for a strange reason, I have found none are as beautiful as where you are from." He hung his head for a moment but quickly and with forceful enthusiasm lifted it back up again.

I gave a slight grin and glanced back at Pierre. "So, France is nothing compared to the U.S.A.?"

"For you, mon copain, not for me. Maybe it is relative, and I am a common madman, but I believe our hearts find a love in our home that can be found nowhere else." He reignited a degree of drained yet not lost fervor.

"Our hearts are the biggest fools," I said. "Who is to say how one feels at home? Some may despise it."

"True, but maybe you must be some kind of fool to enjoy life, and perhaps I am the biggest fool of them all." He smiled half-question, half-statement with optimistic ignorance and leaned back, resting his head on the back of the boulder. "And yes, this is for me. The only person I can ever speak for. Some may wish themselves to be any place but home."

"Maybe," I responded, "Maybe... Then that must mean that they have not found their true home."

"Hmm, perhaps." Pierre eased away from conversation and into quiet.

I went into the cottage, unrolled my wool sleeping mat, and bundled myself up. It was cool that night, but the wool was about all I needed. I was one of the first to head in for the night. I, however, fell asleep not long after I went in and warmed up with my bedroll. As I was drifting off, I could hear the muffled reverberations of the loud Italians staying up late outside gathered around the fire. Against the judgment of his earlier remarks, Pierre eagerly partook in their banter and late-night antics. I, for one, think he wanted to fill his stomach and have something to drink.

I woke up quite early, before everyone else. The dew rested thick this morning, and it was surprisingly brisk outside. I walked outside, with the air feeling fresh and crisp; it was a nice break from the usual heat of the day. I opened my knapsack and ate a small and juicy orange I had plucked from a tree not even a few days ago when we were in a lower altitude and warmer climate. Considering most of the Italians we had traveled with smoked a cigarette and drank an espresso in the morning, I would suppose my breakfast was comparably hardy.

We were supposed to intercept the package tomorrow before it was to be sent out. Devrek was a few good miles north. As a unit, we were supposed to move in and camp in the hills, approaching to intercept early in the morning. The Italian men had their own auto cars with two motorbikes, but we still took our own.

We got into our issue autocar with Charles and I in the front, although this time Charles was driving. We had started to work out a rotation of sorts. There were about two cars the size of ours and a similar model. Rectangular, simple, and without a roof. The two motorbikes were also military-made and thus sturdy but undecorated. I would say a dozen of the Italian men, give or take a few.

Charles, lastly hopped into the car and said, "I haven't directions for you right now, simply follow the others and we should arrive at our camp."

"They better not get us lost." I turned on the car and followed as last in the line of vehicles.

Emir turned his head over to Pierre in the back seat and shook him by the shoulder, asking sarcastically, "How are *you* feeling today, my friend?"

Pierre, with his head back on the chair and eyes still closed, spoke, "Non, je ne regrette rien, I may feel like a damp towel, but I knew what I was getting into." He was visibly irritated, but not only at the question.

"Had too much fun with the gentlemen yesterday, I see," Charles interjected with his short and sharp degree of English wittiness.

"What can I say, we have an understanding." Pierre attempted to explain, realizing his faint hypocrisy of the words he spoke only yesterday.

"What would that be?" I asked rhetorically.

"The sweet life, you English and Americans work so hard all the time you've forgotten how to have fun."

"I think you've forgotten how to work," I said mockingly.

"It is a balance." Emir tried to strike the middle, and he was not necessarily wrong, as is with many things.

The countryside was quite beautiful. The long fields appeared to wave like the ocean in parallel congruence with the wind. The trees would sway slightly too. An old man told me once that is how they avoid snapping.

Each village we saw in the distance felt ancient. Seated far away in the landscape as little arrangements of plaster lime-washed rectangles and clay roofing that perch on the features of the earth. Always having a story to tell.

Finally, we arrived at Devrek, or the light slopes above it, more accurately. The Italians found a small clearing in the hills and decided to stop there. They set up camp with waxed canvas tarps and cordage. They took the deadfall sticks scattered in the grass and sharpened them with their knives, hammering them down into the ground and tying the cords around them to secure it all in place. We had finished our own tents when one of the Italian men walked up behind me as I was sitting in front of a small fire in the center of the clearing.

He came up behind me and what felt like a shout flew close by the back of my head. "Bernardo! And you are?"

"Gerard!" I responded with an artificial and slightly sarcastic enthusiasm that matched his much more genuine enthusiasm. Bernardo was Italian but had the tawny and sun-kissed skin tone of a Greek or a Near Easterner. He was approaching skinny, and he bellowed obnoxiously loud without a care, but one must admit, it was a sincere laugh.

He then conversed with himself for a moment. "Gerard, no, no good. Gerard-O. Yes, *Gerardo!*" He laughed loudly once again. "You, Gerardo are new. I never met an American before!" He stood tall and firm, but his frame shook a little with that hint of former laughter.

"You speak awfully good English for someone who's never met an American."

He stopped to make a point he felt was quite important. "I meet many Englishmen, many Micks, and a few Scots; One Canadian, and he is very nice. Now, an American!" He was quite ecstatic in his speech, and I wondered if it would ever stop.

"You're quite the chipper one, eh." My head spun up and around from my spot at the small but warm fire towards Bernardo standing behind me. He sat down on a log to my left and rolled a cigarette. His thin frame leaned forward, reaching into the fire, and pulled a small twig from the fire. Lighting the cigarette, he spoke with it hanging on his lip and used his hands to push back his greasy black hair that I would call grown out, but not long.

"When you are happy you live longer and live better. How do you think my *Nonna* is ninety-four? She smiles!" He was confident in his words and outlook on life.

"Is your *Nonna* about to intercept a cargo train headed to Constantinople?" I asked rhetorically.

"No, in fact I am not sure where she is now. It has been quite a while since the war began, I know you joined late." He chuckled, but it was a stifled chuckle that covered fear and unease beneath a calm surface.

I backtracked a little bit. "I did not mean to hit that note... I am sure there is plenty of uncertainty right now."

Bernardo was about to dispel the shame in my comment, but the abounding voice of a large round man butted into the whole crowd and cut the steady ambiance of the camp.

"No, but we are." The man expressed a demanding tone as men left their tents or walked up slowly filling the campfire's circle. "I am *Maggiore* Leonardo, your leader in this mission."

With his fingers he combed the varied shades of gray in his beard with his hand as he spoke. One could tell by his demeanor he was a man of the military, even if he were to take off the obvious uniform. It was how he walked, stood, how he looked at things with critical focus and detail.

He addressed the men in Italian first with a rapid and direct intonation which for an American seemed uncharacteristic of the floating and graceful tone of Italian. Afterward he spoke to us in a thick but comprehensible accent giving us the plan and making it clear he was the *Maggiore* of the operation. Charles seemed a little stiff at the thought of it but did not let it fluster him up too awfully. I went to sleep almost immediately after that. I was tired and knew we would wake early tomorrow so I thought it best.

Chapter II

We awoke early before the sun began to climb. I rose earlier than most, but we were all sleeping quite close, so I pretended for a little while that I, too, was asleep. I laid in my roll and stared at the canvas above me until more people were on the move. We quickly put all our gear away and loaded it onto the autocar or in our backpacks. The air was cool, and there was no breeze present. With a piece of bread and a canteen of water for breakfast, we hopped in the car and puttered off.

Pierre looked around and spoke, "That Maggiore seems like he's got quite the stick up his bum."

"An awfully big one, I dare say." Charles was quietly waiting eagerly for an opportunity to get a jab in at him.

Emir became sheepish, "He is doing his job, that is all."

I did not care much for Maggiore Leonardo; he seemed stubborn and uncompromising, but I suppose that *is* part of his job. The job of a major is to be so unlikeable that all the soldiers are united by their distaste. The road down to Devrek proper was bumpy and unsteady as the sky was still a dark purple so we couldn't entirely see where we were going. However, that transparent purple hue sat in the sky and shaved off enough bits of sunlight that were to come. We were headed downhill and the roads were not well-kept or well-traveled. Devrek was in the northwest corner of Anatolia and nearly bordered the Black Sea. In this way, it was rural but still important for some trade routes, especially those that one might wish to keep hidden.

All of a sudden, the autocars stopped. We were a mere mile or so outside of Devrek. We had been told to pick up our supplies and follow the path downhill. There was something that resembled a road, yet the remainder of the trip was to be completed on foot as per Maggiore's orders. It was best this way if we wished for the enemy not to hear us. I was near the back of the line with Pierre, Charles, and Emir. The Italians had the terrain maps; for this reason, on any excursion, we were to follow them on the path. We walked quietly and at a brisk pace together.

Most of Maggiores' men copied his march like mimes. Carrying their guns in hand and belt packs around their sides. Charles seemed uncharacteristically stiff, and Pierre looked as if he were attempting to do an impression of what he imagined a serious man might look like while marching. We marched in rows of two, and I was paired with Emir. I had not known Emir that well.

Emir looked over at me. "So, what is an American doing in Anatolia fighting Turks?"

I looked back right away as we stepped onward. "What's an Armenian Muslim doing fighting Turks?"

"My brother was a *riddah*. An apostate or some may say a convert. Few Armenians are Muslim to begin with, but when he became a Christian... The Ottomans executed him with most of his family." He became quiet after that for a moment. "My family and what was left of his moved to Russia; weeks on foot." He seemed tired from just speaking of it.

"Why do you fight for us now?" I asked, hoping for more detail.

"I cannot vow myself to the flag of those who killed my family, although they have my land. So now I fight for the flag of the country my family now lives in."

"So you are displaced," I said to clarify my own thoughts.

"Something like that. Well not so long as I fight." He smiled very briefly, then looked down to the ground. It was a kind of dull and forced smile that lasted just long enough to convince you there was not a frown underneath, but there was, I could tell. I did not wish to push anymore as I could read men's body language, and he wasn't keen to speak much more of it. I couldn't blame him for it.

We marched for a good while and came upon the outskirts of town. Maggiore ordered us across the stream that seemed to divide the town and a patch of small and winding trees with many low arms... It was quiet, and the air was still.

It was a narrow stream. I came up to it and hopped off the grass across a few well placed stones. It felt eerie and unsettling, moving into the quiet mountainous town. Upon reaching the other side we split into smaller sections and scouted around, looking for the cargo.

Emir eventually saw a man in Bernardo's group find a wagon with ammunition and weapons in it. The wagon was hooked to a horse in the town and quickly evacuated. I was surprised how smoothly it went without attracting any attention. The lack of security played in our favor. The tough part was marching back before dawn. By the time the sun had begun rising over the highland crest, we'd just arrived at the autocars. The supplies in the wagon were discretely transferred to the autocars along with our own utilities. It was a simple task, yet enduring.

We drove the autocars with cargo back toward our camp. The expectation and order was to evacuate Anatolia by next week. We were advised to head northeast through the Caucasus Mountains and finally into Russia. Nonetheless, for now, we pushed east of Devrek further into the Mountains and thus began our evacuation journey.

It was a long ride, but a beautiful one. The dark blue and purple of the sky that was cast like a net over us served as a form of shade. A shade from our enemies and a convenient way out without being spotted. Although, now the light was beginning to peek, and the trees were covered in their emanating orange and yellow hues cast atop the green leaves. The sunlight sprawled over the angled chips of bark.

Finally, darkness receded as the day began. The plateaus and highlands off in the long distance were each painted over with that very same orange and yellow, and it was backed by the gentle touch of pink that outlined it.

I could smell the smoke of fires made by the villagers in the hills. I did not see them but as the fire's aroma danced through the air I imagined it. They had gotten up just as early as us, if not earlier. The men and women high in the foothills and dells were well on their way; cooking breakfast, smoking meats, and creating new again the simple human joy of warmth. They began their day, and we had begun ours, though it was not the same.

The warmth of the fires did not spread to us, but the enchanting smells of burning pine, spruce, and cypress and took me back to a simpler time. A time of campfires, swimming in lakes, chopping logs, and scary stories that aren't as scary now as they seemed when you were a child. I suppose that was because other things had grown to take their place and did quite a good job of it. Things that did not live simply in books, or fantasies, but things that live in our minds and our world. The woods were thick, but there was no underbrush, simply fallen leaves and stray gravel paving our way.

"What are you thinking about, old chap? You seem lost and pensive." Charles shifted my attention abruptly.

"Just thinking, what's the point of all of this?" I asked rhetorically.

"Of what, my good man?" He asked with the quiet patience of a grandfather as he maintained the cherry of his cigar.

"The war and the fighting and the likes of it. It hardly ever brings much good." I said so, matter of fact.

"War," he paused. "I've seen war, son. What is war, you ask?" He stared off into the trees and took a hefty puff. "War is when the young and foolish are tricked by the old and greedy into killing each other." He sighed and breathed deeply.

"You know the game and you still play it?" I responded, expecting a rationalization.

He became firm and still as if he were holding back more raw emotions. "Most men don't wish to fight, son. In my heart I don't wish to fight, but I suppose I'm just still young and foolish at heart."

"The heart doesn't lie." I looked over, anticipating a response.

"Ditto son, ditto." He coughed from either the cigar or the conversation, then recentered himself. Away from the contemplative and reflective, and toward his normal self he became forcibly calm and cool again. I suppose the hard exterior of an experienced veteran had to come back up eventually.

After a drive through wooded highlands, a few of the men spotted a cottage a little ways behind the trees. Abandoned and unkempt, the cottage seemed to have been left not too long ago. Seated a little further back within eyeshot, a barn. It stood beside the cottage, yet resided in considerably worse condition. All things considered, it was still more than livable for what we had come to expect.

We drew sticks and I was in the cottage. There was a small fireplace at one end. It remained simple and undecorated but certainly made a warm fire. The walls were a varied assortment of cool gray stone with a tainted white belt of mortar in between each of them. Old growth pine wood cross-beams extended across the width of the modest, but heartily crafted house. I was fond of houses made with pine. They were often filled with the citrusy and crisp smell of pine sap and raw preserved wood.

There was a flagstone slab that served as a countertop in one of the corners. A few stale loaves of bread rested there alongside some wild herb sprigs that hung from twine which was tied around the rafter beams.

"The bread is hard as a rock, and the herbs are bitter," I commented to Bernardo.

"Gerardo! No worries! We bring olive oil with us. You dip bread in olive oil and it is not so bad anymore! Watch this" He smiled and handed me a small clay cup taken from the inside of one of the cupboards that were below the countertop. He crushed some of the dry sage and basil by rubbing it between his fingers then poured in some olive oil.

"Thank you Bernardo. That's a kind gesture." I took the cup and mixed the bread in the oil until it started to become soft again, and then ate it.

"What goes around comes around mon copain!" Pierre came up next to Bernardo and poured the cognac into his metal tin until it met the brim.

"You are one *pazzo paisano*. But there is one problem *amici me*." He looked over to Pierre.

"Quoi?" Pierre was drunkenly puzzled for a moment.

"I am too Pietro!" They laughed as Pierre leaned over to fill my tin too.

"Bienvenue!" Pierre smiled and took a small piece of my bread and dipped it into the oil, "it is not so bad when you dip it in the oil you know."

"This is what I say!" Bernardo laughed very loud and took a large gulp from the tin. Pierre and Bernardo exchanged stories about France and Italy as well as a few lighthearted insults.

"I am from Villefranche-sur-Mer, you know. It is very beauti-ful and just quaint enough." He spoke as his open eyes gently reminisced for a quick second.

"What a creative name." I teased and Bernardo let out an unrestrained laugh once again at Pierre. Bernardo bellowed loud, proud, and unabashedly as he did.

"Your American cities are no more clever. New - York? New - Hamp-sher? New Jersey? Why not come up with a 'new' name." I could see in his face that Pierre thought his joke was quite clever. Bernardo laughed again. I think he enjoyed simply watching the banter play out more than anything else.

"Those are states not cities." I said, knowing it made no difference to him.

"New York is a state and a city." Pierre stated.

I laughed it off.

The density of the bread and oil as well as the stomach warming pulse of cognac had filled my stomach and left me satisfied. We spoke and jested for a while after this with surprisingly full bellies and an empty bottle. After a while I grew tired of talking and it became hot inside the cottage. This was thanks to the fire of the small cabin, and all the loud men crammed inside; not to mention the warmth of the cognac. I needed to cool off and refresh. Thankfully the outside was autumn-like.

The wooded highlands were unusually brisk that night, not a painful cold, but a breeze that I felt nipping at my face and simply reminded me that I'm alive. I sat down on a fallen tree no more than a few yards from the worn door of the house. One could tell it had been sitting there for some time as the bark had just begun to break apart and fall off.

Above where I sat was a clearing through the dense edge of the canopy and a small glimmer of moon that carved out some spots of light into the darkness of the forest floor. Despite how close I was to the house's voices of conversation, they felt distant as the wind cut through them and the stone walls dulled their strength. I went back inside after some time had passed, then chatted a short bit longer. After that, it did not take me very long to fall asleep.

Maggiore Leonardo began barking orders at the room and we all woke up quicker than I could register where I had slept. My body hopped above me and I flinched awake.

"Up, now! We must get moving. These supplies are valuable to the Russians and our allies! They are also useful to our enemies. This may help us win this war." In all truthfulness, this generous sentence of English came after a beratement of Italian which was all but useless to me. Would it help win the war? Doubtful, I thought to myself.

Why do we want to win this war? I asked myself this as well. What Charles had said resonated with me, either which way he meant it. Why does a man who knows the foolishness of war still play the game? Nonetheless I packed my bags and tossed them into the autocar like every other in our troop. I suppose I'm becoming a victim of the same trap. We got on the move and headed deeper into the mountains. The woodlands became dense and cool. We watched mainly for Ottoman patrols. We also stayed keen on local civilians who might alert those around us. However, that could go either way. It was quite a long ride. The roads were not well kept, and at some points hard to distinguish between road and rural.

We hadn't planned the trip to take as long as it had, consequently we were running out of gasoline. We needed to stop in town. This was a risk and a necessary one at this point. The Italians knew the terrain better than us and so once again, we followed them. We temporarily altered the course to aim southeast. We aimed toward Keban which supposedly had petrol according to the journals and scripts of the Italians and their resources.

The Anatolian plateau felt more like a steppe at first. The wind rushed through clear high-standing fields sparsely laced with trees. Wild rivers broke the landscape visually as I saw the deer line up along the river banks and then flee into the brush the moment we appeared. Like most breathtaking landscapes it was most pleasing to the eye at sunset and sunrise; for that was when the fields seemed to be fashioned of gold and the trees remained encrusted in emeralds. The lands stayed consistent for many miles but were alluring all the same.

"I would wish to paint this if we were not at war at the moment." Pierre breathed deeply as he gazed off thinking about something deeper than what he had just said. "I'd sit myself down and paint this whole damn countryside, you know?"

"I would paint if I could." I gazed off looking over to where Pierre's eyes had been caught. I tried to view it with the lens he had, and I think I came close for a mere moment, but there was no way of knowing. "Where were you before all of this?" I asked.

"I sold my paintings and would do little jobs here and there."

"Did you make any money?"

He smiled at me with his mustache that had begun to grow thick and long, for lack of a razor and proper bathroom. "Off of the odd jobs? Yes. Paintings... rarely"

"Are they at all good, your paintings?"

His smile turned to laughter as if I; one of the artistically un-inclined were a fool to ask that question. "Oh! I would like to think so mon copain, but no artist is ever fully satisfied with his own work."

"So why are you here then?" I wondered like a mind like his was here.

"Les conscriptions. I was, how do you say, 'drafted' to the war."
Bitterness bubbled to the surface and boiled over in his dark brown
eyes. A clench came into his jaw. "I am just another man, so what
does it matter? Another ant in the colony. It's not so big a deal after
all, so for this reason I do what I want." His eyes settled again and
cooled off.

Now his face said more than his words. I knew he had an eye
for the artistic things of life, the emotional and abstract. War,
however, is not art; it is the science of strategy and the animal of
brutality.

Chapter III

Keban still remained some miles away, it was getting dark and gas was low, so Leonardo ordered us all to pull over to camp here tonight. The fields and bushlands did not offer much protection or defense from the Ottomans or the elements, but there were no true woodlands around. Once we found a suitable spot to stop, we pulled the cars around and parked in a circle to create a kind of shield. We grouped up like the mama and papa elephants who gathered around the baby elephants when lions came to attack, except we were the babies. In the center of the circle we tented up and had a fire pit. Everyone was gathered around the fire, smoking and eating bread from the old cottage and other scraps they found here and there.

"You look tired." I said. Charles' face said fatigue. Not a kind of tiredness that called for sleep, but a kind of tiredness that 8 hours wouldn't fix.

"I most certainly am, old chap. I miss my wife, and my kids... and my armchair." He paused for a moment and the light in his eyes tossed through the reflection of the flames as he stared into the fire. "But, Gerard, you're a young man and I wouldn't ask it of you to empathize."

"I wish I could."

"Maybe someday you will, but what is color to a blind man? A vague concept with abstract ideas tied to it, nothing more." He reached into his bag and pulled out a small piece of bread. It was stale, but it was bread.

The sprawling accent of Pierre broke the quiet mood. "Oh la la! Love, romance, it is all a joke and marriage is the punchline."

Charles spoke in a subtle and deep way so that the words would only reach me "I reckon that is what one would call a blind man." He smirked at his own joke and carried on to eat his stale bread.

Bernardo came up to the car Charles and I sat leaning against. One of his Italian friends was trailing him. His friend sauntered behind with a swagger that did not boast. They both sat down and assumed the same position as Charles and I.

"This is Marco! Marco, meet Gerardo!" He seemed ecstatic to introduce us to each other.

"Ciao! I am Marco." He eagerly opened up his military issued canvas bag and reached inside. "Formaggio! For you and your English friend." It was a hard and large block of cheese, about the size of a softball, pungent as well. Marco reached for Bernardo's rifle and unclipped the bayonet off, then carefully cut the cheese into slivers. "For everybody!" He passed it around along with the bayonet.

Bernardo began to eat and chat with us "Who this friend of *yours*, Gerardo?"

"Charles."

"Pleasure to meet, Charle, Char... Carlo!" Finally he put his hand out and looked down at it to gesture towards a handshake.

Charles seemed momentarily confused then he said "Charles, chap, Ch-arle-s"

Bernardo paused then reset. "Carlo! You like some-more formaggi?"

"Charl-" I cut Charles off and leaned my head over to him.

"I don't think he understands non-Italian names or he just refuses them, either way, you're stuck now." I did not particularly mind being Gerardo, but I think being 'Carlo' vexed Charles a little more than I.

"I suppose so." He could not be bothered enough to fight it.

He took another slice and placed it on the last of his bread. It was salty and delicious cheese. The flakey and dense cheese would be the perfect kind for this long distance travel. For only a brief moment I left the windswept plateau of Anatolia and traveled to the coast of wherever that cheese was born.

It sounds foolish, but when you are so far from everything that your heart holds close it is simple moments, like those with good cheese, that remind you to keep going. After only a moment, however, I was back. If you stood up and looked around you'd be able to see until the curve of earth and there were about as many stars in the sky as blades of grass on the ground. I attempted to count them for a few minutes. I did not get far.

"What is America like Gerardo?" Marco was playing with a short twisted stick he pulled out of the fire. It was red hot at the tip and I could see he was trying to spell with it in the air.

"Lots of immigrants; lots of poor people, and those usually go hand in hand." I spoke as a matter of fact.

"My cousin, Antonio Rossi. He leave, goes to America, do you know him?" Marco seemed quite serious. I don't think he knew how big the United States was. "He said he wants to go to ...New York."

"I couldn't tell you, but I know that New York is a big city, and America is a big country." I looked over, "I'll look for him, when I get back. I'm sure he's alright."

"Very smart, and he's a hard-a-worker." Marco was confident.

"Most of them are." I did not doubt it.

I finished the cheese and ate some of my bread, but I had wrapped mine in cloth so it wasn't too stale. Marco kept blowing on the fire stick so the end would occasionally flame up, and then die back down to an ember. Eventually he tossed the whole remainder of the stick into the fire and watched it slowly burn up. I stared up into the sky, and everything was so clear and visible. I sat and let the back of my head rest on the wheel of the parked autocar.

The moon was strong that night and I wondered, with the help of Pierre's cognac, what other sore soul might be staring longingly at the same moon as me at that moment. From then, my mind drifted to the dull sounds of the wind. The wind carried the voices of aimless chatter into the thin air. Small talk of no substance that served to bring any bit of comfort we could conjure up just a little bit closer to us. After that, I was asleep.

The sun, as many times before, crept atop the horizon line and painted the fields with amber. The dew settled on all the leaves and made the air feel cool as it evaporated. I stood up and walked over to the fire. There was nothing left but some ash, charred grass, and rocks around the rim of its remains. I stretched and had a few eggs for breakfast. There was a whole pot of them made, scrambled style, from the donation of everyone's collective stash. It was good, but at that point almost anything tasted good.

Maggiore gathered us all around and started speaking. It was in Italian so I understood barely any of it.

I looked over to Bernardo furrowing my eyebrows. "What's he talking about?"

"He says that only one autocar should head into town to get gazolino." He spoke softly under the boom of Leonardo's voice. He says "The foreigners will go."

"Well, we are all foreigners here." I sighed and sat leaning back.

Maggiore looked over and pointed at the three of us except Charles. Probably because of his ranking Charles was exempt. He then pointed at Marco and said something in Italian to him that most likely meant "get going."

Marco, Emir, and Pierre and I all had to now go into town and silently fetch the gasoline. This was quite the pinch because it was morning and people would be about, but we were quite low. We needed gasoline now. We all got in a truck as we tossed the jerry-cans into the truck and fastened them to the back. I was a passenger and Emir was driving. Marco and Pierre were in the back.

Emir took off as soon as we got the go ahead. For a rather quiet and soft spoken man, he drove like a rock skipped on a lake. He skidded and skirted on the natural berm that lined either side of the road as it went up and down, and swayed left and right. You would worry temporarily, but he'd always seem to also keep his grip somehow. Marco spoke instructions to Emir on where to go, he would also hand the map off to me so he didn't have to do his job, then take it back at a random moment's notice. Altogether the ride was speedy, with little difficulty.

"Will someone tell me what is happening? Where am I going?" Emir asked, curious exactly what the plan was.

Pierre quipped back at him "We have to get gasoline or we will be stuck here. In *a middle* of nowhere." Pierre smiled.

Emir squinted his eyes and smirked "Aren't you the funny one Pierre. This I know, but what is our plan, really?" He said while driving and trying to focus on the path in front of him. "Are we just going to run in and say 'hello there Ottomans, we would love some of your fuel please?"

"No, we are going to steal it, and hopefully without anyone having noticed." Pierre stated his vague plan as if it was truly formed.

"What if we asked really nicely?" Marco asked.

"I think we can steal it." Bernardo responded to Marco.

I chipped in. "I think we are here."

We pulled up on the edge of a dropoff, steep and grassy down about twenty feet or so. We parked there and walked down the side of the slope till it met the edge of Keban in a small field basin inside the rocky drop off. We saw the town, it was small with only 15 houses or so, all made from clay bricks, stones, plaster, and logs, and none more than two stories. We saw two cars inside the village and hoped it meant our gas was there too. Pierre broke the steady and quiet crunch of our boots. "Must we all go to get gas?"

Marco played into it. "Pierre and I can watch the truck! You can get gazolino, eh?" He grinned a little and knew what he was doing.

Emir sighed and looked at me. "So mature they are, ha! So we must be adults."

"That's alright, it's better in our hands then." I responded. "I wouldn't be surprised if they lost the truck." I said, Emir smile-scoffed quietly.

Emir leaned over, just barely a crouch and I walked along the grass trail behind one of the larger houses along the river. We didn't see anyone, which soon became suspicious.

I leaned over to Emir, then whispered. "I think this was an outpost, there's no one here anymore."

We turned a corner and there they were. Standing right next to the river far behind their cars. Emir slowed and tensed up like an ocelot. There were seven soldiers in the shade next to the house around two cars.

Hidden under the angled overhang along the outside of a house we were up against I moved back and said. "We should draw them over here. Do you have a grenade?"

"I might," his hand scrounged about in a knapsack, his face contorted as his hand gripped something, then he stopped. "Yes."

"Here I'll do it." I put my hand out, palm up. "It will distract them, then we'll go to the cars."

Emir sighed in relief but didn't say anything. He handed me the grenade and started running, before the tab was even pulled. "Catch up." He quietly started away, around the other houses until he was out of my sight.

I pulled the pin and tossed it into the window of one of the nearby houses with just enough arc that it cracked through the window and rolled inside. I ran. Those few seconds felt like an eternity. The grenade exploded, I could hear it behind me, and I could see the dust come over my head as I moved out from it. The men started yelling in the distance and running over to see what the ruckus was.

We turned to a tight corner in the direction of the Ottoman cars where the men were moments ago; then headed straight under a parallel row of old willows. They were old and tall. Their dangling vine-like branches reached low to ground, as weeping willows do. The long dirt road drew onto the increasing thickness of the tree lines. We pulled right, behind a row of dense verdant bushes. A single house stood on our right side, near the cars.

I ran into the house first, a handgun held by both of my hands, so in the case I were to fire it, it would be under control. Emir was behind me and we split, each respectively clearing the small house that contained only two rooms. We creaked on the floorboards which were far too wide apart and wood which felt much too thin. The area was cleared quite hastily as all the men who might have been near there moments ago had gone to chase after the grenade we had thrown.

There was a door in the back as we stepped back onto the dusty dirt and gravel. The side of the house was routed on foot. Two neatly parked autocars, side by side, belonging to the Ottomans. Both with deeply tinted windows. They appeared surprisingly more durable than our issued cars.

Emir ran towards the driver side door of the one closest to us. His hairs were stiff and his muscles tense. He was all blood and bone. With a nervous approach he reached forward with his left hand. The pistol in his right. I could see the pistol shaking and quaking in his hand, nearly as much as his left. He squeezed the handle door and turned it...

Metal mechanisms clicked in the door, and the bolt moved back. Metal mechanisms in his hand clicked and the bolt slid back. I could not tell which came first but his right hand swung forward the moment he pulled the door open and away. The gun released its bullet and the split wide open, a single deafening shock of smoke and light. The bullet went into the autocar and fired at a moving figure in the back seat.

It was resoundingly quiet after that moment, and the air stood still. Emir froze and his eyes were more open than I had ever seen them before that.

There was a bass-filled thud like a hammer hitting a bag of sand. Afterward, a soft, but lifeless exhale. I ran around the car, to the side opposite of Emir. I yanked at the door next to where the figure sat and opened it.

"Emir!" I shouted, with a voice that cracked and screeched more akin to an animal call than a name, and I immediately forgot the grace and caution required in an enemy occupied zone. The small and skinny human frame fell out of the car. It lay limp into both of my arms. "It's a kid." Even after having just screamed, these words could barely come out as a whisper.

Emir stopped and stared at me, face frozen. "It's a boy."

Our eyes met one another and said no words, only emotions. Unspeaking, yet louder than anything able to be verbalized.

I pushed the still, warm, lifelessness of a body back in the car and closed the door instinctively. "It's a boy..." I looked to him over the distance of the autocar, "He's dead."

Scrambling and shaking in his hands Emir put the gun in its holster and placed both his hands on his head. He squeezed the fabric of his hat and pulled it off in what looked like a reflex with how tense and quick it was. "Do we leave him there?"

What other choice did we have? "We need to move, now! Get in the other car!"

Emir ran with his head in a spin to the second car's passenger side. I got in the driver seat. I looked in the rear view to the back seat. Both cars were the same model, and for some reason my mind expected to see the young boy here as well. Obviously he was not.

As I sat down, my hands jumped around, but not nearly as fast as my mind. My eyes followed the dashboard to eventually find the spot where the keys go. They were resting, unturned, in the ignition. I twisted it and started up the car, just as I began to hear the sound of the men who were only minutes ago chasing the sound of our grenades. I could hear them talking, back and forth. Their voices got louder as they got closer and their pace increased. My heart began to beat faster as they pushed their way past the very same trees we shuffled and ran through. I knew it was time to go. So I pushed my foot down on the pedal with more instinct than a hungry alligator.

I switched over to reverse, and the car rolled back a good twelve to fifteen feet kicking the ground in a screeching and rubber smoking swerve. The engine was on, there was certainly no doubt about that. The engine puttered to a beat like a heart with arrhythmia. I drove the car into a messy K turn and swerved out from the house, then to the right. Away from the other car. The one that had a kid in it.

Emir gripped his chair, and I gripped the wheel as if to strangle it. Every swivel and turn was a tightly bound and firm rotation. I could hear curious then angry men shouting and sprinting toward the sound of the autocar. Hustling under the weeping willows the men ran to us. We rode the same way back out.

The Ottoman men were running at the car after it completed the turn onto the row of trees they had come from. Sprinting at it. I kept my foot on the pedal and laid the gas onto the straight road. That was the gas we needed, but as soon as I did the men broke. They all split out of the autocar's way in different directions, like a herd of bison on either side of train tracks.

I powered the autocar of gasoline past the men and amidst the low hanging branches of the dangling willow trees. We skid and swiped out from the small town, closer to the drop off. The men would not be able to catch us on foot, yet once they had settled again they turned at us with their guns. I heard the gunfire crack as we passed the houses on our right and saw bullets shatter tiles on the walls. Mosaics of thousands of pieces sent off from the once loved and cared for homes. It took me a minute to locate the men on our left. They were firing from behind the dense green of the twisting wild bushes. Some pierced the bumper and door as we sped out, but not one hit Emir or I.

I spun the car to the right, away from the spray of bullets, then mounted the slope of the hill. It bumped onto a wider ridge that swept into the woods. We both let out an exhale that had been building and it felt like we were breathing again. Emir and I stared at each other, tossing the darkness back and forth in each others eyes.

"He was a boy." He sat silent and expressionless. Then, with no warning or pause, he punched the inside of the auto's door with an aggression I never before saw in him. A mere second later he shamefully covered his face with his hands and started mumbling.

I patted him on the shoulder. It was the only thing I could think to do at the moment. "I think he might've been older than I thought."

"You're saying that so it does not feel as wrong." He cranked the window open and leaned into it. "You do not have to say anything. It was always wrong."

"I am. Of course I am, he was about 14 if I was honest to say." I kept my eyes on the road and gripped the wheel tight. The rest of the short ride was silent, but we felt the same thing, so for this reason not many words need be exchanged.

Words help people reach each other. Words help us find each other when we are in different places. There are two times when people say nothing; when they do not feel they will be able to find the other, and when both know they are in the same place. Emir and I, at least for that short time, were in the same place. It was not a good place, but left no words to be desired. We drove back in the misty guilt, fear, and decline of adrenaline that leaves one mentally disoriented and tired.

I slowed while pulling up behind the trees back at the car with Marco and Pierre. "You brought a car back?" Marco scratched his head. "We will drive both back, haha."

"But where is the gasoline copain?" Pierre smiled sarcastically, looking at the autocar and tilting his head.

Marco laughed. "Do you have the *gazolino*."

"The gasoline is in the damn car right now." Emir barked back and kicked the wheel with force that seemed to Marco and Pierre to come from thin air. His boot bounced back off the tire. "Time for us to be going."

"Other than the autocar, we have no gasoline to show." I responded to Marco with more seriousness and looked over to Emir in calm. "Emir and I will drive this auto back, we'll follow right behind you."

"Oke, don't be late." Pierre turned on the autocar and jolted off on the trail that would lead back to camp. It was dead quiet. The birds and short quickening canopy wind drowned out pure, deafening, *silence.*

Chapter IV

We were in a camp outside Erzican. The huge mountainscapes enveloped the camp within a tiny rest in the Anatolian Plateau. A single wooden cabin fit for simply a few men nestled rare among the titanic crevices and deep mountainsides. The men began setting up canvassed tents on the large beds of dried pine needles. The thick paving of needles were fragrant and softened the ground. We were all seated in a small circle, some on the ground or a boulder edge, still others leaned against a parked car.

The campfire had just been lit up and was crawling its way throughout the kindling, just catching the larger twigs and soon, logs. Emir gazed at it with a pale hopelessness. While he seemed to look at the fire, he was viewing himself.

"Emir, are you hungry?" I split one boiled egg lengthwise with my cooking knife and lent my right arm forward holding the egg face up.

"No." Emir's response was cold and his eyes remained set in the fire, unchanged.

"Hold onto it, it might do you some good." I set it across the rings of a flat sawn tree stump.

"Tell them. They ought to know." He blinked once and tensed rapidly as his somber eyes remained closed for a moment just barely too long.

"It was an accident. That too." His head leaned lower now, covered by his hands, and facing the ground. "Aya." He breathed deeply, forcing the exhale out his nose. You could not see his face but you could feel the distress.

He raised his head again, tipping left near me, but still quite caught by the fire without looking at me. His eyes were glassy as I saw them reflect the fire from the side view. "You think they will come for us, we killed one of them?" Slowly, slowly but suddenly he made exact eye contact with me, careful not to change his expression. Then looking down to the ground behind me, he made fists with both hands rubbing his eyes then stood up.

I began to talk. "No, we are already on the move. They would have had to follow us back into the plateau and..." He appeared as if he were to say something but walked off plainly in silence before I finished answering.

I grabbed half of my egg from the trunk.

Charles sat down and his cheeks climbed up his face. "Chap, are you saving that there half for me?"

"I suppose so." I redirected my arm and rolled the half egg into his hand. He sat down precisely where Emir was a moment ago.

"Thank you." He smiled and met my shoulder with his fist, almost a punch. "Not hungry is he? Emir there." He threw half of the egg into his mouth and chewed it in a single bite.

"I don't think he is, no." I looked up. "Things went sideways Charles. Things really went sideways."

"Tell me of the shite." He smiled unknowingly, and eased forward unto the growing fire. "I had fought in the Boer War. You should have been told, oh." His reminisce and nightmare passed by his mind and he focused back to me. "That is shite there, yes." His head rested into place and he settled his shoulders into his frame. "Tell me now indeed, what is the shite chap?"

With no buildup or cushion, I spoke. "He shot a boy in a car at Keban. I know it doesn't make for much more grace, but it *was* an accident." I inhaled through my nose, and we met our eyes. I held my face still. "He fell dead, onto my arms. I put the bloodied kid back in the car, and we left." I let my breath go in a deep exhale.

Charles' jaw pushed up and out. His brows not yet furrowed yet eyes tightened, to something sharp. "Oh my, truly that is a tragedy. Bitter like many things." His expression soured, using his two fingers and forearm pressed his temple to hold his head to one side.

He lifted his thumb and two far fingers covering his face for a time. Raising his right hand away after a moment, he wafted the worst of those emotions up with the smoke. "A shameful truth that humanity bears in common." He glistened for a moment. "Ironic, indeed. Oh isn't it."

"Yet right then, we ran off with the second car. As if it was not our responsibility, not our fault." My words hardened in my throat more than I intended as they came out. "We had to go somewhere." I softened again. "How are you so calm and matter of fact?"

"Ai. O Good Lord, it can be a blue world. You'd be surprised what people are capable of." Silencing himself Charles paused. "I carried a kid across my shoulder like a log in burlap. It smelled in the heat of Transvaal and buried him in the sands of the desert." He whipped back then slid these embittered words toward me. "The Second Boer War son, yes I was in it. A diabolism of nations."

Charles reached in his shirt pocket to carefully bite the end of a cigar off, spitting away the small stub. He pinched the end piece in his rounded lips and lit the match with his free hands. The rising orange flame on the match danced back and forth until he pulled the hot air through the cigar, then loosened his breath. First air, then the smoke. "You know, after a certain point the ground in a desert even begins to grow cool and damp if you can dig deep enough. Of course, one must note the air becomes frigid at sundown as well."

"Should we worry, do you think?" I looked over to him, and pondered before his response.

"Think of w'hat, chap." He said while the leaving smoke played to leave the nasal in his voice.

"Will they be coming after us or not? What do you say?"

"Well, in my experience." All around him paused for Charles as he attended to his cigar once more. He filled the smoke with my anticipation as well. "Yes." The dense leaf smoke ascended up with the growing pillar of campfire smoke.

"You're experienced." I ended abruptly, as if I were to say more.

"So, do with that what you shall, an old man's advice." He said. I was not quite sure, what even he had thought of it. His face was still and firm.

"It would do well with me, thank you." I thought about it, and became unstill. It was not a pleasant thought.

"Thanks for the egg, son." He smiled, "I'm glad you saved it for me." Using his forearms and hands he pushed back on his knees, until he stood up with the cigar in mouth. He shook my hand and nodded; while gripping the cigar that made way for a soft, but aged grin. Then he walked off behind the log.

Maggiore made his way over to the growing circle around the campfire along with the other Italians. I got up and started walking away from the camp. If anyone asks, I've got to go get more wood for the campfire. However, in honesty it was too crowded. I wanted to get away and breathe; but I could split logs at the same time.

In honor of transparency it was dangerous to go out and not tell anyone, especially after what I had just heard but that is what I did. I just wished to be unknown and alone for a time, if even a short one.

The forest slowly unfolded along the surprisingly gentle

sloping piece of mountainside. Below the forest of aromatic pines, no underbrush lay on the ground. Simply a carpeted needle bedding from layer upon layer, year to year. I went into those sap-scented woods and followed a deer trail down. Downhill always leads to a stream or river.

The trail wisped beside the flat stones that pushed themselves straight out among the declines. I connected through the rooted steps of the trees and down into a gravel path. On the way there were a few fallen limbs by the trail, after hopping over those, I chopped the decent sized branches into a generous amount of logs. Wrapping them in the cordage I carried them around and set them to be hidden behind a rock, then told myself I would bring them with me upon return.

I headed further until I arrived at the stream which meandered and trickled through the thick clay and sand-lined bank. Gently perched over it was a quaint stone bridge. Held together without fracture; each gray stone was puzzled upon one another. I swear by the sturdy age of it, that the bridge had seen Romans and who knows what else.

I threw my clothes onto the base of the bank and shuffled them in the water to wash them some. I then sank myself in the shallow freshness of the spring water. Kneeling amidst the waters, then laying my back down against them. A cool rush came over me and a feeling as though I was melted throughout that clear yet lively stream. Brisk flowing silence finally, and not only that, but a silence of momentary peace not of the other kind. For a mere second of eternity I had been swept up and lifted out of this place. A place that held me so tightly in its grip, temporarily removed underneath a humble current.

I pulled up out of the water and shook my head to air out my hair. Looking over, across the bridge, up the hill to the other side of the stream. Resting silent and quaint among the trees there was a spring house on top of the clear spring that fed into the stream. It peeled over and away eventually tossing down the mountainside in a flow. I put on my still damp shirt and pants, meandering the gravel and trail pressed earth that turned to smooth stepping flagstones in the ground. There was a thin wood door much younger than the deep gray cobblestones separated by mortar. A simple split spruce wooden roof. I went inside.

The spring house was empty. Only a single chair and a small wooden bucket, yet the small canal that traversed the shack continued to flow. The stream breezed under the house clear and quick. I pulled the bucket to me and gave it a bath first in the water, then filled it. I brought it to my mouth, drinking and spilling. I cooled off my face as the water spilled down my back. I leaned back in the chair and sat for a while. I was drunk off fresh water, and sat peacefully in the single chair, alone. Once I had returned to my place I knew I should soon be back on the way.

The sun teetered between scattered clouds and bright light. Now they finally all came in. The clouds gathered and stood tall over my small stream. This is when I decided it best to head back. I went up the trail after I crossed the lonely cobblestone bridge. I marched up the hill among the trees for a while until I passed upon the tree I had laid the logs behind. Creeping behind I snagged the strung together pile and swung my feet back onto the path. My clothes were between wet and damp when I carried them. I climbed the gently layered slopes.

Time got later and the sun was low. I was still tired of course, yet refreshed in a solitary way. When I took my final turn my view finally peaked over a clearing foot rest in the hillside so I saw the camp. The fire that started in the pit had grown. Those who weren't already asleep gathered around the campfire. The drizzle had turned on and off during the day. However it began again, gentle, graceful, and light as mist.

The men made camp with the waxed-canvas tarpaulins, yet some like me still slept humbly in the car. Pierre was lying down in the back seat of the car I sat upfront. It was dark and he began to light a cigarette inside. Lifting the match up, but slightly under the end where the leaves poked out. A plume rose within the car and the orange dot dimly lit the autocar after the match had left us.

"What the hell happened back there? I can read people you know, mon copain." He said in his classic, 'all knowing' fashion.

I cranked the window open and leaned into it. The smoke drifted up and out like a ghost. "Back where, at Keban?"

"Ouais, something was wrong when you got back, you know that."

"You wanna know." I pulled the now dim, dying cigarette from his stretched out hand. "He shot a kid." I dragged it a single time, but long so that I coughed mid pull; then tossed it onto the damp sodden mountain grass and needles.

"He shot a kid... oh Mon Dieu." The thick smoke that was accumulating in the car was not clear, yet his kids were.

The window pulled out the smoke and let in some cooler, fresher air. "Mon Dieu, that's it." I looked back behind the chair toward Pierre. "A boy." I could not keep a straight face.

"How old?" He asked, hoping for me to make it sound, or feel, better. Somehow.

"14, give or take." I sighed "*Take.*"

"Take..." Pierre propped himself up from laying down, resting his head on the back seat. His face slowed up then his body. "How? Did he not see that he was young?"

"It was not obvious. He was in one of the Ottoman autos. The rest were out searching the building we distracted them with." I turned the handle for the window and closed it again, the inside was clearer now. "He opened the door and shot him. It was reflex, confusion, fear? My guess is as sure as yours."

"So his reflexes were too quick. Maybe it was both, all three even. Why would they put a boy in the car?" Pierre restlessly leaned forward with his elbows on his knees and head in hands like a pyramid.

"I don't know! I was there, I was not inside his mind." Now wishing myself to feel better. Quite a bit to ask at the time.

"How is Emir? Like in his head." Pierre ran his fingers through dark hair then rested his forehead onto his temples and fingertips.

"Shock mostly, he hasn't said much since." I placed my hands on the dashboard, then threw them up. "I tried to chat with him but..."

"I will talk to him." He waved his hands like a conductor out at his sides above his shoulders.

"Not, about the actual event."

Pierre pulled his gaze up to me. "Of course not copain, I'll talk about other things."

"What other things?"

Pierre's face wrinkled "Weather, Politics, or maybe how to cook a proper lamb!"

I smiled with less muscles than usual, and gave a small chuckle as the air went out of my nose. I felt like I was pushing it out.

Pierre dipped his arm down and reached into his bag under my seat. "There should be about three quarters of the brandy I still have, oui?" Pulling the crowded bag up and onto his lap.

"No, put that away, I'm going to sleep." I leaned back into the chair.

Pierre dropped the bag on the car floor. "It's not there."

"Good. Good night."

"Non, not good. Where is it?" Pierre's eyes focused. "You don't think he would... He's Muslim, no, they don't drink."

I looked over. Our eyes met in the near darkness. The mortal stare said everything and nothing, we paused to look away in the silence and started again.

"He's human." I said.

Pierre slapped the head of the back of the passenger chair. "Where is he sleeping?"

"I heard in the cabin."

Pierre quietly opened the autocar door, then I did. We walked up the short incline and low grasses to the stone step outside the old wooden cabin. I slid the metal pin to the right and pointed the upward handle facing down. The door almost opened itself and there were four cots, two double decks.

"Un, deux, trois people."

"Four cots. Maggiore, Charles, and another Italian." I turned around immediately.

"Merde." He whispered under his breath, then made a visor with his forefinger and thumb, pulling his hand down with his face.

We tracked behind and back onto the door and closed it again, pushing the central pin back into place. We got outside, and saw a lantern hanging on a long hand-forged nail sticking in the cabin wall.

I grabbed it so the forest could be navigated. Cautiously not to alarm, we worked our way out of the comfort and into the wet wilds. "Emir!" Pierre shouted, and called for him into the dark and shadowy night. A washed ground from days of intermittent rain.

The latest fresh footprints looked like Emir's, if I hadn't seen them marching hundreds of times before. Trekking from the warmth of the campfire and clearing exposed to moonlighting;

and away deep in the high mountain forests. In the day they were enchanting, almost magical with the dance of canopy light. However at night, they feel mysterious and dominating. It was night, and late into it.

We followed a trail we believed to be Emir's, going down the hill. The trail began open and flat. However the deeper in we went the spruce and pine branches the deeper they leaned in. Bunching low and looming over us in the darkness. Only the oil lantern highlighted the path in front of us. We hastily followed the prints in the damp, molded dirt and descended down the rocky inclines. The steps became jagged as we arrived at a creek.

I believed it to be the same one as before, that I had come to alone. The trail Emir took ran us further downstream. There was no footbridge, just deer tracks and a few wolf prints. At this point the creek had grown wider as it was further downhill. It was tough from the rain and icy cold in the windy mountain night.

The few stones that peeked over the thrashing foamy midnight water would not be enough to cross. Pierre hung his head and walked in a pensive circle on the bank. He paused, placing his index finger on his lips, crouched and picked up the smooth glass brandy bottle.

He pivoted over and tapped my arm with the glass. Looking at me and handing it to me. "I found it!" He sighed, just as worried as before. I clasped the rounded bottom while it rested in my grip.

"Putain, where is he? We cannot find him now." Pierre swung at the air aggressively and disappointed, but with nowhere to go. "What are we to do now?"

"There's no finding him across that damned river." I loosened my grip on the now ghostly empty bottle. "Hell, did he even make it across the river."

"He'd better just be alive. Even if it means he is a defector."

Pierre sighed and picked up a small flat stone. He skipped it across the river. The frustration skipped alongside it and some of it settled in the stream-bottom. "Dead or alive, we don't know." Pierre pondered with an almost honest charge to his voice.

"If the Ottomans find him he's burnt toast." I said.

"We can hope he finds us first, unless of course he left on purpose." He thought to himself which would be more likely the case. "Then we will just have to teach him how to lie?"

"It's our luck if we ever find out. Defectors don't always want to be found."

"Too much for him? You think all of this was too much?" Pierre asked.

"I think he thought what he did was too much." I re-established my grip on the bottle in my thoughts. "Would've been for most people I think."

"Not for me, I do not believe it!" Pierre rested his hands at his sides, but clenched them.

"We all say that now, you can never know." I brushed off his statement. "You would've believed Jesus if you met him while he was alive, right?"

"So I suppose, but I would never believe it to be me." Pierre insisted. "If he performed a miracle, perhaps."

"Congratulations for not deserting!" Moving my hands and face emphatically.

"Well, I will wait to do so for at least forty days. Deserting under influence." He looked away, I think he grinned a little. "Why not, perhaps I should as well."

"Keep it together connard." I darted my voice at Pierre, then rested my voice.

"Jesus did it and so did Emir, why is it that I cannot be like them?" He was sarcastic and overly playful in his voice. It did not sound quite right. You could tell he was upset.

The night became deeper than before. The wolves sounded like rustling leaves and leaves sounded like wolves to human ears. We scoured the land around us for anything else to tell us our way. Nothing was revealed. What else were we to do? Go back and tell Maggiore.

In those moments of turmoil, with a dark concentration we stared deep into the haunting woods far away from the camp. The dark concentration that gathered turned glowing pines of day to haunting woods of night; they weren't like this at first, but the abyss had become overshadowing. We were mere ants in the vastness. This grew proportionally with the realization we had no idea where Emir was.

When we got back to camp we had told Maggiore all that we knew. He was sitting in his tent and having a snack of biscotti. He offered me some. I took it. He told us to write it down somewhere, but he didn't mention it much. It was not helpful at all.

It was not one of his men, and he simply did not care as much. Nor was there much we could do, unless of course he decided to make himself known again. Maggiore made it clear he was either a deserter or he's already bloated up in a stream somewhere. I did not happen to think it was that simple, but you don't bring that kind of stuff up with most people, especially your *Major*, so I let him talk. I nodded. Calm and clear.

Some fresh foods on hand were cooked into a delicious soup. The stars and birds were delightful to watch. A few even played instruments they knew and the Italians were tearing through a private stash they kept amongst them. No melody was found among all the instruments, yet they all pleased themselves, within their own rhythm.

One man shouted something in Italian from a ladder while

seated in a tree. He saw smoke rising up and heard singing in the woods.

"They are singing like the Ottomani." Marco looked at me and stated the jist of what the man said in English.

"We heard the small airplanes from time to time." However, Charles was right, we'd had more planes recently. "Back in old South Africa they'd fly planes so often you'd believe they were to be the paranoid ones. Then they would stop."

"What would happen after?" I was playing along with the story.

"They would ambush us." He struck. "Oh chap, did they sting, quite the bait and switch!" His lips clapped back onto the cigar, he puffed it back alive from his brief stint of talking.

Bernardo laughed, "We are so far from the borders, this is not a problem." He played with a small piece of cheese and bread.

"We stole their cars, so I imagine we are on someone's list." Pierre shook his head and shrugged with his legs long and back.

"Well it's better we get to the Russian checkpoint sooner than later." I remarked onto the train of verbal thought. "They'll put the pieces together at some point, or they'll pull ours apart."

Chapter V

The light of a tired sun rose over the hills far away. It gave itself as a sign to us. We began to pack again. You can only travel so far in a day, that is when you're rationing gasoline as well. Many of us were hiding in the barns of an old and decayed Christian farmstead. We could only assume it was probably deserted and never reoccupied.

Some men made jokes so that they did not feel so far from home. They joked, gagged, and shenaniganed their way about, to displace themselves, at least for an evening or two. We packed bags which held rolled up clothes, rarely folded. Some brooded outside in the angry and pathetic silence that does little for circumstances. Nonetheless, we tossed everything onto the autocars which at this point were the closest semblance of a home we had for months. Home was almost out of gas. I got in the passenger's seat and met Charles, who was driving.

"Some more good company, eh chap." He adjusted his circle rimmed eyeglasses and chuckled to himself.

"Do not get too ambitious, I'm not always good company." I pulled forth a smirk, which was the best I could muster at that moment. "How do you do?" I asked.

"I don't believe it." His eyes squinted and he smiled like Santa Claus for a moment. Behind that smile was years of life that made even the very bad things seem rather capable of overcoming.

"You're a high ranking experienced military officer. Certainly you could have opted out of this mess..." I spoke assumingly.

"Well I'd been to South Africa, Caribbean, and figured why not the Ottoman heartland, sounded worth the trip."

"Worth a head in a basket?" Marco interjected.

"Aie!' stop that talk, you are Catholique, no?" Pierre added.

"Yes, in tradition." His voice twisted and turned a little bit as he gently clutched his necklace with its bronze crucifix. "It is always difficult to explain." Spoke Marco. "What does that have to do with anything anyways?"

Pierre tossed away the other remarks but nodded. "It is always difficult, yes."

I returned to the more soft conversation. "Maybe in peace-time. It could be worth the trip." I clarified. "It is magnificent out here, all the more; there are enough of these mountains and forests, you can *almost* forget a war is going on."

"Yes lad, for some moments. But that pensive burn remains for you. A baseline it rests on, ticking." Charles observed, through his particular looking glass. "I keep ticking, this is where I ought to be, simple as that." His words settled.

I thought to myself; then I said "Then someone disappears, however I did not say this." I looked away then back. "Or someone dies."

The car ignited and ran, after Pierre and Bernardo got in the car. The engine clicked for a few turns then ran. Everyone breathed a sigh of relief.

"Say you could really disappear out here." I commented on the staggering landscape, and how much it varied.

Charles proposed. "Who's to say that isn't Emir, seemed awfully shaken didn't he chap?" Charles went further. "Too much for him to handle, he scampered. Maybe if I was younger I might've managed to pull it off?" He reflected. "I am a committed man."

I sighed and looked over. "Well I'd like it if we could talk about this more."

Charles played back, "Well placed sarcasm, yankee."

"Who the hell knows why he went?"

Pierre said with a thoughtful disdain, "Does he even know why he went?"

Charles patronized ever so subtly "I suppose killing a child was the straw on the camel's back."

"A damn big straw." I said matter-of-fact.

"This is indeed true." Charles looked at me, "his mettle was tested."

Pierre interjected for the last word "Maybe it was aluminum."

"Go pound sand if you want to judge. You should not speak on this. You know little of it." Marco stated. "I, included." He concluded.

The car started off again, sinking into the meadowlands, and away from the towering ancient ridges and peaks. Majestic and beautiful, yet at times demanding and dominant. The jagged rock faces and facets transformed into gentle hillside waves. Less daunting, but more exposed. Whistling through bits of forest and woodland; all the while on gravel, or the pressed and packed dirt of the rolling earth.

We careened across a curving stretch of gravel road that pressed up against a moving and swaying field. The land eased down into the field and around the edge of a forest, village was a generous term. It was five houses, one of stone, the rest were log cabins. There was no one there, but two dogs barking at us. Both were skinny, one more than the other. They were walking in methodic circles around the houses scouring for food.

We checked inside the cabins and stone house. No food was found, olive trees began creeping out of the warming cliff edges, alongside cypress and pine, all of which were stirred into a common airy fragrance. We wheeled through carriage tracks and grass. Fields of buckwheat and orchards. You could not help but feel small. Each tree, its own ancient witness reaching in every way up to a sun they cannot reach.

The Italians were getting impatient, so Maggiore ordered us to pull over for a lunch. We saved the good and fresh food, but instead ate some of the long-lasting sardine tins. However, even if it wasn't tasty, bread was always sure to fill the stomach.

Morale was not bad, yet still not good. Nonetheless, lunch, however light and rationed, helped much to loosen peoples strings and let them breathe, briefly. Although, I'm sure no one was thoroughly full, only temporarily satiated. A small horse and carriage passed by, rickety and all wooden; but only for the surface of the wheels, a thin sheet of molded iron. It was painted forest green and filled with vegetables. The man directing the horse stared at us with his neck rotating, and he was unphased viewing the group as he went by. He looked again then once away, then sped up and off.

"Who is this?" Marco said in between sips of his canteen and pieces of bread. The humid pulsating sun painted the scene around us even though we ourselves were under the temporary haven of shade.

I spoke to those in the car. "A stranger,"

"He did look strange." Pierre claimed.

"He looked at us strange." I glanced over.

Marco's face twisted a little, he mumbled italian and said "Grazie... ``You know they do not make bad wine, here you know." He slipped slowly to lift it up, swirling his tin cup.

"What does that do?"

"The legs, a good wine is like a lady, it has long curvy legs." He went on to explain. "You get the air into it, with this, the flavor."

"I guess an American tongue cannot taste a difference?" I

asked.

"Yes you can, but not the same way, you see?" Marco smiled. "About wine and women I mean."

"So what, you have a monopoly on love and alcohol, ha that's a first chap." Charles almost rolled his eyes, and sarcastically looked at us as if he were in some way seriously impressed at the innovation of thought.

Marco was more focused and serious than necessary, "You laugh but are not the same!"

Charles broke the steady banter. "We have not spotted a good water source chap, for some time surely. My canteen is approaching empty."

I remained steadily silent. Unfortunately, I knew there was a spring we had passed some time ago, but I did not mention it. I did not think to, inconvenient.

"Soon good men, we must arrive in the basin toward the Black Sea, then the inlets will be revealed, right that is."

"Of this you are sure?" Marco's chin leaned into his cup and he drank intensely.

"Yes chap, damn well sure on that one." Charles clenched his jaw and released, gazing at Marco and leaning back.

We continued to eat and when we finished spirits were lightened. Lifted and fed, and now on the trail headed north, into the sea.

Chapter VI

The car hit along the curve of the hill's edge and pulled close into the hillside's flat face. The dirt kicked, and a plume followed behind us, although we followed the dust cloud left by Maggiore's crew.

Pierre pulled his gaze away from the landscapes and looked over to me. "What is childhood but the most perfect and innocent lens with which to view the world. It seems to me as though most things all trace back to this, and all after." He pondered momentarily. "Reminiscing or running either way."

"Not much can be done about any of those." I glanced onto Pierre to measure his face's expression. We both sighed, leaning into the chair of the autocar. "It is more about the 'and all after' that's important I'd suppose."

"Indeed." Pierre said, "A curse or a blessing, ça depends. You learn from the past, careful not to get stuck in it."

"I suppose if someone betrays you while you're young...' You'd expect them not to trust, or trust in the wrong places." I contributed another idea.

"Where would be the wrong place to trust mon copain?" Pierre straightened his eyes and pursed his lips in slight contemplation.

"Government stability, a bad partner, or a cult." I grimaced a little and then pulled back. "Plenty of things."

"Ah yes for the first I must agree." Pierre wagged his finger once and smiled. "Any Frenchman worth his Francs cannot say no to a good protest."

"It's important to shake things up, a few well-placed demonstrations can go a long way."

Pierre paused "Should I say an American worth his bucks!?"

"Buck, bill, dollar, and yes." He was impressed with himself for employing American slang, and I found fondness in it. I reached my arm out of the car into the wind. "We do like a good revolution, but we try to keep it at a minimum. When necessary."

"Have your way, however I for one think it keeps society healthy."

"Cults?" I jokingly looked at Pierre with disapproval. "I'm joking."

"No, government, it is like a tree." He explained as if he were detailing something important. "You must trim the old and hanging branches."

"What kind of branches?"

"Old politicians, bad laws, and all the rest comme ça"

They were last in line in the stolen car. The two autocars from the military were in the front. Maggiore was in the center car behind the driver.

I smiled at him and we continued to make conversation as the trail and sometimes road wound like string around each sloping hill onto the other side. We were getting closer to the grip of the Black Sea and things became windy. In circles and swinging waves, the wind slipped over each grainy and grassy dune. Pushing up and over like hair being played with by a pretty girl. The wind picked and slammed down every few miles or so. The sun would peek out and hide, nearly taunting us as to its intent. The tops of the witness trees swept and swung restlessly aside the rushing air.

"Are we safe up here? Ami." Pierre stared at me for a moment.

"It would not push the car over. That I know." I said.

"How do you know this?" Pierre glared again and at everyone

else,

"Stop. You need to bring this down. Tu Comprends?" I set my eyes on him and shew a heavy understanding.

"Entendu." He stretched his legs and skinny body with his arms and head pointed high in the sky like a diver. Then dipped into the chair and rested his head back. He was jittery, and I knew that Pierre got sharp when he was jittery.

"How are we doing back there folks?" Charles spun his head giving us his cents.

"You're just telling us to quiet down. Politely, I admit." Pierre flicked Charles' chair and smirked.

It became quiet and the air slowed, yet it was still lively outside. Humid and warm.

"Indeed there is a time for quiet and noise, yet we are never pleased with the one we are doing." Charles puffed a cigar and coughed lightly.

"Ouais, when it rains, we wish for snow." Pierre looked over, "When it is sunny we say it is too hot, yet when she is gone we cry like fools wishing her back."

"Do you speak of weather or women?" I gave a verbal target to follow.

"I suppose you can never be satisfied unless with yourself, but that itself is one of the rarer things." I nudged Pierre's shoulder and we were close for a moment, but like most men pulled ourselves away again. Retreating into the silence temporarily.

Pierre breathed and looked away, "This is where the many mediators come in."

"The mediators?" Marco gave a sharp but confused look.

"Such things men do when they are not occupied, as to stave off that slow and pathetic burn that kills all of us." I scratched my head then pushed my hair back into place.

Marco laughed "Such things as wine and spirits?"

Pierre sighed and gripped the side of the car door with an animal clasp. "Yes, these among other things."

"Such as, chap?" Charles asked, full well having known the answers on his own.

"The wilds, vocation, pursuit of knowledge..." Pierre paused, "making love, the greatest of these." Pierre loosened his grip to relax, yet he entered a melancholy.

"There are many things that we say are the greatest. One must find *their* greatest." Charles left the word hanging as he further nursed the cigar. "I'll say, most of these would kill you all, a matter of time is all that is in question."

"Rather to die doing something notable, no?" Pierre's eyes darted and narrowed. "Or at least notable to you."

"Making love *will* kill you, but it is slow, chronic, and torturous." I breathed and let the wind hit me. "It can be notable."

"Not making good love will kill you too, eh?" Pierre fished out a notepad and wrote something for himself.

"Death by a thousand cuts, however, it is undeniable those deepening grooves feel quite amazing sometimes," I spoke in return. "Other times they burn long after they cut."

Charles turned solemn and focused as he dragged a heavy puff. "I wouldn't dare wish to say that is the way of things, but it is true." He let the smoke out and became nasally. "No one's heart and logical mind are congruent in the world of love, at least never entirely."

Marco slipped back in again. "Love is not simple, never simple, this I say!" He paused to catch his own feelings. "It was the wrong time, wrong place, but she was the right lady." Once more, he gave himself a moment. "This is mine to carry."

"It is much like that, the world is a complicated place. With too many moving parts to understand." Pierre sipped a small bottle of gin Charles had seated next to him. "Paola was brought back to Lisbon for what?"

"Who?" Marco asked.

"A childhood friend, she was Portuguese but we lived down the road from one another in our youth," Pierre said with a tone of remembrance that soured him just slightly enough to be noticeable.. "We could not have been more similar, but the world was simply not for us."

"The world is a grand, but aggressive place." I smiled

Charles flicked the ash off the side of the autocar with the gravel in his voice coming out. "That! Chap is why the world trumps the many lesser things within it, unfortunately, we are often the lesser things."

"To push against the grain of the world is a difficult thing." Pierre laughed at his own thoughts, then pulled back to reality. "Near impossible."

"It is worth the price!" Marco sparked, "If you are willing to take the splinters."

"Splinters must be removed," I said

"Love cannot be removed, jamais. Not fully." Pierre took one more sip. Before he returned it to Charles, Marco grabbed the neck and took some.

"That is all." Marco handed it over. "It is not easy, not simple."

"How does one know when to give themselves splinters?" I asked in intrigue.

"When they are willing to not only take splinters but die," Pierre responded with furrowed brows.

"To die?" I asked, not out of a lack of hearing, but in confirmation.

"To die." He said, matter of fact.

To this day, I still do not know if I mean literally or figuratively.

Chapter VII

The sun was low and the orange, pink, and pastel red pierced the scattered and patterned clouds. They sat on the edge of the world in the green and rocky prehistoric mountainscapes that grew ever farther and farther away. It was without a soul, yet not desolate or lonely but quiet. We all pulled away onto a gravel road and parked. Down the road was a simple inn, fashioned of old aged wood. Wooden doors, banisters, and architecture not furnished simply by oils or stain, but by human hands, and the wind of time.

"They would not care if we stay here. Yes?" Marco asked.

"It should be said they probably need money more than trouble of any kind." I said. "We should pay them somehow. That is if anyone is there."

A short dark olive-skinned man came out of the inn. He was built firm and stocky, with a large nose and wide lips, and was stepping onto the same wooden porch. One could tell by the way that he walked he was not a proud man, however he most certainly knew his worth. He waved his hand flat above his head, pulling it up towards him. He waved us closer and then pointed to the door with his dense workmans fingers.

"Here, you come here!" He smiled and hopped a little, moving his short frame in a boisterous and confident way. "I am Adri!" "Adri!" He tapped the sternum of his chest with three fingers and a vigor, nodding a little bit, and exposing the hair he still had left from his balding head. "Who are you men?" He was interested and inquisitive.

"We are many things, mostly Italians. I am American, my name is Gerard." I shook his hand, but he squeezed mine with his short but firm fingers.

"American! American! Gerard." He laughed and swung the door open. "Inside, yes? You eat, then you drink, then you sleep... *and* maybe laugh a little in between."

"I like the sound of this," Pierre said as he walked in taking the invitation at face value.

The man ran in circles, picking things up, putting the same things down, and moving others. He was hasty, yet deliberate. "My wife cook, she is best of all." He threw his hands up and down. Then he looked up. "Ok, I lie! Guilty! You sit first... then you eat?" He smiled and chuckled loud as he smacked my shoulder in a friendly way.

The man was friendly, albeit a lot to handle, but he was nothing but kind. I backed out onto the porch to avoid the preparation of his controlled chaos, and sat in one of the armchairs. The dark and storied wooden beams that strutted out in an overhang held us in-between the outdoors and the homely inside of the inn. Bernardo sat down in a chair beside mine and took some bread out of a wrapped burlap cloth.

"Bread for you, would you like it?"

"I will eat soon, no need to ruin the appetite."

"It prepares the appetite, some may say this." He tossed a piece he had ripped from the body of the loaf into the air and caught it with his mouth. "Loosen the muscles, try to relax while we have the time."

"Ok then, go ahead and prepare your appetite, and I will chastise mine."

"Why should you do that?" He questioned.

"Because I've decided so." I folded my hands and rested them on my chest, settling into the chair.

"We do not eat often enough, and you decide to do this still?" Bernardo ate the bread, satisfied.

"Not here I suppose, on other things yes, I believe so." I took my hand out and took a piece of bread, ripping it from the loaf.

"In what things?"

"Those of larger consequence, as in those things that make us and others regret, and those that make us satisfied." I paused, "not in the stomach."

"You mean to say what?"

"I will not be sad in the ways of my heart and mind if I do not eat your bread." I sipped water from a canteen.

"You would if you shot me. Yes?" Bernardo said while chewing the bread with its hard crust and light interior.

"Yes, I would if I shot you. Although this goes as well for things on a smaller scale." I took another small piece of bread that he had preemptively placed on a small stool out between the two chairs.

"You are taking the bread," he looked at the now-empty stool. "You are hungry, and a liar!" He said while laughing at his half-hearted attempt at acting angry.

"A liar, but only on the small things."

"Not on the large ones?" His gaze squinted and he sharpened.

"No."

"How does one choose?" He said in interest.

"One always knows, even if he chooses wrong he knows," I said with an unexpected degree of certainty. "Especially so then."

"Sometimes one suppresses it."

"Suppress the gravity towards good." I finished the small piece of bread that held me over. "It is easy to do habitually, and much of the time it can help you."

"It helps to get you ahead." Bernardo waited to think, then continued, "few know that you are sacrificing something."

"Either that or they ignore it. It is easy to ignore all else if you ignore what comes first, that being the right and the wrong."

"In that place, there are no rules."

"If there are none of these; then there is no sense of progress." I looked back and forth between the scenery and Bernardo. "There is not much after that."

"It sounds to me like there is nothing." Bernardo wiped his hands together. He discarded the residue on his fingers, and then he set them in his lap.

"You could say that, and I would not disagree."

Adri came running out onto the porch and stopped immediately at the threshold of the door. He turned stiff and looked over to us in excitement with shoulders high.

"You close that, wrap now, we bring you the good food, eh?" He gestured to the door and lifted his hand swift like a paddle pointing to the second floor. Bernardo began walking in and as he passed the door, the old man slapped him on the back heartily. "Time for a meal! One you will like."

The house smelled of ancient wood, burning fireplaces, wax candles, and spiced aged meat. A giant steel basin the size of a large sink, it was seated on a stone box on the first floor. Perfectly fitted, and a small fire was burning underneath. In the basin were meats and vegetables, each was individually unidentifiable, but it looked to be delicious. A short older woman with a floral headscarf that seemed to be his wife was vigorously stirring. She was strong and tough, hardened by the demands of her life. As she stirred, she reached over into a clay pot and pulled a handful of spices out. Her old and wrinkled hands, far from weak, waved in the air like a spell as she tossed them in the basin and kept mixing. Adri stood at the base of the staircase and nodded once for each man who walked by onto the first step. He slapped some of them in the arm and grinned, looking up to the room. Mostly the skinnier ones.

"We eat, we eat! Come, my beautiful wife!" He held one side of the basin and she, the other. Together they tipped the food over into a wooden bowl of a slightly smaller size. They lifted it and carried the food up the stairs.

"So very generous of you!" He thanked his wife for us and smiled like it was the first time he had seen her. They came up the final step and placed it on a stand at the end of the table. "Thank my wife! Greatest of food!"

He stepped back behind her, tilting slightly, and gestured her forward in a formal pose, with hands pointed at the floor. She gently nodded her head, leaning in a little. We all thanked her at once and some clapped lightly. He ran downstairs without a word. We saw him come back up in haste with wine bottles pinched between each of his fingers. Some opened with the cork still on, and others still sealed. He passed quickly down the single, long, wooden table that extended throughout the room and placed one down incrementally until he finished. Finally, he sat down at the end, as his wife was sitting opposite. He took the last bottle, set it firmly in his lap between his thighs, and uncorked it with a wine cork that looked like it could have been forged by a neighbor or family friend.

"I say eat too much - With no eating... Now eat!" He was calmer immediately after that. Moments later he slowly then poured the wine into a single small wine glass. So we began to eat.

Pierre looked over to Marco across from him. "Do you still think of her?"

"Of who?" Marco bit his lip, then went on. "Of course I think of her; you call me a liar if I say anything else."

Bernardo popped his head up and looked at me. "Is this a bad lie? What do you say, Gerard?"

"He didn't lie, did he?" I said.

"No, he did not, but tell me, if he had?" He ate a forkful, "would it be wrong of him?" Bernardo's eyes darted and gave me that rightfully questioning look.

"I suppose it depends on the reasoning." I drank a few sips of water, then the wine.

Pierre interjected after a heavy sip of wine. "If he lies to you, he may have his reasons." He ate some food but held attention with his hands and eyes. "If he lies to himself, no," Pierre repeated with a sobering seriousness and clarity. "No one, no matter how tempting it is, should lie to himself. This is categorical." His eyes stole our gaze for a frozen and careful moment.

Marco returned to the conversation. "I joke, but I do not lie."

"You are right. There is a difference." Pierre continued to eat. "It is good food." He raised the glass and glanced at Adri.

"Good Food!" Adri raised the glass and finished what was left. It was not a question or point of conversation, but a statement.

"I thought you did not like the spices?" I asked Pierre.

"I did not like Emir; the spices were not bad. However, now I miss Emir." Pierre's lips pursed themselves as his face bittered at itself. He dove into the food and let us alone, but mostly for himself.

"Absence makes the heart grow fonder." I tagged onto Pierre's thoughts in an effort to dull the edge of them.

"It does not make the mind any clearer." Bernardo sighed.

"It can make the mind clearer." I argued. "As long as we don't feed the past, and maybe just learn from it."

"Sentimentality keeps people in the past, but we always let go or hold on for a reason." Pierre thought about it nearly as he said it.

"Of course." Bernardo was anxious to get to the next point. "Sentimentality can give reason to things."

"Some things are better left without a reason, better yet, no explanation!" Pierre felt he made a good point. "They are easier to leave that way."

"Sometimes it is worth figuring out, even if only in *retrospecto*." Bernardo admitted.

"It can make you go mad. That is even if you do not lie to yourself." I said. "I think there is always a meaning, but sometimes it's worth more to just keep going and not think about it too hard."

"Do not lie to yourself." Pierre finally declared. "You always want to know don't you?"

"It is a sin of omission." I said, giving him just enough.

Marco finished chewing a piece of chicken or lamb. "I think of her more than I wish to, but less than I used to." Marco looked down and away and anywhere but at us. He brought the conversation back around one way or another.

It was quiet for a second, and the emotions grew thick but unspoken.

"Absence makes the heart grow quiet?" Bernardo said in a contradictory but cleverly contemplative manner.

"Hearts grow where they are supposed to, not where quotes say they go." Pierre had stiffened and turned stale but honest. It wasn't quite pleasant, yet still, honest.

"Who the hell knows anymore." I looked down the table at Adri's wife. I raised my glass, next looking over to Adri I did the same. "Damn good food and tasty wine! Thank you fine sir!" I congratulated them on their food and hospitality, yet I really meant the life they had created.

"Tasty! Yes! Thank you, my beautiful wife! Maryam!" Adri raised an empty glass, as the lamps in the room played off the ring of red at its base and bounced light out of the glass.

"At least there is one fond heart in the room." I grinned and ate to be full, as I had not been in some time.

We finished eating, and many of the men went right to sleep. A few rooms were up on the second floor. Most were on the ground floor. I was sleeping in a cottage the man owned on the other side of the road. The air smelled of flowers, fireplaces, dew, cigarettes, and windy, warm evenings.

Pierre and I walked back up the old handcrafted wooden stairs toward the top floor where we had eaten. The slanted roof crept in on me and imposed. I stepped across the old creaking floor to the table. Reaching for the wine bottle and a few pieces of meat that we could see, sucking its nectar for a mere moment, then chewing the meat. Taking the bottle with me; I traced back down on the rustic stairs and down to the gravel path that became a road crossing. Pierre carried the other in his hand.

We arrived at the cottage again and went inside. I pushed my left arm as support against the cool stone walls inlaid with mortar. We went down the steps through a red dutch door and out into the back. There were benches in the back and I sat down—Pierre beside me. We were silent and at ease.

"Do not think too hard mon ami." I said to Pierre, in a non-judgemental and relaxed but clear, precise manner.

"Je sais ça … 'I know this." Pierre let his tense and tight breath go. "I cannot stay here, yet I do not wish to return home. Paola is also dead."

"Why can you not return? For the second, I suppose there is not much you can do about the second." I leaned back into the folds of the bench and looked up into the many stars.

"I can, but I do not wish to." Pierre's voice split like a pine log, as he tried to push a sentence through.

"Why?"

"It is empty, there is nothing for me waiting." He broke. "Pas de parents, pas d'amour, pas de chez, rien. Vraiment rien."

"What happened to all your talk of home, and how it is like no other place?" I asked, "Nothing..."

"Home will always hold a special place in my heart, but that does not mean that the things that made it home are still there." He contemplated. "You can return to your special places, but the things that made them special are not guaranteed to be there."

"Then, they are not special anymore?"

"Ohhh, they are always special, in a different way." He became a little bit melancholic. "They are special because of what they were."

I sighed, knowing it to be true, "Then we must go to new places, meet new people, do new things, and pioneer again until we find something special once more."

"Some things stay special, at least I believe this... yet still I cannot stop my scribblings." He tossed the notebook onto the bench next to me. It was filled with paragraphs and pages and drawings.

"You think, but you create. This is a good thing. No, it's a great thing. It comes forth from you." I said to Pierre in comfort. "There are many, if not most who think but do not create. Then and only then is it a waste."

"I know, but this is what frightens me. Among other things." Pierre was distressed, and not in a simple way.

Not in the way that is tangible, no not that way. In the way that crawls about, and teaches you each and every emotion in the strongest way. This you cannot stop, but only ride alongside and learn from.

I rested my arm on the top of the bench so that it touched Pierre's shoulder. "You will leave here, and that I am sure of." I looked at him. "You will go home, but the home you have not seen yet." He did not belong here; he belonged in Paris or Madrid sculpting and painting, but that's not so.

Chapter VIII

We awoke, and all was quiet except the birds. The birds were awake much longer than I, and they would not stop their songs. However, I did not complain, they were pleasant and comforting. A dull yet ignorable enough headache came not long afterward. Pierre came into the room with a large ceramic pitcher of water and a tall clay cup.

"Bon matin, mon copain." He stepped across the cool tiled cottage floor onto a small handmade woven rug next to the end table of the bed. My body was shocked to have woken up in bed. It had been some time. He stopped in front of me, then he placed the cup on the table.

"Bon matin." I said. We spoke in French about the man from last evening as if he were not a man but a character, which in some ways he was. Beyond our simple conveyance of things. "Tell me of the many things you have done."

"What things have I done? Many ask me of what, and I would give you the honest answer." He sat on a petit three-legged stool in the high ceiling room.

The aged beams sat neatly on top of the cool plastered stone in a smoothed eggshell white hue "Tell me of Paris and the cafes and the cynical philosophers who point fingers at the dreaming artists."

"The peacetimes, before war and these modern tools of death. This oh this." He lifted his hands, and as if they were heavy he dropped them again. "I smoked far too many cigarettes and drank enough coffee to give a statue shaking hands." He laughed and settled into a hunch, with his head resting on his hand. Legs crossed on the short stool.

"How did that treat you?" I sat up and kicked my feet off the bed.

"Well I did a lot of notebooking, and I did a lot of writing, painting, talking." He spoke a little less jokingly and more factual.

"It was well, you had good fun, I suppose."

"I wandered down many alleys. I saw the stars in the sky above the monuments. You could not see them all, even if you were born there. There are stars everywhere, so perhaps that does not count."

I walked outside after finishing the glass of water in a single hasty gulp. Just that simple cup made things better. Seated on the same bench as last night, I breathed in the sun and the loving clouds that wisped across a cool orange sky. The grass mingled with the morning dew cooling and wetting my feet gently. It was comfortable and I looked off to the house we ate in last night. It was surrounded by tall narrow cypress trees and playful light grasses. The world was quiet, but only for a moment and things were simple. The sun was warm, the air cool, and I had slept in a warm bed.

"It is the simple things, n'est pas?" He walked out, standing a few feet behind the bench I was in.

I sat precariously on the edge of the seat on the bench and spoke in the rhythm of the cool morning. "Bread, cheese, and eggs." I looked back over to Pierre. "These are the best and simplest things in the early morning."

"Well let's stop talking about them and eat them."

Adri came and knocked on the door. "Come now! We have the juice and the eggs and the new bread." We heard him from the backyard and went back through the house to open the door for him.

"More water?" I asked, shook by his booming and welcoming voice in the morning.

"More water indeed!" We were in agreement.

We followed Adri out and back across the same road as the night before and went inside. It smelled like morning, with cooking meat and fresh bread. The fumes mingled through the air and created a melody. I followed the melody back and up the same stairs as yesterday. There sat poached eggs, bread, and many other delicious breakfast foods. I drank the other glass of water in haste and then poured another which I drank marginally slower. This was accompanied by another slightly smaller glass of juice. Both of which went down quite easily. It was some of the best breakfast food I'd had to date.

"It is best we begin to get a move on." Pierre folded his napkin and scooped the last piece of egg onto the corner of a toasted slice of bread.

Bernardo leaned over to me and said in a hush tone. "We don't need to put Adri and Maryam in danger."

"The sun is risen after all." Pierre looked over to the window and gestured at it with his hands while chewing the remainder of his food. The sun peeked through and cast onto the boarded flooring.

We all finished our food and stacked the plates. Bernardo and Marco put the forks and knives into the glasses at the end of the table. A few of us paid Adri what we could for his generous housing and feeding of us.

Chapter IX

A few days had passed and we were a good while from Adri and Maryam. I was waking up slowly but surely. The hood of the car was pulled back, and my feet were stretched out across the back seats where I slept. My feet went off the edge out and over the side of the car. The woolen blanket I had pulled over myself in my sleep was just now below my nose. My eyes squinted, and I looked up and out into the world. The sun was just beginning to rise.

The flowers were fragrant and gentle in their movement, and the storm was gradually rolling in. The clouds tumbled in over the sea between the orange ombre and compounded over themselves into a wave that collapsed and built upon itself. It was cool but not cold, and the ground was dry and rocky, with grasses and wildflowers splendidly filling the land. The clouds grew thick and full and turned from white to a deep gray, with the pure white only casting out as a frame on the edges. Sharp windy breezes cut the cool air with warmth, and each played off of one another, as the broken wind shuffled down across the meadows once more. The large boulders and edged rocks pushed up from the swaying earth like ancient monuments.

Pierre looked back over his shoulder behind the chair I laid in. The roses shook with the wind and all the cars were lined up off the side of the road in the dust and coarse dirt.

"Are you going to get up or what?" Pierre puffed his cigarette smoke into my face and smiled dearly. "We must pull the roof before the clouds push in."

"I've been dreaming too much." I pushed the wool away and pulled my legs in.

"Tell me of this when the waxed canvas is covering us, but for now, work with me, please." He placed the butt of the cigarette in his mouth and swung himself over the door, as he headed toward the back of the autocar.

I hastily rolled up the blanket and reached around behind me. Gripping the metal frame, I pulled the convertible top out of the car and it clicked. The clicking continued incrementally until the navy green waxed canvas slid across the jig and over my head. Pierre walked about the car on the outside, pressed the front into place, and made sure the whole piece was locked in.

"Now we will be dry, I can be sure of this." He smacked it one last time as his body pivoted on the door handle and he saddled back into the front driver's seat. He pressed his tongue on the butt of the cigarette to put it out. He flipped it out of the car with his thumb and forefinger and cranked the window up until it was closed. Then he cranked it a little more and looked intently at the seam between the window and the top of the autocar.

"About your damned dreams?" He said jokingly and softened his face as he asked.

"I thought you'd never ask."

"Said we would come back around to it."

"Well, that's just about it," I paused and looked at him as if there was nothing left to say. "I've been having many of them, and they keep showing me things."

"What do you see?"

"I see the things I think of, but the things I do not know I think off."

"This makes no sense."

"Once I see them then I know they have been there. As if I slapped myself in the face."

"Don't we slap ourselves. Slap us all?" Pierre pushed his straight black hair out of his face and looked at me quizzically. "The key is to get someone to slap you. Or kiss you, if you are into that as well." He joked. His face changed immediately. "At least you can see the slap, it is the subconscious after all."

"So you believe in all these things?"

"Believe in what things."

"Signs and symbols, those things which present themselves into our world." I caught my breath. "That which we do not fully understand with logic alone."

"The supernatural and the spiritual?"

"Yes, in one sense, among other things which present themselves."

"The coincidences and happenstances of the universe that are indeed not happenstances or coincidences."

"The things that beguile us in confusing enchantment, that is what I speak of." I attempted in an all too human way to clarify.

"I feel as though my reality is supernatural at times." Pierre opened his cigarette tin and held it, then squeezed it and put it away. "Some things just line up in the most illogical way, but it somehow seems to make perfect sense."

"There are ways to try explaining it, yet none can offer to encapsulate it."

"This I also find to be true."

After this, the rain began to drizzle patiently. It was hardening itself towards what might come soon. The other auto cars pulled the tops closed and all huddled inside as we were near no established building or dwelling place. The road became damp as it was dry for weeks before this. The clouds poised themselves above us, domineering as they clumped together and began weighing down. They were heavy and it began to rain even more until it was forced down upon us. The rain became dense and pushed into the earth.

We turned the car on and I crawled up into the front passenger seat next to Pierre who was driving. The car clicked and grunted then started running. We waited as each of the cars in front of us pulled forward onto the dirt and gravel trail. Pierre pressed gently on the gas then bolted forward when the car picked up on his action. The road was straight for a while and weaved curves around the monumental boulders that changed the path.

The rain was now aggressive and unyielding. The rain would've soaked you faster than a shower. Pierre's knuckles turned white while he clutched the steering wheel, the water slapped the windshield like buckets and he pressed his body back into the seat with his arms stiff and extended. The wind would appear to whip the rain up into the air and back down. All the while we were inside the thick and sweaty car. It was dense and felt foggy inside without looking the part.

As we drove in the wind it teased us. A sharp turn came up on the other side of a boulder and Pierre pulled tight on the wheel. It was fierce and instinctive, like a threatened cat. The car and all of its parts screamed anxiously in the tenuous strain of the turn. Time slowed and the car became uneasy. It pulled on the right side until it gave in and spilled over to sit precariously on its right side. The car was heavily rolling on its angle. Tossed in a shark cage. The car was pressed by the rain and the rush of the water and air overcame the side laying in the earth. We fell off the roadside and rolled away into the bushes.

Tossed onto our side, as a rubber ducky in a bathtub. The car went off tipping into the grasses interspersed with rocks. I could hear the outside of the autocar crunch and bend. It was slapped against the earth by her. Shifting into place as each dent and crush folded in on itself. I could hear each damage done, but could not see from the inside. The right window shattered to my side as the pieces meshed with the mud that seeped in from the graveled and rocky grasses.

I pulled myself out of my seat and looked over to Pierre. He was in a daze. I pulled him out of his own seat and drew him close to me. Climbing into the back seat I took him with me. The car was at its side and so we were not safe, but there was nowhere else to go as far as we were concerned. Anywhere else would be deep into the heavy rainstorm and that guaranteed our danger. In the back seat I attempted to rest, yet did not sleep much that night, and once Pierre had woken back up he did not either.

Chapter X

On the next morning the air was thick and dewy and all the car was damned. Our eyes and head were still shaken and ached from the crash, yet we were glad that neither of us were seriously injured to any degree. We climbed out and stepped into the cracking and slushing of damp mud and onto the trail. It was wet and everything around was soaked or in a puddle. The both of us thought we were lost for good. However, one of the cars had turned around and picked us up. We squeezed in among those within the car already. We went along the road heading close to the coast but among the trees. Now, not far from Rize.

Charles grinned and punched Pierre in the shoulder. "I suppose I'm glad we came back for you." He winked

"I think I know what I'll do when *we* lose *you*." Pierre smiled and pushed his hair back.

The car in front of us was fast and we attempted to follow.

"We are heading north, are you ready to follow?" Charles asked with a degree of silly suspicion.

"Yes, we are on our way." Pierre was excited and eager to respond. "No crashing this time."

The sky was cloudy and there was a constant breeze that fought through the air for its life. All of the people in the car were silent and not ready to talk or answer any questions. Pierre opened his cigarette tin and sighed. It was dented and the cigarettes inside were bent and crumpled. The tobacco was loose in the tin and broke open throughout his pocket. He was peeved. He took the large parts that were still wrapped and sent them to his mouth; as he smoked on them he pinched the tips to his mouth, yet burnt his fingers nonetheless.

"Are you going to smoke all of that?" I leaned closer to him and my feet shook, tipping back and forth.

"Yes, or at least as much as possible. It is all broken, and it will not stay good." Pierre held a second match up to the bits and pieces of the cigarette. Pierre smiled half-heartedly at what I had said, as well as what he imagined he might look like doing what he was doing.

"You need to talk?" I gestured up to the sky and leaned in with my arm around his shoulder.

"Look copain, I know all too well that this is pathetique to watch." Pierre laughed at himself with the painful irony of self-awareness.

He threw down each increment as late as he could. After each toss he stepped on them and evened them down into the ground of the car. Once he was finished with his turn burning all the pathetic ends Pierre cracked open the car door while we moved and ushered the ashes out with the sole of his boot. They fell and disappeared into the muddy dirt trail.

The air was temperate, just about perfect. Probably no higher than an average spring day. You could feel almost nothing but the breeze as it filtered through your skin. There was a silence in the air, not a demanded one, but one that felt deserved for the beauty of the day. We all leaned back into the chair and just breathed so that we might be nearer to something we could call peace. Moving north in the summer, we felt compelled to force ourselves forward to the coastline. It was close and I could now see the rocks and the dunes as they passed by us in the warming of spring and summer.

We could not stay too close to the shore too long as the troops would likely be there as well but it was nice.

Bernardo pointed off past the road and over the dune, and he slapped me in the arm. "Do you see this? Look Gerardo, out there in a car."

I squinted and saw just the very top of the car and the heads pointing out, but the rest of the frame was blocked by the rolling waves of land. "Are they allies?"

"I do not know." They went out of view, but were approaching us and we could hear the car speed up along with the wind.

Charles had heard us and eavesdropped for a moment. "Prepare your weapons lads, but do not aim." He had shifted tone and tense in his voice. "Keep them steady on your lap."

Pierre anxiously pulled his handgun out of the holster and laid it on his thigh. His hand shook within the grip, and I could not tell whether it was the cigarette or the gun that was doing the shaking. Possibly both.

The car turned the corner as soon as we turned ours and the man in the passenger's seat put his arm up and swung it in a circle then pointed to the side of the road. He shouted something which was not Turkish and then the car slowed down and pulled onto the grass from the rough gravel.

Charles looked back and slowed the car down to the side of the road as well. Their car and ours were side by side but facing opposite directions as the drivers met one another. Charles looked at the man across from him and waited one long moment while staring at him intensely. He said some formal greeting to the man in an indiscernible tongue then asked him a question. Charles looked back at us and grinned with a face that captured relief and simultaneous hesitation.

"Russians, they are Russians lads." He breathed out, resting his hand with a sigh on the passenger's seat next to Pierre and gripped the leather with satisfaction.

"What do they have to tell us?" Pierre asked Charles, waiting for a response.

The man across from us in the Russian car seated in the driver's spot interjected and spoke in quite palatable English. "I am Dmitri, and you are the group I have been told of. This is true?"

Charles removed his attention from us and returned. "Hello Dmitri, I am Charles. We come from the west, from Devrek and we are headed to the border."

"This is what I am told as well." Dmitri's hands waved in the air as he was explaining to us. "You should stay sharp, Englishman. There are lots of people who have gone missing out here. Not the safest."

"I will make note of this lad." His head bent forward and acknowledged his words as he focused. "What is your business here?"

"Security. You should not ask so many questions, old man." He gave a hollow dead stare at us.

"Watch this! Get a move on." Pierre lifted his gun from his lap and ... I gripped his wrist.

"We don't need any theatrics." I loosened and he became quiet again.

Dmitri mumbled something in Russian.

"Oke, we are leaving now, and we shall see you at the crossing?"

Charles nodded and turned the car back on with a vigor. "We shall see you soon, yes?"

"Depends on your skill, Sir." Dmitiri gave a dirty smile and winked at Charles then looked back at the rest of us, "As well as your luck."

Charles glared at Dmitri then eased his gaze at him and looked away. Finally, he revved the engine and looked forward, indicating his direction to Dmitiri. Dmitri waved us onward upon the trail. We left first and as we took off his car went the opposite direction while watching us slowly and carefully.

"To Russia now, I should suppose." Charles said as the wind picked up and so did the car.

The wind was warm but the settled air was cool. We saw off high in the distance the crags and bluffs along the oceanic shore that rose above the dunes of grass and led deep into the evergreens and the plateau above. I saw the deer running through the grasses until they ascended into the high hills. Houses in the distance daubed with clay. The orange and brown tiles that sat atop the house settled upon the roof. It was a small town and I did not know the name of it but I could still imagine it now. We rode closer and saw the discomfort and the hesitation as we drew nearer to the border. All were on edge and we could not see the motion of the horizon as it faded in our face. We only saw the edged cliffs and overhanging trees that funneled us closer to the sea. We were the ones who should surpass and prevail.

I saw Pierre as he danced an orange around in his hand and I could see the dimples in it as it rolled and pivoted along each of his fingers. He took a small canvas bag out that the orange was in and he rubbed it until the orange was shiny and clean. He grabbed his knapsack and pulled out a knife and sliced the orange in half from where the stem met the orange to the bottom. Pierre lifted up one half and bit into it.

"Are you going to eat the whole orange?" I looked down at the half that was still seated in his lap atop the canvas that he had used to clean it.

"Not if you want it." Pierre smiled and lifted it up gesturing toward me until I opened my hand and I took it from him. He bit into it once more, and chewed the peel and pith along with the meat's juicy fruit.

We approached a town and once again it was empty, sitting close to the Black Sea. We maneuvered down the slopes and merged into a dell hidden gracefully between the grasses and dunes of the coastline and the woodlands sloping incline of hills and highlands. As we entered we could see the old houses made of the very same kind of rock they rested precariously on. Some are higher than others. We drove down the main dirt and gravel street and on either side the town broke down into small narrow alleys entangled between one another. We stopped the car and a slightly salty damp sea air ran through the town. The pines and other trees bent with the echo of the winds.

We searched for a place to house ourselves. I walked and followed the street toward a minaret that sat high above the rest of the village. The town itself was plain but the mosque was ornate. Pierre came up behind me and we walked up to it together. There was a black metal gate that went high above our heads and encircled the mosque. To the right of the light blue wooden painted door was the grand minaret with a crescent which matched that which was also atop the dome. The mosque had large arching doors with mimicking arches on either side as windows. The window was made of empty pentagons and triangles filled with glass of varying colors. Above the rounded top the wooden doors were alternating keystones of beige and burgundy and the same was laid around each of the window frames.

I could hear the seagulls yell as they rode the misty cool wind above the mosque and the sea. It was not raining but the air had a thin mist dwelling within it, not so much as to make one wet but to moisten the face as one pushed through it with their walk. We pushed on the gate and it creaked open, then swung away all the way around to hit the fence it was hinged on. We walked on the tiles and up the steps onto the smoothed clay that made the floor in front of the door. I raised my hand up to knock on the chipped blue paint, yet before I could, the door opened. A tall and skinny man who appeared as though he had not eaten opened the door and stared at us blankly.

"Asalamu Alaykum," I said, somehow he managed to look even more confused. He stared at me with bewilderment. The man put his finger up as if to motion *one moment* and looked away behind him.

A short bearded man in a long gown grabbed the door and motioned the other man away. He opened the door further and gazed up at the both of us. "Wa Alaikum Salem! I am Rabi and I run the mosque, but I should like to know, who are the both of you?"

"I am Gerard and here is Pierre. We came from Constantinople and we are headed to Russia."

He squinted his eyes which were deepened by his thick eyebrows. "Russians?"

"No, we are headed there, and we want to leave. It is getting dark out and I thought it wise to stop for the night."

"Come in, you sleep here, but first take off your shoes." He pointed down at our shoes and swung his hand up like a paddle. "Is this all of you?"

"No, there are more." Pierre admitted hesitantly.

"Ok, more, bring them all to sleep here tonight. I insist."

"Understood." I said.

Pierre walked off and went to get the others as I knelt down to untie my boots. The boots were muddy and damp and had scratches and abrasions. They had seen better days, but for my only shoes that I had been wearing for weeks, they stood up pretty well.

I untied them, alternating the knees I leaned on as I pulled each off.

Both times a small amount of water spilt out when I turned each one upside down. The wool socks I wore were wet and reeked of hiking and spoiled dirt, that is if dirt can spoil. The inside of the mosque was more decorated than one might expect of a rural seaside town and I was impressed. I saw the tiles on the ceiling and the same windows from the inside. The tall blue pillars were covered in white ceramic painted with ornate blue and green designs. It was cool inside and the dome had calligraphy written from top to bottom in rings.

"The town is abandoned, why are you still here sir?" I asked while scanning up and down the detailed interior of the mosque.

His head swung back and we made eye contact at the same time. "I must stay, it is what one must do."

"There is no service to perform if the village is empty."

"No service?" He said as if I clearly did not understand. Which I did not. "There is always service to be done as long as Allah is present." He paused then nearly chuckled to himself only to look me right in my eyes. "Young man, He is always present." His underbite moved his spindling beard up and down as he nodded his head and closed his mouth.

"There is no one here, and you do not know if they will ever return." I slowed my walking as he looked back, hands folded and seemingly always contemplative.

"My great-grandfather built this mosque. He might as well have built the town. If I am to leave I can be sure not a soul will return. However, If I stay, the people will have someone to return to." He smiled an innocent smile. "It is not the building that makes something holy, it is the love of those who are within it." He put his hand up as if to touch the walls of the cavernous interior, yet it simply met with the air as he stepped across the intricate stone floor.

"Well I hope for them to return one day, and sooner rather than later." I followed him to a door in the back of the mosque.

"Inshallah son, Inshallah." He turned the knob carefully on the door and opened it for me to go first. "Are you a man of faith Ger'ard?"

I sighed and walked through the door. "Thank you, and I try to be. I practiced when I was back in the United States. I don't know if it was for comfort or true belief. Although I am happy for those who believe in something."

"Have you tried asking?" He followed me in and closed the door gently.

"Asking what?" I wondered out loud.

"Asking which one of the two it is." He started as I sat down in a small wooden chair and him on a stool.

"And who am I to ask?" I retorted with a subtle undercurrent of silliness at the question.

"Allah. You may be surprised. Sometimes he has an answer for you, and you just have to be willing to ask."

"I'll ask him." I said

"No you won't. I know that kind response. Heard it a thousand times young man." He grinned as if to pierce me with wise innocence.

"I will." Him calling me out was ironically needed for me to steady my response enough to actually mean it when I said it.

"Hahaha, now I believe you, at least give it a chance." He put a kettle on top of a metal rod and hook that hung atop the dying embers of the fireplace. "Tea?"

"It would be my pleasure." I titled my head down and forward, and he grabbed two small glass cups.

The tall skinny man came through the door and stirred a pot that was sitting next to the coals of the fireplace.

"This is Ahmet and he does not speak your tongue, but he is a very good cook and a gracious man." The soup stirred flagrantly with the sauce slapping up and back onto the soup with his vigorous stirring, as Rabi licked his aged and wrinkled lips which seemed to curve inward. "Where are your friends? They must be hungry."

Pierre pushed the door open and peeked his head in. "Oh yes, there you are, my favorite American." He switched his gaze to Rabi. "I have our company!"

"Good! Bismillah, and be prepared to eat." He put his hands on his knees and stood up giving a large exhale. He walked out the door to meet the group and raised his hand as high as an old man could to wave at them. "Make yourself comfortable and please remove your shoes, this is all I ask."

For most of the men it was their first time inside a mosque, and still for others the first time they had seen an Imam. They tossed open their bed rolls and unfolded blankets, lining them up on the fine floor. Marco flicked a cigarette into his mouth and grabbed a matchbook from his pocket, ripping one of the matches from the paper and then preparing to light it. Just as he was about to light it Bernardo snatched it from his mouth and as if a mother talking to a child who had made an error, aggressively whispered something in Italian to him. Marco reached for it sheepishly, but before he could Bernardo pulled his hand back.

Bernardo stared at him, brows furrowed. "Would you smoke during mass?"

"They smoke incense during the mass." Marco complained and half heartedly attempted to explain it away. "Is like incense, you know?"

"Just don't smoke it, capisce." He threw the cigarette onto Marco's lap and laid down into his bedroll. "Go outside, we are in their house, and I don't make my own rules in other people's places."

"Sounds like you are the one making up rules now, eh." Marco opened the tin and put it back inside with the pack of matches, and a defeated look remained on his face.

He eventually got up and walked outside to smoke, and Pierre went with him. I dropped my backpack on the ground of the main room of the mosque with the others and unrolled my sleeping bag, then I sat on top of it and opened my notebook.

I wrote for a few pages, then scribbled for many more. Then I got up and walked back into the room where the fireplace was. Rabi was just pulling the kettle off the hook as it whistled loudly. The sound of the boiling water took over as it was removed from heat. He stood up and shuffled as an old man does to the kitchen counter and grabbed a small clay jar with a petite lid on it. He reached in with his hands and sprinkled a little bit of loose tea in both glasses then poured the water in. The tea swirled up from the bottom to float as the water rushed in, yet after it had been steeped the leaves sank to settle on the bottom of the cup. This signaled they were ready to be drunk.

Turning around slowly from the counter Rabi leaned over as he handed me one of the cups and sat down again. "You will eat with us, yes?"

"Yes I will." I sipped the tea, it was aromatic, piny, smooth, and a touch bitter. It was exemplary of Anatolia, for it tasted as Anatolia's high foothills felt.

The younger skinny man, Ahmet, came back into the room we were in, which was a building separate from the mosque but connected via one short hallway with a few steps. It was a low ceiling with wooden beams on the ceiling and walls, and a single small window for a single small room. Ahmet leaned down as the coals slowly died and pulled the lid off, and a plume of steam arose. It filled the room and my nose. Charles walked in.

"Good lord chap, what are they cooking in here, it smells divine indeed." Charles wafted the room up and into his nose.

First, smoked paprika that was fresh and robust, followed by herbs, sage, rosemary, thyme, all perfectly absorbed and mingled within the stew. The body of the stew being lentils and kashi or buckwheat as some call it. He walked down the few steps further into the room and his belly lunged forward as he stretched and leaned backwards in satisfaction. The Imam, Rabi looked over to the both of us and began speaking.

"We will eat soon, as of now. Yes?" Rabi stirred the pot with a spoon and looked up to Ahmet pointing with his crooked tawny pointer finger to the cabinet with bowls in it above the counter top. They doled out the bowls and spoons and all ate well.

"This is very good, I am quite the fan." Pierre ate fast and enjoyed it.

"I thought you did not like the spices." I asked rhetorically expecting some valid rationalization.

"Ok so maybe I am hungry, maybe I was not an hour ago?" He dug in with the spoon. "Or maybe I have changed my opinion. So what if one changes their opinion." He said slightly defensive but mostly honest.

"One has every right to change their opinion. My life experiences are always happening." I responded.

"Well our experiences decide us, and change us non?"

"Our experiences change us, yes, but we also choose how to react to them; we are not simply clay molded by them. Besides, when you put clay in an oven it is stiff and uncompromising." I paused to eat my soup. "That is no way to be."

"Our experiences will change us invariably my friend." He put his hand out palm up as if to accentuate his point.

"We often have the power to decide to which degree, and in what ways. However, that is a question of will power."

"Not always."

"Not always what?"

"If I lose my hand I do not decide how much of it is lost." He finished chewing then swallowed to let me speak.

"You decide what you will do with your other hand."

"You still have a missing hand."

I conceded one point. "Yes, you still only have one hand. One to slap you with." We smiled at one another, and finished eating before going to sleep.

Chapter XI

It was an early morning not only for us but the earth. I could hear the seagulls and the birds outside the mosque. They made their many sounds, the sun rose early that day, sweeping away the mist and dew of yesterday with the broom of the wind. It was warm and tidy out as the rain was washed and evaporated away to the shining embrace of the sun.

I was one of the first to wake up and I went outside. The early spring sun had risen. Its warm embrace was akin to that of a loved one and it showed you the love of one who had not forgotten you when others did. It was kind and endearing, and the sun hugged every part of you that faced it, and where it did not reach you felt warm. When you sat on the rocky outcrops of the Black Sea, the hug of the shores came upon you and you were immediately transformed and understood by its love and warming power, yet great might. For what is love if not mighty, not in its taking, but in its giving?

I sat on the steps of the mosque and smoked one single cigarette that had been offered to me and I had felt bad about it. The mosque was beautiful on the outside and demanded respect. As the sun rose it gently expressed itself upon the graceful figure of the mosque and mingled its bright grace with the exquisite beauty of the mosque. We packed up and began to load our vehicles. I walked up to Rabi outside the door of the mosque.

"Thank you for your gracious hospitality Rabi. You are a

generous man."

"Thank you for your presence. You are a kind one." He laughed in such a way that made you smile.

"Thank you, but.. we must go on, it would endanger the few locals you have if we rest longer." I adjusted my backpack and knapsack on my shoulder.

His short and old figure shifted around and then looked up to me with the eyes of a grandfather. "This village is near empty, but the hills are not." He looked both ways as if to pretend he saw something. "Be careful, you and your men."

"We will do our best."

"I know you will. May Allah guide you safely."

"I pray he will guide us." I said in a manner of conversation, but not true prayer.

"I *pray*, he will." Rabi leaned closer to me and his hands rested in front of one another near his stomach. "Allah will guide us when we are ready to ask him."

"Fair, nobody likes unsolicited advice." Pierre said.

After some time the cars started up again and we were getting ready to leave.

They would brew espressos and they would invigorate us so as to move along and plow forward. The caffeine would penetrate my brain.

Bernardo made an espresso for Rabi and held a small cup for him. "This will be good for you, yea."

Rabi took the cup and sipped then gagged and swallowed eventually. "Ohhh, now that! It is strong, I will climb the walls, yes."

Rabi had not enjoyed the espresso, yet he was too kind to admit. He would have been much happier with a simple black or green tea in his cup with its more subtle flavor. The coffee felt bitter and harsh in relation to his regular taste buds. It was strong and robust. It was also time for us to leave. The men rolled up their supplies and stuffed their backpacks up once more. It was to be a warmer day but not a hot one. The wind outside was stagnate and only occasionally waxed or waned. We had to get a move on and there was only so much time before we would be able to safely leave undetected.

I stuffed my backpack and clasped my bed roll into it then walked out of the large arching blue door. "Thank you for your generosity Rabi, I am grateful for you and Ahmet." I gave the proper measures for a respectable and amicable farewell.

"Thank you for your time." He stood right behind the door of the mosque and smiled at no one in particular but let it float into the crowd of us as we left. He then focused on me. "Be sure to ask him, I don't know what he has to say. But it might be important." He sounded like he was letting me in on a little secret.

"I'll keep an ear open."

"Sometimes he whispers and sometimes he yells." His words bounced around inside my head.

"Sometimes he slaps you." I retorted

"That too." We hugged and he patted me on the shoulder only to hold me for a moment longer than I expected, then we said goodbye. Into the hills behind the trees it is steep up on the right but on the left it is steep down.

The air was tense and we could feel it.

The men woke up on time and the cars ran at about average pace. It was all too well orchestrated and shewn to the nature of the plants which drew the men's most energetic self forward through the coffee of the Italian men and the daily tea provided by Rabi.

I tossed my bag into the car like all the rest and sat down. Maggiore had given quick orders and their car took off in front of us and we followed. We were not too far from the border by car, but we had to go back into the hills. It was thought to be safer this way. Charles was driving and he revved the engine. It clicked a few times but eventually turned on. We took off. The wheels turned and we sped forward.

The hill was soggy from days of rain. The dew once more lifted away by the rising sun, yet it still remained moist all the same with its damp clay grip that stuck to everything like unkneaded dough. The enduring sludge sloped down into the valley and coastline until it picked back up and led deep into the foothills once more. Men fought for those foothills and the land revealed itself to us. It had passed through many hands, and was laid claim to by many people. Each and every one claimed it for themselves. Every rock that was sat behind. Every stone that blocked the brutal embrace of each and every bullet was a smart one and it told us the way to go above all else.

The hills were steep and unforgiving as long as the mountains were true. I did not know the fight that the mountains gave, or had seen. The hills closed in and the trees loomed over us as they were taller and thicker than the group of us. The gravel mixed within the road gave a grip to our car as the axel strained to pull up the aggressive and steepened hill. You cannot outrun the necessary dwelling of fate in so much as you can overcome the urge to breathe. I could see into the far yonder hills which had become engrossed in their own presence, as they decided where the sunlight rested and how the clouds would gather around and above them.

The sun was peeking, its orange warmth embraced intermittently throughout the countryside as it peaked throughout the trees. Higher up, the air rose and warmed, but the warmth only offered to loosen the mud and gravel from the roadside and above. The forest was alive and you could hear all the animals, yet only some could be seen. Soon we had reached a plateau on the mountainside and the cars slowed, but did not stop. Those in the back carefully monitored the woods and kept eyes peeled as if they attempted to look around the trees and through each bush. We drove on the flat and remained on high. However the side that ran off trail and down the side of the ridge was steep, and the bushes, rocks, and trees helped to make it not seem so. They crowded the heavy and daunting slope that lay to our left. A deer crossed in between Maggiore's car in the front and ours and some of the men preparedly drew their arms only for it to scaredly pass through and back down into the woods.

"Is it the destination or the journey?" I asked generally.

Bernardo looked over to me and began to explain. "We have a saying in Italian.."

"We have that saying as well." I nodded and glanced over to make eye contact. "I say the journey, yet the destination is rewarding all the same."

"We do not enjoy all our journeys, some are grueling, painful even, yes?" His hands went up and down as his intonation changed.

I noted his thoughts and offered a response as I saw fitting. "Yes, fair. But I should say, even if we do not enjoy the journey it is insightful. I would argue the most enlightening experiences are some of the most difficult to undertake. Physical *or* otherwise."

"Otherwise. You speak of the mind and spirit." Bernardo agreed to an extent but did not offer any rebuttal or alteration to my point.

"If life were full of destinations I think I'd be pleased, but I wouldn't have learned much, or anything for that matter." I built on my point a little. "A life full of destinations is a meal made up of only dessert."

"It tastes good, but does little good for you." Bernardo agreed.

Pierre interjected, "A life of destinations is a life of satisfaction."

Bernardo began to uphold my point in response to Pierre. "Is unearned satisfaction, true satisfaction?" He furrowed his brows and pierced Pierre with more intent than he normally spoke. He paused then concluded. "Noo."

"Many things in life are unearned mon ami, but we still enjoy them." Pierre lit another wrinkled cigarette. "Many things are rightfully earned, yet those who deserve them seldom get to enjoy them."

"True" I said in contemplation. "Should we speak of this now?"

"Non, it is too sour a subject. We should forge onward." Pierre dragged on the cigarette, and it ashed and drained quicker than usual.

The clouds quickly closed in and they grew over the trees. The sky that was blue and gentle as it carried the sun across the sky was surely enveloped. The heavy weighing clouds gathered and became white then gray. They were not rain clouds and we did not yet fear the rain, but as was with the Black Sea you could never really tell what weather was to come next. It shifted slowly but surely mingling around each cloud until the plumes were round and swirled around one another.

The dense clouds had killed the breeze that traveled up and down through the forest. The wind settled and felt stale. The woods grew quiet. The firs and pines rested and did not sway as they had a little time earlier. The birds were silent and their music was not to be heard. Neither could we hear the frolicking and rustling of squirrels and deer. The road ahead met a gentle but new decline and Maggiore's car weighed down on the brakes to a roll.

The autocar pulled forward and we followed some meters behind. It seemed that, for a mere moment, Maggiore's car had slowed and in my mind nearly stopped. The tires became eerily slow, then a second of pure nothing. The front of the car flew violently forward into the air as we could see the back wheels kick up and jump. From our own view the back tires spun uncontrollably up in the air while the front wheels followed suit. The axels bounced left and right, soon the entire car was suspended flying through the air. I saw one man fall out of the car as it was held in space and he landed face first into the tread mud and grimy pebbles. As soon as he landed he would not move.

The car had landed finally on its head bursting at once into aggressive oily flames whose dense black smoke filled the air contrasting with the dull gray sky. The car jostled and settled topdown into the ground as the flames shook and grew around it. The fire shuffled off as it burned with a glowing red aura. Men quickly came out of the bushes on the right and crouched on the rocky overhang above the road. From the boulders on high they shot down at us. One of the Italians in the burning red car crawled out through the grime, yet the bullets had pierced him before he could attempt to stand up. They shot at him and the man who had first landed lay motionless atop the broken earth. They then focused their attention shooting at us and fired without reservation.

"Landmine!" Charles' voice boomed as he clutched the wheel and sped up.

They fired at us, one of the bullets had hit the back tires. Charles turned left off the road and away from the men who were firing. The car shook violently as we veered away. It felt as if it might fall apart, but did not. It split the bushes and broke through the smaller trees and saplings. Grinding and catching debris as it did so. I grabbed the bottom of my seat with one hand as we crashed down through the mountain slopes. The other hand pushed against the chair in front of me so as to keep me still in the car. The car kept rolling and simply would not stop. We eventually ran into a large tree trunk whose branches loomed over the car. Upon impact the car collapsed and the front crinkled to fold in on itself. The bent and mangled metal sat there with smoked branches atop it.

The clouds rolled swiftly; there were no blue skies remaining, all gray. I saw Charles' head jerk forward. He hit the wheel with his face. He was bleeding red across his whole face. Bernardo reached over to him, cradling the back of his head. Charles looked over. Charles feebly lifted his hand up to his mouth, and then ran his fingers up his face.

The blood came off onto his fingers and into his palm. "Oy, that is quite the nosebleed lad." Charles pulled his hand away and stared at it a moment. His red face mustered a slanted half-hearted grimace as the dark red trailed down his beard.

Bernardo looked at Charles then his hands. His expression contorted with shame, disappointment, and that feeling so uncomfortable that you cannot help but give a pained look which did little to balance the emotion. "That's not a nosebleed signore Charles."

I leaned up and looked at Charles. He was not present, at least not entirely nor consistently. I put my hand on his shoulder. "Stay here, you're safe, you're okay."

"Non, we are not safe, and no we do not have any time!" Pierre said, flustered and in an angry stir. "We must move it."

"We!" Bernardo shouted, staring at Pierre's life, with the intensity of a wolf.

"We." I said, simmering down the heat of Bernardos stiff yet boiling words. Charles' forehead was gashed open and he was bleeding profusely. It was not his nose. "Still we must get a move on nonetheless." I opened the door.

Pierre with a reclaimed sense of what could be considered

remotely calm in a situation such as this reiterated. "The men are on their way down the mountain, they'll be here any minute."

"And Maggiore is certain to be dead." Bernardo focused and took a cloth roll out of his pack wrapping it around Charles' head.

Charles was in a daze and we could hear the gun fire, as chambers slammed back and forth it echoed through the rocky ledges and wooded slopes.

"We must hasten, for Pierre is of reason." Charles' eyes flickered and he reached for the door handle on the car with little definitive skill.

Bernardo and I lifted him up and shouldered him carrying him down the hillside as the gunfire became louder, and consequently closer. The crunch of the leaves and twigs below our boots would sometimes give grip and other times slow us, or yet still near us to slipping. We carved our own footpath and headed down the mountain. The gunfire was deafening and we sped ourselves up as much as we could with an immobile passenger. Pierre was behind us and carried our bags as we propped Charles up. The car was ruined and there was no sure way of getting anywhere except on foot.

Forthward we moved with a fast pace that could not be considered a sprint. We went through the narrow glens that sloped, and held soft beds of leaves and needles at the base of our heels. I think a few men hiked into the woods after us. It was long after I saw the last bullet fly by that I still heard only the sound of the gun firing and its chamber slamming back. We hiked for some time and eventually the guns sounded like fireworks and the air smoothed out.

It was dutiful to carry Charles down the hill, and heavy. We stumbled and twisted away under the weight, and while treading the uneven and downward facing ground that demanded so much of us. However, Bernardo and I did not fall and refused above all else to drop him. We walked down the hill further and further. It was through the fragrant trees and decomposing brown leaves that began to mingle as a scent somewhere between leaf and dirt. The ground had remained for the most part wet, and the sun slowly began to dull as the day passed us by. We traveled on foot until it was dark, and then walked further past sundown.

Once we had gone far enough so as not to be near the search of the Ottomans we stopped and settled. Our camp, if one could call it that, was beside a beautiful little stream that bubbled and danced around the small stones. The stones in turn were hugged by the pebbles.

Most things were lost, left behind, or burnt to a crisp alongside Maggiore and his men. I did not know where Marco was or any of the others, and I did not know if I would see them. When a man is chased by a wild animal he does not think of his next meal, he can only see what is in front of him, until it troubles him no longer. When it troubles him no longer, then he, like all men must find something else to trouble him. It may sound raw and grotesque, but at this moment it was not something I could be terribly troubled with what was behind me, there was enough trouble in front of me. For when it rains we say we need sun, when it is sunny we wish for rain.

I had started a small fire, one that was large enough to emanate warmth but not so much that one could see it through the woods and occasional clearings. The roads were safe no longer and neither were we. No tent, and no building desolate and abandoned by the dead or displaced to sleep inside. So as those who ran from wild beasts once did, we sat outside. The bedrolls spread out in a circle around the fire, and backpacks, or knapsacks as pillows.

I admit sleeping outside is raw and I felt exposed and unsafe in the highlands. It had felt primal and basic, as if nothing else mattered but that present moment. This is the appeal, if one could be bothered to find one in such a thing. However, the first point remains. I had not merely felt, but been primarily reminded that I am within a food chain, one that has existed forever and will continue to do so. The large mountains of snow, the cliffs of stone, the wolves, snakes, and bears that can maim or kill any man without a gun. One that I and all others have desperately attempted to remove ourselves from in an effort to consider ourselves distinguished and powerful. Though this effort only creates another food chain, and one where man is a cannibal, one where man eats man. Not his flesh, but his strength, ambition, money, and freedom.

There were other things on my mind that night. The future was unsure and now we were reduced to our most basic and simple selves. No car, and no one else, if one were to die here, it would not only be his body that had perished. I heard the animals in the distance and was reminded of this. Their sounds were interspersed with the sound of the closer insects and other creatures, as well as, of course, those hauntingly ambiguous sounds that one was in no way sure of. This may have been what our ancestors called spirits, monsters, and gods. I was on watch that night, although it was not hard at all to stay awake. I think it would have taken me more effort to try to sleep.

Chapter XII

It was a deep night now, and the moon gave its somber attempt to shine on us. It was thwarted by the branches and high leaves. I was on the night watch and as Bernardo and Pierre slept, I sat up cross-legged in my sleeping bag leaning up against the cold hard rock. There was no pillow but my back was straight and I looked over to Charles.

I doubted Charles could sleep, his pain and his wounds could not allow something so gracious. He lay, head up so as not to rush blood to his head, and stared off. His eyes locked as he looked high up into the trees, but he was not looking at the trees. Charles looked past the trees, blinking only occasionally and seldom turning his eyes or head anywhere else.

Debilitated and drained of all energy he remained, propped up, and the blood did not rush to his bandaged head. One of his eyes was bloodshot and the blood from his head had dried into the cloth. To remove the cloth would mean to open the wound, and to open the wound would bring the uncertainty of being able to close it. The cloth was now crisp and the dried blood almost a deep burgundy or brown. It collected on the now beige and yellow white fabric that protected his strained and torn face.

"I am not in good condition, this much I know." Charles gave me a shit-eating grin as he slowly turned his head to me. It seemed to have taken a good bit of strength.

I responded, surprised at his attempt at conversation and

tried to entertain. "You went into the steering wheel when the car crashed. Mostly your head, but we carried you. I think you might manage."

"Hahaha, no chap, you would manage." He seemed to laugh at my lack of comprehension and inability to relate. It was slight mockery but mostly reflective on his part. "You are young my lad, and the young can endure most things. You can take a dent or two when you are young. It is youth that shapes us, and it is harder to destroy something that is on its way to being made. You're sick, sleep it off. You cut your finger, wrap it up. The old have no such luxury."

"You are quite tough for an old man. You have been through worse, as you have said so yourself." I restated, in an attempt to remind a man of his own creed.

"Ahh, yes chap. I've been through worse indeed, much worse in fact. I was young then as well. When I was more akin to you. My flesh was tight and my muscles firm. My beard was brown and not yet a beard, but settling in." He reminisced at his own words as they bounced throughout his mind.

"You doubt yourself, why? It does no good to doubt yourself." I responded while switching my gaze between the pained face of an aging man and the fire. The latter was easier to watch.

"I do not doubt myself, I doubt who I am now. I am realistic. When I was a young chap, I thought I'd simply get old. Gray hair, a deeper gravel voice, and the quaint little cane to go with it. I would tip my hat to those along the street and people might go on to hold the door open. I did not think of the muscles aching, the forgetfulness, and the memories that have left me so long ago I do not even know I have forgotten them." Charles conjured up those memories which still rested with him.

They did not rest easy and seemed to ask of him, yet I could not see those memories. Like all memories only those who have lived them can see them. Those invisible but all too real moments, captured forever in the mind. This makes them special, but they like all things that must be lost. Perhaps that makes them more special? All life is lived through our own eyes, and even when we know someone well. When we think we know all about them, we do not. For their memories are endless as ours.

I returned to a drifting Charles, his eyes fluttered, not as if he were tired. It was as if he had ceded himself in the slightest. As if he had just barely for a moment ceded himself to that eternity that absorbs and devours all.

"Charles!" I lifted my voice and the determination of it. "Is it the war that troubles you so? Is it the things you have done? The things you had not done?"

He looked at me as if I knew nothing, and he was not wrong, yet I suppose acknowledging that proves I know one thing. "Oh lad, son it is not what I did in war, it is the war. War pulls men away from who they are and turns them into what others want them to be."

"Do not say that. You are an honorable man who has done honorable things. You served your country when needed and have been around the globe." I tried to comfort the man, but one cannot change the mind of those who are decided. "Besides, think of your wife, your children. Your armchair."

"Yes, yes, I miss my armchair dearly." Charles was not saying something and he breathed deeply, coughing and gagging slightly until he could speak to me. "Very good indeed."

"You told me you had missed them. Why do you refuse to speak of them now? If war is untrue, then surely they must be, or at the least something within them." I searched for the good and the positive and I had thought he had not wanted to give it to me.

He mustered his words forward in a fever of shame. "Gerard, my good man. Of course I miss them. I miss them all too dearly. Why do you think I had spoken of war as I had? My wife is long since dead and it is not much different with my children, for they refuse to speak to me. So I suppose I should say I am more dead to them." He seemed to have lost his words and all the same did not want to find them again.

"Most things can be reconciled. This could be most things, when you return this can be written into the good. Your wife is truly gone, yes, but your children have children and wives and husbands of their own. Wouldn't you want to hold a grandchild in your arms? Not all is ever fully lost." I realized the irony of my words. Memories can be lost. Lost into the eternal, the after that which comes from the beyond.

His breath became heavy and his words dense. "One life young lad. I had one, you have one. I spent it serving the British Empire and her people. I would like to say, for one I served it well; and, I may have put a ring on my wife's finger, but I married the service of my country. I decided as well in doing so that her soldiers are my children."

I sat and paused for a moment. "Tell me about your beloved armchair then."

"Fine upholstery lad, and the frame is a solid and good wood. Made of fine stuff, it is the work of craftsmen from the past century. None of this manufacturer rubbish." He thought surprisingly fondly of his armchair and I smiled at him.

"Tell me about the room that armchair is in."

"Well lad, I shall tell you." He looked over, "If you have truly asked?"

"Yes sir."

"Deep walnut on the walls, the ceiling is tin and silvery in colour. Of course you know it would be floral. The armchair is placed in the corner next to the double window and the window looks out upon my garden." He recalled those memories, the fonder one, and there was a brightness in his eyes I seldom saw.

"Speak of the garden. That is not the room, but your home nonetheless."

"Tulips, daisies, roses, and vegetables being the most important. You cannot always eat pretty flowers, but you can eat a carrot. Now a carrot is not always pretty, but you can always eat it. Potatoes too." He spoke as if it was somehow artificially important in one sense or another, he spoke in far more detail than I expected, but it was beautiful to see joy reside ever-lightly. Soon after I could hear him hum a tune to himself.

A humble English sounding tune. It meandered slow and melodic while it searched for a peace that once settled and rested in the past. A peace so far behind it would no longer be peace if one even attempted to capture it. To awaken peace from its rest is to rest outside of peace.

I sat in a modeless silence, and did not know what to say. "You give your all to one thing, right? All other things must take the wayside?"

"Yes, It is not a delight to hear but true nonetheless my good man. When Thomas learned to walk I was in Burma fighting rebellions, against those who have lived there for a thousand years or more." He paused to catch himself. "When Elizabeth had cancer I was on Crete shooting the same Ottomans that shot at us just now. When Analise had her first word I was in South Africa, firing guns and cannons at men with spears and woven shields." He coughed over his sigh as he exhaled and a spitlet of blood flew from his mouth onto his lip. He pursed his lips back into his mouth and licked it off, then gave another stiff cough that settled in his throat.

"While war has not been kind to your mind. It is still a noble pursuit."

"You believe this because you are young. The reason that I am noble is because some of those wars were won, chap. If we had failed you would stand here today and call me a barbarian and savage slaughterer." He said, confusedly frank. "Some might call me both."

"It is those who succeed that write the histories."

"The victors decide who is righteous and who is evil. Oh good lad, all I mean by this is that you should be happy. When you return, make yourself satisfied and be happy if not for yourself, for me." His eyes, one bloodshot and the other still white pierced me with intensity I had not felt in some time. The powerful gaze was altered and expanded by the fire's swaying light.

"What would that be?" I asked

"Young man, that is not for me to decide. If I had your age, looks, and all that comes alongside I would find a fine soul and give her children you will raise yourself. Make good love and feed your children well. Keep a hobby if you can manage it. I would damn my sense of duty to hell and live well." He exhaled and mocked the very word of duty.

Charles looked up to me and lifted his arm gradually drawing his one finger to a point. He gestured to his knapsack flicking his wrist. His old skin folded as his wrist fluttered in the gesture over. "Would you be a good man and pick up that bag? There should be a small wooden box on the inside."

I folded open the canvas on the bag and reached inside, and there it was, a small box with a sliding wooden lid. It smelled of coffee and earth. I slid the lid off and there were cigars inside, along with a box of matches. I lifted it up in the air gesturing to him that this was the right box.

"Yes lad, there should be a few good cigars in there. One is darker than the rest, would you light that one for me?"

I pulled out the dark cocoa colored cigar, which was longer though slightly thinner than the rest. I leaned up and away from the cold hard rock which supported my back as I placed the cigar into Charles' mouth wedging it between his dry and wrinkled lips which had grown tough from years of smoke. I placed the box down and picked the match box out of it. The matches were from some English restaurant, and I supposed he had taken them with him. I unfolded the front cardboard and ripped off one of the matches from its base. Swiping it quick but precise on the outside strip of the matchbox it sparked for a moment then snapped and fell to the ground. I tried once more, it lit and burned bright for a mere second as the sulfur fizzled off then simmered back down to the flame of a normal match.

He spoke, nearly mumbling, "Light me, would you, and for hell's sake take one for yourself my good man." The cigar sat unlit between his lips gently seated on the right side of his mouth, surrounded by the gray beard accented by the white stripe down the center.

I took a cigar, this one was light brown like the foam of an espresso and placed it in my own mouth. Simultaneously I stuck my arm out with no need to shield the finely rolled leaves as the air was dead and all but still and silent that night. It quickly caught and I could see the glowing orange and red swirls on the end of his cigar alight like rings on a tree. I did the same for my cigar and we sat in a quiet moment. A moment, and a memory, one like all else that was destined to be forgotten one day or another.

"A simple life is not one to be frowned at or scowled over. I should know, I spent my whole life avoiding it." He rested his elbow on his chest and his hand on his cheek as he lifted the cigar out of his mouth occasionally only to put it back in. "There should be a flask in the bag as well lad, my scotch I believe."

"I'll get that for you."

"For you too, chap. We've nowhere to go at the moment, have we?" The burning leaves settled in the unmoving air, slowly rising but filling the small valley with coffee grounds, nutty aromas of the earth, and clean warm dirt that reminded one of a toasty and dry summer day.

I sipped the flask and the scotch was mossy, wet, woody, and tasted like a bog, but the kind of bog that you would love to smell and walk about. I handed it over to him. He gave more effort than should be necessary to grip the flask. He clasped it and drank while laying halfway down all the while smoking the rolled plumes of leaf.

"I see. That is something for me to decide myself altogether." I commented on what he had said, delayed in response but still valid in my acknowledgment.

"Authenticity, son, Authenticity."

"What do you mean?" I inquired not for explanation, but elaboration.

"You must make your path, if you follow someone else then whose life are you living? Surely not your own." He laughed again, this time I could not tell if he was laughing at what he had said or just himself. "If you doubt your own actions, well how the hell do you expect to trust someone else?"

"You can't." I said in between puffs as the thick smoke rose through the canopy.

"Exactly good sir." He said with definite certitude.

"Sir?" I asked

"Sir, you've damn well earned it at this point. You are a sir now, not just a chap." He smiled and for the first time since the crash I saw through his bloodied and scarred face to see another man. It may have been the man he was in his youth, it may have been the man he wished and longed to be. I do not know who I saw, but through the scars, smoke, and scotch I saw a hopeful man hidden behind an old face. "If you are to trust someone, trust them. Trust does not come with caveats, and it cannot be faked or imitated. It can only be given, in its entirety. With trust comes pain, but that is what makes it valuable."

"Can one come to trust oneself by trusting others? Would one know themselves better if they were to place trust in the hands of another?" I saw the wisdom in the man. I saw the regret and frustration. However, it was only through regret and disappointment could I find the ability to trust that very same wisdom. For that wisdom would be cheapened if it had not come with failures. Failure is itself cheapened when no wisdom is harvested from its ashes.

"Why of course they could. Man is not a vacuum and is not separate from the world. For he is called to trust others this is how he learns others and himself. Still, there must be a mirror, if one has no self to start there is no trust to be placed."

"One must give of themselves."

I agreed with him. "What does one give to others?"

Charles paused and thought deeply as he looked first into the fire as it shone upon his face, then into the darkness of the woods. He touched his bandaged head and thought much but said nothing as he digested what I said. The night was dark and it was late. It was so late one might call it early. However I found it to be early enough that one would not know the sun was to come up. The air smelled of the cigar smoke, the air was moist and heavy but did not sway. Pierre rustled and moved in his sleep, and Bernardo did not move in the slightest.

"To trust you must give of yourself. You give those whom you trust your uncertainty, and you give them your fear. Not to give them fear as well, but so that they realize that when they too fear they are not alone in such things." He seemed to have approved of his words as he was speaking them. "Above all sir, you must give of the parts you wish least to give. You should offer the things you yourself often shun."

"How does one do this? Why would one do this? Trust is compromising and induces fear of itself." I took the flask as he passed it to me and tasted the Scottish countryside once more.

"My point exactly son, that is what makes trust as it is, its ability to compromise your armor in the hopes, no, the belief in another that it will not be pierced." He smoked the cigar fast and coughed as he did so, I was not sure whether injury or the smoke induced his coughing. It must have been both. "Trust is a principle of faith, not one of fear. Change this and it is no longer."

"One will see your failures."

"The reflection of trust is not pure or flawless, but true and genuine, that is the goal. To trust someone who is perfect does not require much, that is why it is hard to trust at all." He was tired and ached with pain. "Authenticity is the legacy of a man."

"Then what do you regret? You have lived authentically, authentically to the best of your knowing. You did what you believed to be true, and that is noble. If that is no longer true to you then so be it, but to pursue it is honorable regardless. That cannot be said for most."

He conceded himself, aside the usual stubbornness and decided answers he had often fashioned. "The pursuit is noble. I no longer believe that war is noble by its nature, but what I simply ask is that which my father asked of me. You must leave behind what I have done wrong and take what I have done well. Your children must do the same." He was losing his physical resolve but his mind wished to speak more. "One must push death out of his mind until it is no more than a thought. It is still a thought and a daunting one at that, but it is easier to do so when you are young. When old it is not only death that haunts you, but those things you lacked to do in life."

"Sleep well, you must heal, and we are not far from Russia." I said in an attempt to comfort and soothe?

"I will finish my cigar, and you will finish my scotch." He handed the flask back and I uncapped it, finishing in a single swallow, but there was more than a swallow left. "You are a good man Gerard, and for an American you know a thing or two. Make something of yourself and take a few of those cigars, but save one for me." It was not an ask or a question but a demand.

"Thank you, and you as well Charles. Regret is for those who have not learned from their mistakes, yet you have learned. So I ask you this, please do not regret. At least not so deeply." There was hope, but a pinch of futility in my request.

"I shall try, good man, I shall try sir." Charles sighed with relief and from his sigh came the feeling one gets when lying in a warm bed on Christmas around the fireplace.

Contented and free for that moment he remained. Charles sat there in a quiet contemplation and finished his cigar. Puffing to the bone, the leaves burnt and became hotter as they approached the stub. He finished, smoking as much as he could without burning his fingers. He tossed the end into the fire and it lit up like an incense. My cigar burned fast, and I smoked it faster after the scotch had hit me. It was not for the weak. The cool moist air was calming with the graceful contrast of the fire and cigars. We sat there occasionally looking at one another without words, understanding what the other had meant. It was strangely peaceful sitting out vulnerable to the elements and ourselves.

I had felt exposed to the outdoors, yet not as before. Not as prey but as an instrument. An instrument in the orchestra of mother nature playing his part, not fighting her, nor attempting to conquer her. I was simply surviving, being with her. The scotch dulled my senses and yet amplified my emotions. I felt fine and settled my back onto the coolness of the stone. Falling back gently onto the rock I watched the fire as it waned. Eventually fire became coals, and they shimmered. I would throw smaller sticks on until It felt silly to continue. Finally, long after Charles had fallen asleep, I could feel the night become lighter, for the sunrise was not many hours away. I shifted down from the rock until I was flat to the ground and fell asleep.

Chapter XIII

I did not sleep much that night, I was to be watching in the unlikely event we were tracked down, attacked by animals, or I suppose any other dire circumstance that might've arrived. It was safe to assume they thought us dead, or lost to the point of no return. Afterall, we had little left but what we carried with us. All else was behind us. I woke up and looked over to the fire which was now nothing but charcoal dry and chalky. I grabbed a stick, and the last remnants of heat exhaled as I spread the pile apart. I made sure there were no live sparks left in the residue, then woke up Bernardo and Pierre.

"Time to get up. We must be on the move." I shook Bernardo's shoulder.

Bernardo's eyes flickered and he stretched inside the bedroll before pulling himself forward so he sat up. "Ok, ok, I awake now Gerardo."

Pierre was already awake but he stayed lying down, staring at me. He rested his forearms on his forehead and did not move. Pierre looked up into the canopy before he mustered enough to get up. It was one of those mornings where everything felt dull and still, too still for any degree of comfort to be more than transient.

"Should I wake up Charles." Bernardo asked me as he looked over Charles while he lay down on the sleeping mat. He was peaceful and calm as he slept.

"No not yet, before we leave. He needs all he can get." I swung my hand through the air as if to waft away his idea.

We rolled up the beds and packed our bags. Before long, we were finished. I watched the sun rising once more as it fought to stray its beams through the dense and heavy trees. The stream swayed and rolled over the river rocks smooth and round from years of water running over them. It was clear and cool. It was spring water. I splashed my face with it and saw the dust and dirt in the creek bed rise up as I lifted the water to my head.

I waited until the dust settled again and went to a different spot. Dipping the metal tin cup into the stream. The water bounced around on the inside until the air in the cup was displaced by cool, clear, water. I went over to Charles and put my right hand on his right shoulder. Ushering the cup of water forward with the left.

"Charles, we are to leave soon. Have some water before we get on foot again." I gently squeezed where my hand was resting on his shoulder. He did not move. I tried once more and shook him lightly. "Charles, you must wake up, the time to leave is now."

I did not hear from him, nor did his body respond. I shook his body more vigorously this time, in an attempt to get some sort of action or reaction. That which I did not receive. He was still, unphased and looked more rested than I had seen him in some time. However, I was worried.

"Bernardo, would you wake him? He will not do so as long as I try." I handed him the cup of water.

Bernardo did the same as me and received the same response. "He is silent."

Pierre snipped. "Of course he is silent, he is asleep."

Bernardo looked as if he was angry at Pierre. "He is dead."

"What do you speak of?" Pierre's eyes shot over to Bernardo, in a way of assuming he made a mistake.

I went back over to Charles and stretched my frame over his sprawled out body, only slightly warm and comfortable inside the bedroll. Extending two of my fingers I reached down to his blood stained, dirtied, and dried sweat covered body. His facial muscles were loose and calm even with the bandage and dried blood he still seemed serene. Static and passive on the Turkish ground. The two fingers I situated on his neck. I reached behind his dense and wide beard until I found his jawline, and below this the wrinkled and worn curves of his throat. Between those two, my finger was planted, and within that groove I felt nothing. No pulse, no beat, no struggle, just the pacifying yet absent energy of the dead.

"You speak the truth, he is not here. Only his body." My gaze remained fixated on him, and then when this could be done no longer, the ground.

Bernardo and Pierre, and I had become silent and not silent out of duty. Silent in the way that we did not wish to speak. This was because all was said. When one dies there are no words, only emotions and actions. Words may give an abstract form to these words, but the words serve no justice when compared to the air which surrounds them. So oftentimes quiet is the loudest one can be in these still and frozen moments in time.

No speech was required to know what was next. It was only action now. We walked about performing that ancient and unchanging ritual that is eternal through the truth that all who undergo it are not. All who came before you have done this and all after will do so as well. I am simply yet another who has not yet satisfied or quenched the ever hungry jaws of the eternal.

I folded Charles' hands over his chest and he remained in the bedroll. His flask I snuggled into his breast pocket, and pulled the backpack out from under his head so he stayed flat to the wet leafy ground which he now would rest within. All the while Bernardo and Pierre used their spades to dig a grave.

Their shovels traversed down through the coarse and mulchy

dirt of the highlands. They pushed long brown and orange needles aside that were almost bedding. Ever so infrequently they would pull out a large rock and toss it to the side. The hole was dug under an old and tall pine tree. It was wide and firm and had one long root that struck out above the ground at the head of the grave. The tree shaded the earth.

After a while it was deep enough. Pierre grabbed one end of the sleeping bag and I grabbed the woolen fabric around his head. I watched his face as I led him down. The dirt loosened as we lowered him and specks would fall off the sides of the pit onto his nose and in the crevices of his cheeks, within and atop his beard. It seemed mother nature had already begun to bury him.

I took the box of cigars which held the matches as well and placed them inside my bag. He knew what he was saying when he said that yesterday. I slid the wooden lid and took a single cigar out. I lifted his fingers and nestled one final chocolate deep brown cigar in between his hands as they were interlaced and rested easy on his chest. We stood solemn and contemplative waiting for nothing to happen and accepting that was the case.

Bernardo in his Catholicism spoke his prayers. "Santa Maria, Madre di Dio..."

The rest of us listened to him. I did not understand what he had said, but it was beautiful. We took our spades and pushed the dirt down upon him. We filled him in until the dirt that had been tossed met the same level as the ground, and then some. The stones that were lifted out from the dirt earlier as it was dug up were placed in a pattern around the grave as if to signify who was and is here.

Was it that moment? Was it that moment that it was decided, and was it then exactly or another time? Was that the moment that all of his memories were sealed away forever. Sealed behind the door of eternity. Every second and every minute of his. Each triumph and failure. Every walk to church on Sunday, and every time he skipped. Every love, loss, and decided indifference. Were they all simply to fade away?

His comrades in war would remember him. His children would remember him, not fondly but regardless. Maybe when they hear of his death they will pull from themselves and their own memories, and conjure up visions of their fondest moments. It is easier to hate someone who is alive, but often to hate someone who is dead feels guilty in a strange and unsettling way. However, they too will perish and alongside those same or slightly differing thoughts and aspirations. Some of those aspirations will be met, and others cast aside in the need and requirements of the day to day.

So when the dirt was clad and the stones placed with solemn and contemplative concentration we stood silent and still in the atmosphere as it simmered among us like a boiling pot. It was strange, surreal even. Charles had been alive one day, dead the next. What was the expectation, other than to let him remain there, to be eaten by the earth and return to her as all things inevitably do. For us to walk away seemed the only course of action. To be silent, strong, and unphased is what some say. To do that would be to lie and to lie is wrong, but to lie to the self is evil and nothing short of it. However, regardless it did not change things and our mission was no longer to serve or win a cause. To survive and to leave was the goal, and only after such things had this dawned on me. To march onward ceaselessly forced into the future like all else does under the crushing foot of time.

Chapter XIV

Now we were deep into the woods and the day was high. We had carved trails through the forest. On the edges of the mountains nestled in between the rocky bluffs pierced by trees and the stone tossed shrublands that would lead down to the shores of the Black Sea. Pierre, Bernardo, and I would go through phases of making conversation and intermittent lulls of silence overtaken by the sounds of birds and animals in the distance.

"How far do you think we are?" Pierre asked

I looked back as I stepped around the grasses and ferns bedded above the dried needles that had fallen year by year from the trees. "Far from where?"

"The border." He said as obvious as ever.

"Not very far." Bernardo said with a rather certain degree of assurance.

"How would you know?" I asked expecting no surety of a reply.

Bernardo stopped walking for a moment and flipped open the canvas latch on his bag. He reached to the inside and pulled out a small notebook. It looked familiar to me, but I could not pick out where it was from. I watched Bernardo flip it open and pass through the pages until he seemed to arrive where he needed to. It seemed important. His finger centered on the paper and I could see his eyes as they focused in.

"If we head north from here and hug the coast we can make it in good time." Bernardo's dirtied fingers continued to page through and his eyes furrowed, pulling in his tawny and tan skin around them to inspect more closely the blueprints contained within.

"Where did you find this?" Pierre leaned back to look over his shoulder and peek at the book and its scribbled and sometimes printed pages.

"The maps and routes. It was of Charles' belongings." Bernardo shook the book to reference it. "We go to Batumi then we are safe."

"Even then we are not safe." Pierre commented, pushing his dark straight hair away from his face . His lips smacked contemplatively as the mustache moved, surrounded by a dirtied and unshaven face. "How long before we are to be arrived."

"A week give or take. It depends on our speed." Bernardo said. "We should make it if we are smart and consistent."

I looked over to Pierre and then Bernardo, "I would say go hunt something, but we have no bullets, just empty guns."

"Well at least we are alive." Pierre bounced back in response.

"We are. Some are not." Bernardo lifted his eyes from the journal but his head remained at a downward angle.

"Now is not the time." I interrupted before tension could build. "We."

"I bet a nickel Charles may have had a few traps up his sleeve." Bernardo said towards Pierre.

"Stop, I am not here for this, and we will not make it anywhere if it continues." I said. It seemed stiff and unfeeling, but to harness the solemn feeling brought about by pondering over Charles would slow us down in many meanings of the word, not to mention others. Morale to begin with.

Bernardo returned to his journal. "I see a bridge coming up."

"I see clouds." Pierre said.

"Ok." Bernardo shooed us forward and continued to glance up and down from the journal, which was once Charles'.

He was right. I could see the clouds and the wind was picking up. It was about halfway through the day but the sky became darker and more blue. It was a deep and alluring blue that seemed to tell of the weather. In front of it I saw those dense gray clouds that seemed so thick you would be able to walk upon them with ease. It reminded me of the days that we might say gods live up there. I could see where one might get that notion. It was a valid one.

The forest made things dimmer, but the sky helped to further this. It felt like it was not long before evening yet it was still midday. The large stones and fallen trees that lay rotting in between those that were still living.

After some time had passed we approached the bridge that Bernardo, or more appropriately Charles' journal had spoken of. It was no small bridge, but we were still far from a city or town for that matter. It passed over a high and steep ravine. The stacked and mortared stones which were clearly local had gone about a tree or two high above the base of the ravine, and those same stones passed across to the other side. Each of the edges of the mountain pass were jagged and deep. Far down below us a small modest stream trickled down, probably to the sea. I could also tell this bridge had not been used regularly in some time. Stones in the footing were missing, and the sides of the bridge had lost many of their shoulders. Open mortar and crumbling stones pitting out from either side.

"Now my friend, What happens when I push a fool like you in?" Pierre said this jokingly but with enough force to draw attention.

"That's a not funny, jus' stupid." Bernardo laughed in Pierre's face.

I stepped down from the pressed dirt and onto the bridge. I

could feel the land settle over it and crumble where it wished. It was weak, walking across carefully and soundly, but not fearful. Cautious but not hesitant. Minding the holes in the bridge was important as I went across. I had soon arrived on the other side.

The rain came in, and it was heavy. It took some time to pull down through the woods and the canopy. However, after not long I saw and felt that moisture slowly spreading and building. Heavier than I was before. Once again I felt far from civilization. So far there was no place touched by man for us to rest. No shed, or farmhouse, no cottage, and no cabin. Simply land, untamed. Bernardo took the head glancing up and down from the notebook. The book had become wet with water, but the more wet it became the more Bernardo cautioned to take pause as he turned the pages. The leaves turned from light to dark green, and Bernardo pointed forward up and down the slopes of the wild countryside. They wavered like a flag. We hugged the side of the hills in our foot stamping. Here we found a flat place, a place of rest.

Our civilization was a perfectly organized geological formation. A corner in a natural clearing. A corner of stone that fits so perfectly for a corner of people. A ways back we saw a fireplace. A fireplace. Not a fireplace of ruins or remains alongside a house, but simply put, a fireplace. A house had been there, yet there was no remnant. No remnant but a small fireplace and an old wooden chair that did not belong. It was painted baby blue.

"Should we turn around and rest at the fireplace?" Pierre asked as time wore on. "We are only on foot."

"It has no walls or sides, there is nothing there." I said frankly.

"We can start a fire there, and we can take turns sitting in chairs like civilized folk." Pierre mocked his own words and laughed.

"We are not sleeping there." Bernardo was sure.

"What do you mean by this?" Pierre was tired and growing

irritable, but we all were, and had been for some time.

"We cannot turn around and retrace our steps. It is not a good idea." I spoke.

"There is nothing good there, it is heavy and dark there. I do not like it." Bernardo said with hesitation in a way I do not think he could or wished to explain.

"We will go forward." I settled back into pace.

It was placed so close to the pit I can only assume it was used by one man. A sad and lonely man. Although it would have provided warmth, it was a sad and lonely place. I spoke of this and they had agreed. I do not sleep in sad and lonely places. Those places sleep within me. So we hiked onward, and lest we found a piece of earth willing to shelter us. Thank you, that piece of earth.

Here we found a dense bed of pine needles. Needles that were brown and orange, and felt as cushioning as snow, but nowhere near as cold or damp. We scraped off enough layers of the needles so as to be dry, but not reveal the worms and various bugs and crawling things. The former leaves and needles housed the worms and they came from there, when there was something to come for. I piled some needles behind my head and relaxed into the ground. There gently embedded in the earth a small leather notebook. The very same that belonged to Charles once. I picked it up and paged through it.

Maps, sketches of landmarks, drawings. A few cut outs and glue ins in different places that show us where we should be and where we should go. Maps made by hand and notes about how to arrive safely and in time. Notes to others, about others. About himself, and to himself. Journal entries, containing thoughts that sat suspended in his consciousness, but without rest. Thoughts I will never answer, and would not be disclosed, yet deep ones indeed. I lied in bed till my body took me to sleep.

Chapter XV

The night was rumbling and restless when I could hear the leaves tapping and the branches snapping. If there were a worse time for us to sleep outdoors, this would be it. The wind and the rain were tearing through the high woods. We could feel the air breaking through and it was aggressive. The air became demanding. The air demanded more of us. More than some might give.

It was early in the morning, and it was dark. My vision would not pierce as I might have hoped it would. So for this I did not see much. We were close enough to the shores and the ridges that we could hear the skirmishes that you would intermittently hear between the Ottomans and the Russians. There was no way of telling who had won, but you might have imagined it to yourself to feel better.

I was awake for hours at this point and was not in one place. Left to right, as the droplets of rain fell my body would not compromise. Bernardo leaned over and poked at me.

"Hello thee Gerardo!?" He inquired in the late night, I suppose he noticed neither of us were asleep.

"YES." I joked, but he did not notice the nuance.

"Are you awake at this hour?" He asked while looking into the canopy.

"No. I'm asleep at this moment." I looked him in the face and I chuckled. "What is going on my friend Bernardo?"

"Oh, mio fratello I cannot sleep."

"Me too." I spoke matter-of-factly. "I'm brother now?" I was surprised at my imaginary ranking.

"Well, we have slept outside together, no?"

"So this is true," I said.

"We have hiked and eaten our meals as one, yes?" Bernardo laughed at me and with me at once.

"So what would one say what is required to be a fratello, or friend Bernardo il grande?"

"Compassion, a welcoming heart, and someone willing to listen as much as they speak, and speak as much as they listen." His long and thin hand made a paddle and flipped towards me and I saw as he thrust forward to emphasize his point.

He lifted the same hand, cupped it, and swept that hair aside. His slick and layered black hair. I liked Bernardo, he saw life as a big play. A stage, a cinema. Something to live in and burst out of through the seams. Even the late nights, even on nights when you slept in the rain. Nights when you could see nothing. Nights when the mind, body, and spirit were all equally tired and lonesome.

"What sits on your mind, Bernardo." I asked him, not for simple talk, but to get to know him. When I like someone I want to know them. "You cannot sleep, what is the reason?"

"Home, it was home. My family, my woman, my land." His over-enthused voice dulled and pulled to the side to see the true weight pass through. "And death." He was silent, "I believe this requires little further explanation.

"It was You?"

"It was not Me.. It was life. It was my life." He commented, "I miss what my life was. Of course this is my life, but it is a different piece."

"So what is you?"

"What I believe and do, alongside that which I mentioned

before."

"What do you do?" I sent my gaze to Bernardo and my eyes asked intently of him.

"My woman!" Bernardo laughed. "No no no, haha, I like cooking, and gardening. His voice did not fit his frame, but still, he boomed and then resigned himself to a chuckle.

I laughed alongside him. "What do you believe then?"

"Family, and friends, only, the faithful ones." His verbiage carefully expressed sensitivity to each and every word to convey the severity of his claim. It appeared he was one who had spoken from experience. "Where are you from Gerardo?"

I looked back, "Delaware. I'm from Delaware."

"Dela'ware?" Bernardo jokes.

"Do you know Philadelphia?" I asked, hoping for a sense of recognition.

"This is America, And it is near New York?" He was pretty sure of what he had said.

"Yes, that'd be right." I nodded, "goodnight Bernardo." I attempted a swift close.

"Goodnight? Where are you going, my friend?" Bernardo was confounded that I would go to sleep. After all, it was only pitch-black interlaced with random unnavigable rays of moonlight that managed to creep through the melody of branches above. "Where are you going?"

"To tomorrow." I readjusted myself on the ground. "And I plan to be there before you."

"Tell me something. What is the weather like in Dela'ware?" He added. "I have never been to the States."

"We have the seasons, snowy in the winters but very wet. Humid the whole time around. Hot and swampy summers where you feel as though you are marching through wet soup up a hill. However, the autumn is a cascade of orange, red, and yellow. The air smells of decomposing squash, leaves and extinguished campfires." I paused and glanced over while speaking. "Tell me something."

"Yes."

"Why do you not want to go to sleep?" I asked him, for he had been chatty. Bernardo was always chatty, this I knew for sure. However, this time he was quite chatty, aggressively so.

"I fear. For my life, I fear Gerardo, I see death once. Now I find her everywhere."

"You fear, are not the walking miles enough to tire you?" I asked half-joking half-serious; knowing it to be true for most that when the body is worn the mind often feels weak as well.

"What happens if I die here? Nothing. Potential. Stale and crumbling potential." Bernardo said.

"Then you must not die."

"It is not so simple, Gerardo. You see this?"

"I know, it is much more. Then again to think of everything now is to distract. When this happens we make our minds open, and also our guard. That is where the problem lies."

"One has a mind and a body," Bernardo said.

"The mind and the body cooperate, when one is used principally the other is quieter."

"What do you say?! May you tell me what you mean? Simply put." Bernardo's words rolled over one another to convey his laziness to the description.

"If you think of not dying and not dying only, then there is much less to think of, and less to distract."

"I see what you mean by this."

"That's a way to look at it. At least he was not shot." I thought of the pensiveness of Emir. Where had he gone? Has he gone anywhere? He deserted, that is his business. Although in some ways

I empathize with his reasoning. "Go to sleep, would you?" I said.

"I will try this, I can make no guarantee."

The night remained dim and heavy and I had become entrenched in its presence. The darkness took over, as well as the rain. I was distracted by the falling and wetness of the rain. However, I was not distracted so much that it had overtaken my tire. So I, long before Bernardo, fell asleep.

I woke in the darkness of the night. Soon I became more still and drained of all effort we had at that point. For we were tired, and we could not hold ourselves. A wet body with nothing behind it. The early morning laid atop us like a cloak that held me down. Although I had heard sounds, and I had heard the angry call of animals in the distance. One I had heard again, and it was loud. It was close and I could tell it was close enough to know where we were. So for this reason I had acted as if it knew where we were.

I rolled to my side and I grasped Bernardo's shoulder with my left hand and pointed. "Wake up, Bernardo there is an animal here."

"What animal?"

"An animal that would more likely eat us than us it."

"Bear?"

"I do not know, for it is large."

"What do you say, are we to arm ourselves." He responded

"We have no bullets so our guns are not of much use." He looked at me as if surprised I wanted to react.

"We stay quiet."

"Yes we stay quiet."

We could hear the animal in the distance and it growled. It was loud and branches snapped in the distance between each sound he let off. I did not see him, but my ears had told me he had grown much closer. Bernardo leans to wake Pierre as well. Bernardo had a walking stick he had picked up after the crash and he lifted it like a rifle. Pointing. Pointing out to the darkness, as the stomps and sounds grew louder. A growl and a roar and I know he is here.

"He is here." Bernardo tilts his head to speak to me, yet his gaze is fixed and his words technical as his body is steady.

I grabbed a nearby stick as well. It was long and about as thick as a large wrist. It was not sharp. We formed a small unit, like a pack of elephants in a circle on the savannah facing out to defend from the lions on all sides. Another roar then the forest snaps, and the ground shakes. It was a bear and he had released himself and his rage upon us. A brown bear galloping and lunges from Bernardo's side. He lets out a scream, a primal scream.

The bear kicks up on his hind quarters and stands tall. Bernardo backs his body but he jolts his arms forward and under. He thrusts the wooden spear back and forth, but it does not penetrate the flesh. Clawing down so fast and heavily, the air was cut, the brown bear's front paws landed and the ground shook again. Bernardo jumped away before this, pulling his back out and higher on the grass. However he did not clear, his calf was shredded by one of the paws. He was not standing and the beast began to move toward me. I checked my back to make sure I was not cornered, then I steadied my weapon, if one would call it that. I hollered and yelled at the bear, and pushed my spear into the air in front of the approaching behemoth.

Pierre ran over and took Bernardo's spear and he came up behind the bear jabbing at him from the back. The great giant stood once more, and this time over me. I felt truly small, and I ducked out and away. Then six bursts of light broke through the dark purple shadows of night. They were small and the air cracked open as they passed us. He had been shot and we had no longer become meat. The bear whimpered and let out a grunt, flaring his nostrils then pulled back. He stopped, looked at us then ran off. Back into the darkness and away from us, but in all odds we were in his territory.

A man appeared out of the solid night where the gunshots came from. He looked familiar then I realized it was "Emir?" I shouted. Relieved, yet now with more questions.

"Hello! I am here." He said as a familiar face.

We all ran over to Bernardo. He was gashed and cut. It was one quick motion and it fell sweeping throughout him. It was deep, but he was swift, the bear did not clear bone. We were relieved but that did not matter. I cut part of my shirt, and told Pierre to check our supplies.

"There is not much left, hopefully enough to do." Pierre pushed the items around and searched the rolled aid pack.

"Hand it over to me, I have the shirt too." I put my hand out to the side for him to place it in as I continued to stare at the wounds and attend to them with my free hand.

We had minimal first aid bandages left, so we used a good bit of them as well. First, I wrapped it with my shirt-cloth, though that became so spoiled in blood it became more like a stuffing. I wrapped the bandages around it from the aid bag and taped over it with what was left. Even with the wrapping and the packed shirt you could see the indent where part of his calf had been.

He groaned, he groaned and he sighed. For the first few moments Bernardo was moving and lively. His body was warm and it tingled with rushing emotion. All that had subsided as his surprise faded. Now only the pain. The natural simmering and seething of pure force isolated to a remaining and equally dulling yet much more painful feeling. Bernardo was bleeding and I saw some of it seeped through the cloth and shew red on the outside.

"Woah that is some shit there." Bernardo sighed, he bit and

growled at the air.

We washed it with what water we had and wrapped him up. He had a stick and one of our shoulders at most moments. Bernardo was light and looked pale as a ghost so we gave him some water and food we had. Bread and some nuts and berries. We all managed to stand up and began to simmer down a little bit.

Emir walked up to us as he was putting the gun away and ran the last little bit. "Hello once again, my friends." He put his hands out at his sides. "What is new?"

"I thought you were meat?" I said, embracing him around the shoulder as I patted the center of his chest with my hand. "Nice to see you in one piece man."

"No, no, you were meat. Then I came here and fought the bear. That is the story, right?" He smiled because he was charmed by himself. He had a gun, and well earned some grit.

"How the hell are you here?" Pierre said, he paused then elaborated with a touch of awe to his voice as well as look. "I mean how are you living?" He was astonished. "And where are my spirits?" Pierre interrogated.

"Nice to see you too Pierre. I do not have any of your liquor anymore. I finish most of it the first night." He laughed and pulled Pierre in by the shoulder as Pierre passively accepted it. I think I saw a smirk hidden somewhere in there.

"He's right. How did you get here to us?" I was curious how he traveled alone through Anatolia and made it to us in a single piece.

"After I became lost I walked alone. On nothing for a few days. No food. Well of course I drink the springs." He drew us in with the breadth in his voice. "Soon I found the Ottomans hiding in low tents and small outposts. They travel between and behind us, but I do not think they search for us any longer." He spoke, ironically relieved, but strangely isolated and hurt. "We are not worth their time."

"And you tracked us down?" I urged him on.

"Well I hear the squadron talking about Italians in the mountainsides. So I follow the men who talk about this and they lead me here, to your graves,"

Pierre interrupted. "We are not de..."

"Oh right, that is correct." Emir smiled at us.

Bernardo came closer and spoke. "Thank you good man, we must all get a move on now. I am so proud of us all, yes?" He spoke then moved about like a shepherd dog to get us moving again.

"Funny it was the bear and not the Ottomans." Pierre jested at Emir and us as well.

"He still saved our ass anyway." I added.

Bernardo hung onto Pierre and held a sturdy walking stick with the arm that did not brace his shoulder. We began our descent, and made course for the hills and dells in the eastern crest of the Black Sea.

"You see, my plan was to make friends with the bear." Pierre said sarcastically.

My plan was to feed you to him." I retorted.

"Friends do not eat friends Gerard." He was hurt by the hypothetical insult.

Emir smiled. "Being lost with friends is much more fun than being lost alone."

Chapter XVI

We awoke inside a new camp. It was a long hike downhill the other day. In the lower ridges we were vulnerable. However, we had Charles' notebook and Emir, and so now knew the trails fairly well. According to his calculations as well as the journal that belonged to Charles our best call was to descend. We had set a small camp about halfway down the decline. The next morning we regrouped and continued down quickly setting foot. We uniformly moved pace. In the mountains which lead to a valley I enter the fugue. My feet push in front of one another. The world of reason and mind. The world of complexity and simplicity. It overflows and the world is broken. Only for a moment. Then I returned to the place. My opinion of peace. Refuge and solid ground. I returned

The hillside creeps and winds into the valley. We headed down the passages, and as it would be for most old travelers we followed the small trickling springs that headed unfailingly downward with gravity. I stopped every once in a while and sipped, or washed my face. It felt as though I was being refreshed and ushered down by the mountain itself. The cool, crisp, calming, and clear water that tapped into the heart of thirst.

"Where is everybody, where is Charles?" Emir asked us. "Are they ahead of us?"

Bernardo spoke between breaths while he paced his walk. "They are above us."

"We were ambushed in the mountains. Landmines went off."

I sounded guilty, though we were not to blame. "The car crashed, and well, Charles died the day after."

Pierre went on. "Maggiore's car blew up and they shot anyone who crawled out. The men creeped out from over the very roofs of the rocks and rained down. They tried at us of course, and we nearly hit a mine head on, but Charles steered us into the bushes and he took the crash."

I looked at Emir. "You did not need to know all that." I then switched over to Pierre. "You did not need to say all that."

It got quiet and Emir broke the air. "It happened, I am not going to keep you from telling me anything." Still, after all he had been through he was visibly shaken by the facts of our circumstances. "Charles is gone, yeh?"

"He held on pretty well." I stated, offering my moment of remembrance as well. "But yes."

Pierre kept going. "Did you want to know any more?"

"Are we the only ones who made it?" Emir asked with a sour squint around his cheeks and eyes.

"I think so." Bernardo sounded like he was haphazardly admitting to a crime. His words came out tight, nearly pinching as they left his mouth.

"Hmmm, well we ought to do a pretty good job then, right?" Emir put his head forward and stepped on the path again with ever so slightly more definition.

"No other way." Pierre said to us and himself while staring down on his walk.

"Aren't guns terribly loud?" I asked.

"Ugh, tell me about it." Bernardo let out an exaggerated sigh. "That is my least favorite thing about guns." He sounded exasperated, but then seemed to tire himself a little from the acting.

"My least favorite thing..." Pierre sounded somewhere between a politician and a comedian delivering a line. "When it is cold outside, they are cold as well; given that they are outside."

"I don't like how they pinch and wear at your fingers while loading them." I stated.

Emir was understandably quiet, so we made idle conversation to stir him from the facts that needed to be known. We resorted slowly back to the sound of the trees and animals.

I hated the damn hills, as they would not leave me alone and I was on little good food, even so with the water. We chatted and some people spoke in favor of charting the course for the closest village, however this was not easy. Should one stop in the Ottoman lands or in Russia. We were not far. Our feet could take us in a few days time, but would we be of enough haste to most adversarially conjure a success?

Eventually it was decided that we should wait until arriving in Russia. Emir had persuaded that it was the most coherent and best option at our disposal. We remained in the hills, for two or three days at least. This way we could pass the border in the shadows. So we simply continued to walk onward.

A man torn from his home once is homesick. A man torn from his home ten times is traveled and eagerly urges for more, but a man torn for so long he forgets the smell of his own yard and bathroom is not homesick or traveled. I thought to myself that man is like a song, and each of us chooses our own beat. How fast. How slow. How high, and low. A man of a decided mind has a tune that is upbeat and harmonious and it swings and sways to make one move his feet. When said man moves his feet he moves his life.

The same song over and over becomes monotonous and drains the composer and listener. My sentiment had begun as a simple homesickness, but now I think of my song. I want it to be loud, and I want it to be rambunctious, yet at its most striking and piercing moments that shake me it is gentle. The moments that reveal my vulnerable self, not because I decided to expose it, but because I cared to hide it no longer.

I looked over to Pierre and asked him. "When will we get out of this damned hellscape?"

"When you die or cross that border." Pierre channeled his inner pessimist, but still seemed careless about that too.

"Wow you are fun." Emir said while rolling his eyes, both of which eventually landed on me to convey his discontent with Pierres commentary.

"Have you ever tried Limoncello?" Bernardo distracted us from the petty banter, or more precisely the banter between Pierre and Emir which had overtaken us.

"Yes." I said.

"Really, where?" He looked at me puzzled as ever. "You are an American Gerardo."

"I know I'm an American, and what are you?" I grinned under my words.

"Italian!" He slapped his chest and his spirit lunged forward a foot from his injured body.

"I know this. This was my point Bernardo."

He disregarded my words and looked over to interrogate the truth of his semi-rhetorical question. "So where have you tried Limoncello?"

"I traveled, but regardless I get homesick from time to time." I thought for a moment. "Bernardo, I get homesick from places that are not my home." I then asked. "What is a home?"

"A home is where you grow and pick the cherries or feed the dog. Yes." Bernardo seemed to have a well defined idea of home, at least for himself.

"Will I know when I have lost home?"

"Yes." He said without a doubt.

"The smells of home will seem as though they are forgotten."
He paused. "One cannot help but to know when he has lost home.
A home is sacred for most and it inspires the joy or pain of the
childhood that followed,

"Where do I find home?" I asked Bernardo.

"That's a nice idea." He looked over to me. "Where to find
home?"

Pierre interjected, "Do you find it, or do you create it?"

"I will do what I will."

Pierre called at me like a suspicious mother. "That is not a
damn answer Gerard mon ami. You know this. I know you."

I responded with something closer to my true opinion. "Home
is an opportunity. Just like trust, or a good person."

"What do you mean, my Americano?" Bernardo latched onto
Pierre's inquisitive interrogation.

"Would you stop sharing so much you damn yankee." Pierre
sarcastically attacked me. It was true, and I had understood what
he meant.

"Someone good, and their trust. If home is an opportunity it
is something to be taken hold of. A home is only truly yours when
you take a hold of it. One must make their mark. Hang a painting,
roll a rug, hell, even buy a chair." I said plain and smooth, but with
no elegance.

"Now, tell me about women, and men" Pierre smiled and this
was the moment I knew that Pierre knew he was sharp and right
onto something. "And trust, talk now of trust."

"It is the same here. When you are close with someone you
part from a piece of yourself and leave that with them." I looked
around. "The lighter you bought for your friend, the hat your
woman stole. All the same."

"Trust now, Trust!" Pierre seemed to demand now, not for knowledge, not for conversation. For entertainment.

"I can talk every ear off here individually, but it means nothing. If one does not care one will not listen. Drown the horse, they still will not drink the river water." I left my commentary there.

"I will drown you." Pierre joked, then his edges softened and he came back to me to ask "Why do you speak so little, of yourself, and life, of people?" I started to respond then he cut me off again to elaborate the specificity of his points. "You are a good listener, a great one even. Observant and careful, yes this much is true."

I'm not sure what you mean?" I pretended to be confused at his aim in the hopes of getting him to continue fleshing out his thoughts, or possibly trip over one of them.

Pierre's teeth clenched and ground alongside his mind. "You are keen about learning everyone else, yet you do not reflect the same keenness around sharing."

"What do you mean?"

"Exactly." He started again. "My point is exactly that, Gerard."

"What do you wish to know?"

"Nearly anything." He said back to me as if to be obvious. "Those stupid little things that no one cares about, yet for some reason they remember."

"I hate liver. I've never liked the flavor of it and caraway seeds for some reason."

"Yes, that's about it."

"Cold weather is nicer than warm weather sometimes."

Bernardo's eyebrows jumped. "No. Better? no!"

"This is not about you." Pierre waved Bernardo's words off.

"Sunrise or sunset."

"Sunset, but I feel sunrises are more relaxed."

"Then what is a sunset?"

"It is calm."

"Calm and relaxed are the same thing." Bernardo said.

"When I am calm I am not worried, when I am relaxed, I am not thinking about my worries." I said.

"This brain of yours works in interesting ways." Pierre smiled and tapped the top of my head playful and light, not knowing exactly what to make of it, but still pleased.

"Maybe this is why he does not share." Bernardo broke back into the conversation.

"What do you mean?" Pierre asked.

"Because people like you say things like this." Bernardo shook his two pointer fingers, and his thumb in a twist.

Our brains had been fried from days of walking and all we wanted to do was arrive. It felt as though our feet were heavy and the air was heavy when we pushed through it. In the grass we walked down the sweeping hillsides. Our feet dug into the slate and loose bits of rock and gravel that sat upon the padded stone dust and light brown dirt.

Once we had found some wandering creeks we followed them. It would lead us to streams and rivers, or at least this was the idea. It zig zagged alongside the creeks that gathered down into the basin of the sea. We could see the fog of the sea from here and the flowers were purple and orange. One particular stalk reached high above us and the tan fields with small yellow flowers on all sides high up. It was a spear sticking up through the countryside. Down beside these streams we meandered and the closer we drew to Batumi the closer we drew to the sea. If all went well the Russians would be waiting for us in Batumi.

Chapter XVII

We had found a road. Not a trail, path, or road. Albeit one not greatly traveled. However after the bushwacking it was a relief to see a man made road that went *somewhere*. Walking beside the three other men, I would chat with them. We had watched now as the summer sun rose high. It was shedding its light over the land. The orange adorned the bald dunes of earth and grasses in loose dirt waiting to become sand. By now I had seen these plants.

I knew and could spot them one by one. Some should be eaten. Some you could cook and then eat, and others would kill you. A select and often rare few were edible and managed to taste fantastic all at the same time. The most common flavor profile on a wild edible is *bitter*.

The rubble of the ancient houses lay only a few miles from the coast. Positioned after the pass, right as the mountains pressed us to the sea, and on our left the sea pushed us onto shore. Between both great behemoths was a barely bruised but balding plain filled with ancient stories. It slowly graded downward to the Black Sea.

We were hiking on the road, and a cart came up behind us, actually a wagon. Two horses pulled it. An oiled tarpaulin draped then pulled tight around the frame, ending behind the driver's spot. The wooden wheels slowed when we turned our heads back. On the driver's seat was a priest and two young women. Pierre waved his hand to them and stepped out in front of us to ensure that the priest saw him. They stopped and Pierre began to speak.

"Hello, you are Christian, yes? You appear to be a priest." He asked and stated at the same time.

The priest had an enveloping brown cloak on, and a chain with a crucifix adorning the front of his chest. The crucifix was mostly wood with a little metal inlaid. It hung from a corded rope, not a chain. "Yes, I am Father Vasil."

"Are you headed to Russia?" Pierre said.

Father Vasil nodded his head and his white beard bounded and danced with each motion. He coughed. "Yes. Russkia."

Pierre responded to the man. "How long have you been traveling?"

He was solemn and his deep voice gave way. "Many weeks, maybe 2 months." Then he thought some more. "They have not been with me this whole time."

Pierre spoke back again. "Ahh I see." Pierre seemed a little bit stumped.

Emir stepped in and began speaking to the man in a language I could not understand. It was either a dialect of Russian or a local language. One way or another, it was a territorial tennis ball of empires. They spoke for a few moments and I saw their faces contort and their intonations change up and down. Then Emir looked back at us expressionless.

Vasil stared at me with his sunken brown eyes. "Yes American, yes to you all. Come, we will take you. I do not know how far."

We each thanked him and the women as well. The three of them were sitting on the bench at the front of the wagon. They were both young and had soft olive skin tones, one had deep brown hair, the other black. They both wore hijabs which covered the top of their head, and much of their hair. We were ushered around to the canvas bed. I climbed into the back and there was a child in there. He was about ten or eleven. He looked at us in curiosity.

"Yes we can come with him, and yes, be respectful." Emir said.

"Thank you Emir, this was opportune." Bernardo stepped up and inside the wagon.

I gathered that the priest did not know these people well, yet they seemed more or less at ease. "Where are you from?" I asked father Vasil.

"I am Georgian, but am I from somewhere?" He said rhetorically.

"You do not have a place of your own?" I attempted to anticipate him, so he might not have to explain.

"There is no Georgia on maps? Only Russia, her Empire." He looked overworked and overthought.

Where are they from?" A simpler question, I might've thought.

"South from here." He did not truly know.

When everyone was seated we continued on the road. Bumping and bouncing on the inside, as well as hearing the wood creak. There were crates and boxes that moved into and past our legs. The wood is painted brown on the baseboard, connected to the oiled tarp above our heads. Bernardo lay down on the single long and narrow bench attached to the cart. His long and slender body even laid tight on the plank, with his arm draping down. The rest of us sat on the floor or a solid crate. Bernardo immediately fell asleep.

The child scanned his eyes over us in what felt like quiet judgment. He seemed confused and slightly annoyed by our mere presence. "Where do you go?"

Emir spoke to the boy and they went back and forth. It did not sound like arguing but the discussion seemed like a back and forth more than anything else. Pierre lit a cigarette and the smoke was whipped out and away to the trail that began behind the carriage. We were tired and worn and it was nice to be on the move. Pierre watched Emir and the kid while they were talking. He reached into his bag and without saying anything, handed the child about a quarter of a loaf, the child smiled. It was not the smiling child on Christmas, but a scared child who was suffering in search of food and a place to sleep for more than three days. The things we wish a child should not need to worry about.

The child began to rip apart the loaf and ate one of the pieces with haste.

The boy pushed his hand through the slit at the bottom of the canvas that opened up to where the priest and two women were seated. The sunlight cut in and went out through the open back. We saw the road ahead of us with the mountainscape above. The boy tapped the arm of one of the women. It was the one with longer black hair. She was wearing a soft coral green gown and her hair was draped down her back tied near the end by a bow in a darker green, but much of it was covered by a smooth and soft looking pale brown head gown. She turned around and her head, dipping down slightly to see and find that we were all seated.

"Come here sweetheart." Her arms spread out from her gown and she hugged the boy, clasping his neck and behind the ears with her fingers to peck him on his curly little head with her lips.

The boy said something to her. She laughed, then the boy laughed again at seeing her smiling. After a minute she passed her gaze to us. It was resolute and focused, and then her face immediately resumed and made contact again with the child. He handed her a few ripped pieces of the loaf Pierre had given him. She spoke back to him and rubbed her hand on the top of the still thin brown hair on his head.

She kept her head in the frame of the open canvas as she leaned back and the boy sat down again. "We can take you all to Sarpi, then we go east. So for you, that is where you stop. Lamara. This is my name." She said while gesturing her hand up to herself.

"Mzia!" The second woman identified herself, seated to Lamara's right, we could not see her.

"We have bread." Pierre gave another piece not unlike the boy's to Lamara

"Thank you. There is not much for us to offer other than passage." She smiled to her own surprise, then nodded, tilting her head slightly. She wrapped the bread in a piece of cloth. Her right hand took it and it disappeared into her shoulder bag.

Lamara went on. "Gogi, tell you to the gentleman."

"I Gogi." He blurted mid-chomp on a portion of Pierre's bread. He was a nice kid, just simply quiet, quiet to start. Like many kids would be with a stranger. The question is how long?

"I am Pierre, pleased to meet you, Gogi." Pierre smiled while the very small bit left of his cigarette dangled out of his mouth. "Bonjour, enchanté Gogi." He grimaced to himself, fully aware it would make absolutely no difference whether he spoke in English or French.

"He is young, and you are big. Set good example, men. Understood?" Lamara looked at Pierre, he was the closest to the front. We all nodded in unison, more or less. Her eyes did not waver and the longer she looked the more you understood what exactly she had meant by what she said.

Gogi was young enough that any one thing we did could be a memory or not and we might not know. That single unimportant detail that is strangely yet specifically recollected.

Gogi poked at us and spoke words, none of which we understood. Only some of which Emir had understood. So we talked to one another and watched him as he made sweeping declarations or said something else which sounded equally important from his intonation.

The view caught me for a moment. We had walked down from there, as my eyes followed the now abstract strokes of green and white and gray in the chiseled frame of the highlands. We passed by a number of lakes and streams. Each was gently cradled by the mountains. It was an interesting sight. To follow through from the west to east. To see mountains become valleys, and valleys become fields. I told myself that one of those rivers or lakes had the same water as before. The same spring water as the ravine we crossed, but who is to say? I watched the scatter of warm hues as the sun grew lower.

Pierre had begun to nod off after having been so tired. His head would lean back from its pivot and then his neck would kick up again and his eyes would open. He pretended to be awake for about 2 minutes, and then continued to nap.

"Bernardo" I looked over to him as he was propped up on the bench. He had raised his elbow on the bench so his back was up. This way he could look at us.

"What."

"Are you awake?" I said, forcefully jovial as ever.

"Yes." Annoyed and not entertained, he waved at my words and looked out the back of the wagon where the tarp was open.

"What does your leg feel like?" I pointed at it up and down.

"Throbbing and heavy. Like there is a pulse in my leg and it jumps out into the air." Describing it caused him to focus on it more, then he grew distracted.

"Painful." I glanced down at his leg once more.

"Like, how do you say? Shit."

"Exactly." I cheered him on.

"Like bullshit."

"There you go. Well done Bernardo." I thought for a moment, then realized the child neither understood the word bullshit nor would ever have to use it, especially in English.

According to Charles' journal there was a large enough lake to stop at and take a respite. The lake was calm, clear, and cold enough for a hot summer day. The wagon had stopped on a low-lying ridge right up above the lake. I got out and trudged down the rocks and dirt and finally onto a patch of moss.

All of us got into the water, with our underwear on and washed off. It had been quite a few miles since we had the chance to wash off. I waded in the sandy gravel, which was just about the smoothest part there was to find. Once I had gotten to that spot it was deep enough to dump my whole body in. I tossed myself forward into the cold water.

Feeling clean for the first time in a while was strange. It felt like you had been wrung out and all the brown water was squeezed right out. I could see it dissipate into the lake water as I sunk down. I suppose this was how the ancients may have felt. Bathing in flowing water.

"It is like one layer of dirt off and a quarter layer back on." Pierre said.

"What do you mean?" I splashed up at Pierre and he moved slightly.

"There is dirt and sand and many tiny tiny animals swimming about here. Where do you think they settle? On your skin, and they dry again."

"And we are supposed to despise these little animals that clean out dead skin and dirt that grows the tree?" Bernardo was seated on a rock and his legs were draped over into the water. He dipped his hands in and spooned water on himself with his cupped hand.

When I was in the mosque I was told by Rabi that if it is time to pray and you have no access to water, sand can be used in its place. It was necessary to wash beforehand and sand could perform if need be. I suppose this was if you were in a desert, but I needed a double blessing. I leaned over in the water and felt the bottom with my hand to search for a pocket of sand. Upon finding one I dug through it, washing my arms and scrubbing my legs. It was possible to feel some of the grease get caught by the clumps of sand, along with dead skin.

I had felt truly clean for the first time in a while, as for my physical detriment and debris. However, the other feelings cannot be washed with water. I felt fresh in the cool water. There were flagstones and small pebbles on the shore around the lake. Bernardo gently and precisely cleaned his legs from the bear chomp.

"This is the way it should really be." I commented on washing myself in the water and sand that I could manage to find.

"What do you mean?" Pierre said to me confused as he splashed the water up to his chest.

"This is the way it ought to be. This is the way God had intended it." I lifted more sand and used it to scrub my legs and my arms.

"Washing ourselves in lakes and walking miles on foot?" He said sarcastically.

"Well yes in some sense, but no. Not the war and hiding from people."

"But what do you mean when you say this?"

"The simplicity and the animalness, not wild raw animal, the calm kind."

"The bear would count against you then. Would that be God's intention as well?"

"I suppose in one way that would be true. Some people would suffer and perish at nature's will."

"And that is good? A good thing for a god to see over."

Bernardo cut into the conversation. "You're not getting his point. If I may, Gerardo."

"Yes you may."

"He is speaking of our humanity. We were intentioned for a simple and beautiful life, and that is what he sees here."

"Intended. Thank you. It is the automatic man that is too much, we are to be slow, not too slow, but a slow enough pace to breathe calmly at least."

"I will breathe slowly when I am dead."

"Then you will die slowly."

"Then you may."

"That is not my choice." Bernardo said. "I will die with a sword at hand."

"Fighting a dragon?" I asked jokingly.

"The largest one you can imagine." Bernardo looked down at his leg. The pain he felt was desensitizing and he felt numb radiating pain.

"Yes, the largest one I can think of." Pierre said as he confirmed his point with the conviction in his statement.

"How many heads does this dragon have?" Bernardo asked.

"All of them."

"That is not an answer." I said. "What do you fight the dragon for?"

"For the same reasons that I fight the Turks and Germans."

"And why?" Pierre waited for a response.

"This is because they are the bad guys." Emir spoke then he wafted off, out of conversation.

"So this reason has no true reason." Pierre seemed dissatisfied.

"A motive made of itself has no motive?" I half-asked. "What decides a motive?" I asked again, but this time more acutely.

"You tell me." Pierre lifted his hands and threw the subject to me.

"The meaning behind it."

"What meaning must it have to be a valid motive?"

"A meaning that precedes itself."

"Like what?" He would not let this go easily.

"The virtue that embodies virtue. The quest that is the quest. A good deed that is done because it is good and nothing more."

Pierre smirked and then acknowledged the growing confusion on my end and accepted it. "For this reason I have decided to be the arbiter of my choices."

The sun came down on the shores as if it had a place to be. I bathed and scrubbed with the sand and water until I felt clean. It was summer warm and I had felt cleansed by the sun and water together as they mingled. The heat picked up as well as the humidity but that was of no mind due to the water.

We all kicked around in the sand and danced. We washed and for that particular time it was simple and nice and fine. I had not thought of the war during this time as the moment was too wholesome to distract me. We had, at once, felt like children. Children, not of this time, but primitive children. Children who had no other recourse but to wash themselves in the beauty of the lake.

I tossed the water onto my chest as I felt the cool water pass over me. I paced fully into the embrace of the lake as it overcame me. My body shivered on each advance, from knees to groin. The lake came up on the water to my chest or collarbone area and once more the coolness enhanced. I fought it subtly then became one and our temperatures equalized as so happens.

I saw a figure off in the woods. It was running closer to us, and around the trees. I looked over to Pierre and silently gestured my hand and eyes at it. He was subtle enough to catch my motion for him to notice. The movement came closer as my senses heightened. I sharpened and the figure came into focus. It was Mzia. Emir was farther out and ran over to his gun. I said who it was and he lowered it. She came up to us. I had no shirt on yet and she was breathing heavily.

We came in closer to the shore. The ground was a fair mixture of dirt, moss, and grass. It was not difficult to walk on, but remained scattered with stones. "Where did you come from?" Pierre asked Mzia.

"We come from another part of the lake, but we should move, Now." Her hair was wet and it stuck to her shoulders when she slowed her pace as hair now dampened the back and sides of her tunic dress.

"Why is this?" Pierre asked as he put his shirt over his head and adjusted it onto his skinny frame, with his legs still in the pooled water.

"I am not sure, but I think there are Ottomans in these foothills. I saw some on the other side of the lake."

"They are suspicious of anything at this rate." I said, as I waded in toward the foot of the embankment.

"You are Muslim and a civilian woman, they will not target you." Pierre pointed out, not serving to nullify or bolster her point either which way.

"I am traveling with a priest, and do I look Turkish to you?"

"No." Emir interjected, "You look frustrated."

Lamara rolled her eyes, and then her hair, covering the bun hastily with her hijab scarf. She spoke plainly. "If they see you, they will kill you, and us as well. We have aided you." She waved her hand to usher us onto the shore. "So we must leave, come."

We all got dressed and put our belongings in our bags. Hiking to the wagon with haste, returning up the hill and onto the road. The little boy ran up and into the back. He ran with spirit and fear, but I don't think he fully understood why he was running, or the whole effect of his condition to begin with. As far as he was concerned he was with his family and was going somewhere. The car was packed and we continued to move.

Pierre reached his hand forward to lift away the folded canvas that led to the front and asked Mzia who was sitting up there on the wagon bench. "Did you see the Ottomans? Were they close?"

"I stumbled across a hut near the lake. A lady, how do you say? A seer." Mzia was still a little bit shaken.

"This is why we leave in such a hurry, because you have seen a witch." Pierre was skeptical and a little bit peeved.

"She is a seer, you must pay attention." Emir nudged Pierre in the shoulder, while not necessarily adding much.

Pierre was confused and vexed, but he then gave way to indifference. "Faster we get out of here, no problem for me."

"Lamara said she saw them on the other side of the lake?" I added.

Lamara leaned across the wagon bench and into the gap in the canvas, then interrupted to clarify. "I did. They were on the other side, Mzia only told me after."

Emir responded. "How interesting." He found some strange aligning of intrigue in this fact, and to a certain extent, I did as well.

"It is good we left then, for both reasons." Lamara spoke fair and clear. "If it is chance? I cannot say, but it is strange." She said, admitting one of the things she was not sure of.

"You do not believe in witches, or seers?" Bernardo looked at Pierre and Lamara to ask.

"That was defensive." I laughed then inquired back to Bernardo. "Do *you* believe in wizards?"

Bernardo sounded playful. "I think we should hear what the mystical has to say. I have had too many coincidences in life for them to be coincidences." He admitted as his voice rose up, then back down. "You?"

"Yes, the world is awfully strange. I can't think it just *happens* this way." I assured him I agreed. "What exactly is influencing it is a mystery to me, but it is something to think over."

Lamara answered Bernardo's question. "I do believe them. I think they should be avoided, because of this." She thought some more. "The djinn and temptations and all of these, they pull you from the world."

"They pull you from the world?" Pierre was confused, but curious.

"They distort our world?" I fished for the idea I thought Lamara was getting at.

"Then we do not know right from wrong, head from tail!" She went on. "That is just a mess."

"The Jinn." Emir commented, knowing full well we would ask anyway, now that it was brought up a second time.

I looked over, curious how and whether it would relate to our conversation. "What is a Jinn?"

"Jinn. Spirits, they walk in between humanity and spirituality. These we cannot see, but they surround us and we can allow them to guide us, to evil or good." He elaborated and I was interested.

"Do they have to eat food?" I asked.

"I do not think so, unless they feed on energies. Gerard, I do not have the science behind it." Emir threw his hands up and chuckled.

Mzia continued. "They feed on bones and old flesh." She was serious, with a small tinge of flair.

Father Vasil spoke while looking forward and still holding the reins steady with his firm posture. "Of course there are demons, they do not feed on flesh and bone."

"So *you* believe in spirits as well." Pierre became interested.

"What do your spirits feed on?" Emir inquired.

"The conscience. Then, when you are hollow, it spins you around without a compass." Father Vasil sounded like he was offering us a warning above all else.

"That is more frightening." Mzia glanced over to Father Vasil, ever so perturbed.

"There is much we do not know." Father Vasil stated plainly.

"I know." I smiled and had a small bite of bread.

"Very nice." Emir grinned.

"Thank you." I acknowledged.

"It is simply all superstition." Pierre tossed even the consideration of the supernatural to the side.

"What is stition?" Emir peered over to Pierre and asked him.

"What? I do not know." Pierre looked confused.

Emir was piecing the conversation back together. "Well I know what super means, so I figured if you know what stition is then I can know the whole word."

"Why didn't you just ask what superstition is?" Pierre's face became puzzled again and he gave Emir a strange glance.

I butted back in. "Superstition means taking signs and coincidences seriously."

Emir identified with my definition. "I take them seriously."

Pierre concluded. "Then you're superstitious."

"Ok." Emir said.

"It is meant to be an insult I believe." Pierre contributed.

"Very nice." Emir seemed unphased.

Pierre felt disappointed at how flat it fell. "Come on."

"You can't even shoot a bear."

"I did not have a gun."

"And it would have helped? Why didn't you make one?" Emir started giving him a hard time.

"What the hell does that even mean?"

I cut back in again. "He's playing with you."

Pierre scoffed then smiled. "Why don't you teach me to make a gun with sticks and rocks? Eh."

"What would you need that for? I have saved your ass already." Emir pushed again.

"So I can shoot you with it."

"Well this one is made of steel."

"You are made of steel." Pierre said.

"I'm surprised you could muster a compliment." Emir was artificially cordial. "Or was that an accident?"

"May I ask you? Now that you are here." Pierre's eyes narrowed and gave way to curiosity.

"Certainly." Emir looked over to him and began to offer genuine attention. "What was your question?"

"How the hell did you survive out there with simply a bottle of liquor and intense self-loathing."

"The self loathing part is easy if you've made enough mistakes in the past." Emir grinned and then stared into his words with the same loathing he had described. A subtle, but frankly true contempt.

He was distracted but Bernardo sharpened his thoughts into focus to get Emir's attention with words of the same quality. "Oh, I see. So you mean being a human?" A sincere criticism that floated into a soft chuckle amidst the group.

"Most people do not shoot a child." Emir admitted.

Bernardo's face soured, then he responded with his empathy and equal understanding. "Most people have not been in your position." He sighed as he finished speaking. He took a heavy drag on the cigarette he was smoking. The smoke trailed out the back of the wagon, whispering through the canvas opening flapping like a ghost.

Pierre looked over to Emir, sympathetic and pathetic. "I know this is difficult, but try your best not to be so difficult on yourself please. One who is good can do evil. You, I am sure, are good, you have only done evil, yet evil has not become you."

"What do you mean by this?" Emir asked.

I cut in with a simpler orientation of words. "You did not wish evil Emir, evil happened."

"How does one cleanse themselves?" He said rather formally.

"You mean how does one forgive themselves?" Pierre said, clarifying his point.

"They forget themselves before they forgive. You must realize you are less involved in yourself than you may think. Set yourself to the side."

I commented on top of Pierre. "You do realize that switching words around does not make them more true."

"It makes them more poetic." Pierre shrugged and waved his hand at Bernardo, ushering him to pass the cigarette. He dragged it then returned it.

"I am not keeping this leg am I?"

Pierre exhaled. "Speaking as no professional whatsoever, yes. Your leg is absolutely mangled."

"I had thought so, but I simply wanted a professional's opinion." He gave a dull smile at his own dry humor and gazed over his leg again himself.

It was wrapped well by now, but even within the wrapping you could see the concave that had been left within his flesh and I saw where the skin became a hollow of muscle and meat. Bernardo was stretched across the bench with his head at the back end of the wagon. Bernardo finished the cigarette down to the stub and pressed it dead on the coarse wood palette that made the floor of the tailgate. He tossed it away from himself and the last glow of ember fluttered out in the night air.

Chapter XVIII

Of all the possible combinations of humidity and temperature, we got what I believe to be one of the worse ones. Hot and wet. The hills and shores were soggy and the air was humid as ever, carried onward by the delicate salt of the ocean. The wagon carried us on and a soft but barely detectable breeze pushed its way inside the wagon by way of our movement. We rolled slow and steady to the approaching village in Sarpi. Father Vasil was an apt journeyer and wagonman, we had very few hiccups on the road. We remained in motion, and were not terribly far from the village. Nonetheless, it had already felt like far too long. The mud and puddles caught the wheels when it could.

I had not truly slept in some time. I did sleep, in some sense of the word, but to call it a sleep was generous. Eight hours was a memory, by this point it was an hour here and two hours there. Small lapses of time where I captured brief respites of rest. Rest, yes, restful, not so much. The stress of our situation tended to pull me from my sleep, my focus, and to a certain degree, myself. A natural stimulant all by itself.

The wagon bounced rigidly and then the corner collapsed to the ground abrupt and without a touch of gentleness. "What was that?" Pierre asked.

I saw Lamara's hand reach around the fold of the canvas that opened from the bench in the front of the wagon. The spot from which one would control the horses. Her hand was tougher and acted stiffer than Mzia's, from this I was able to discern. She pulled it and peeked at us. A gaze that scanned at and around us, then she spoke.

"Wheel is stuck. You must push it for us." She lifted the same hand that opened the fold to us and she drew a circle in the air, then she made her hands flat and pushed to the ground.

I believe she wanted to make sure that we understood her, if we had not already gotten the message. Of course I could tell the problem, not only by her words, but by the apparent lack of movement. I looked her right in the eyes and nodded, standing up then hopping down onto the ground through the backside of the wagon.

My boots landed in the mud and it all splashed up, but I was still on my feet. I stood like a child in the rain that had made some massive ripple in a puddle. I suppose that for a child, to make a ripple in the puddle is to shake the seas. Not only are you smaller, but all other things feel much grander.

The rest of the men came out and onto the gravel and mud. I could hear the mud and gravel splash and settle, jostling under them. Lamara came around and pointed at the wheel.

She wafted her hand forward and swayed her fingers to point away from the puddle. "You, Gerard, behind the wheel. You Italian, sit down, you are weight. The rest, push."

We had comprehended the intention of her words and we pushed. She spoke with such directive and graceful decisiveness it had simply made sense to push the car. In one life or another she may have been an officer. The wheel was dipping down nestled back and forth cradling in and out of dirt paste and rain, and we pushed it out and onto the road. It was not much work for as many bodies as were working on it.

"What is it to one man that one should call another bad? We

wish for the casualty of others, but are they truly the evil ones? Are they the ones that want to kill us?" Pierre asked rhetorically.

"They are the ones with guns, of course they are here to kill us." Bernardo dropped his answer as a given.

"We are the ones with guns too." Pierre objected.

"Well, not so much at the moment." I responded.

"Ahhh, well that changes my viewpoint." Pierre said sarcastically.

"They are here to shoot us the same way we are here to shoot them, don't you see. If there is one thing I have learned from Charles it is that we are all fighting the same war, and all are within the crossfire. It is the tyrants, the bitter ones who have laid themselves as the true opponents in each fight, yet they are the only who do not fight. Does the moon get angered by the sun shining over it? Does one weed hate the tree that grows above it? We are men, they are men, we are pawns, many of the Ottomans, the same." I released myself quicker than I had imagined into a tirade that I had not seen on its way.

"Charles is old and dead." Bernardo said to us, but most profoundly me.

"No need to be so starkly dark." Pierre was cut by the edge of Bernardo's words in a way I did not expect.

"We will be too, if we dig our shit covered feet into this mess." I quipped with more emotion than I had intended. "We are not heroes, and yes there are heroes, or at least I believe so; but even then, we are not them. We are soldiers, we are lemmings, and war is a cliff. I've found myself at the edge and realized that the dive is not into a sweet and nectar filled ocean. There is no glory. Simply another dune waiting, one rock hard beneath its deceiving sand."

Pierre looked down at the wooden floor of the wagon like he wanted to punch something, but was not sure what. "That is a broken neck, that is a broken neck and a wasted life."

"Don't you want to save your homelands? Don't you give a *merda* about your family, your brother, your mother, your sister, father?" Bernardo seemed at a crossroads with our thoughts.

"Yes. That is why I don't want to fight this damn war. I want to see them. I want them to remember me, not as some abstract hero, but I want to be their brother, their son, alive." I said.

"I do not have such luxury." Pierre sighed, critical of himself, but also cognizant of how little was truly his fault. "I am a man about. I float without a family who'd remember me. If I die here I am a memory, and certainly no more than the abstract you describe." I saw the pain in Pierre. I saw the orphan. I saw unrequited love. I saw the questions he had asked everyone but himself, and the questions he asked himself but never anyone else.

"Everyone should know this feeling. If one does not know this, then one has a responsibility to understand and respect those who know it." I pitied Pierre, but he hated that, so I held it behind the curtain of my face.

"*Quoi?*"

"Family, friends, and occasionally some good fortune."

"Those tend to cross over themselves." He paused in no neat way.

By now, we all smelled like shit and ash. The bottom of my pants were torn and dethreaded, yet the loose threads were pulled together by the mud and dirt that had been caked on so severely that the threads were stuck in place like clay and would not unwind further. The top of my pants were no longer held together with a belt, where a burnished cow leather belt once stood. I had placed a thick piece of string and wound it around the loops of my pants. I smelled, and worse, I knew that I had smelled. It was worse than my nostrils had imagined it to be. We all did. The night had come and the road was clear and empty. The little boy fell asleep with his head propped against the palettes on the inside of the wagon, then so did I. Drifting into the rocking lullaby of the wooden floorboards in the wagon on a thin wool mat. We rocked back and forth in the wagon bed as it moved and the night took me over.

. . . .
. . . .

Chapter XIX

I woke before dawn and leaned in towards the front of the wagon. I peeked up to see animals pull the wagon as it rolled with us inside. They moved attached to the carts that gave us a study of the land. A simple viewpoint of the weeds outside in the gray of another dying night. In the early morning I peered over the lands, for the vignettes of figures and forms who reveal themselves from the broad strokes of things still intact. The rounded canvas rooftop glowed from hugging the bent wooden frame tight above my head as the sun broke and filtered its simmering warmth and light through the fabric. Like a sliver of ivory with a candle behind it. The warmth shed on my face and I sensed the heat.

I pulled the tired and strained body of mine up and forward. Seated in the wagon with my legs still down to the floor. I looked out the back and saw small houses. Some houses were made of brick, but most remained fashioned in an ancient manner using dark and finely aged wood. The roofs were straw and clay more often than not, the former. On the very edges of the wooden beams that peeked outside the depth of the house, sometimes it was possible to see the resin and the sap collected neatly at each end. They were as fragrant as the dry icy forests of winter and appeared like amber icicles but shorter and rounded in form. Stubbier. Sarpi? I thought to myself. Have we arrived in the town? If we have, how much longer to Batumi.

The wagon stopped, and I heard the noises of the animals

upfront. A slight jostling and subtle tilt of the wagon told me someone in the front on the bench had gotten off. "Gentlemen... We are in Sarpi." Pierre looked around at our dirt decorated, smoke stinking, fatigue plagued faces and gave that shit eating grin that said 'we may be in deep, but we made it somewhere. That has got to count for something.' As much as I dreaded our circumstances he was right, something had changed, and as far as I knew for the better. It was a step by step process, I had to remind myself to be glad for each step before rushing into the weight of another.

I saw the old houses and storied streets and began to think of the other towns and cities we visited. Each building, in its quaintness and unique beauty, expressed itself. Simple as we are, being human beings we found that thing. There was some fondness in it. No place is quite the same. Maybe we are generous, or perhaps I try to find interest in those minor observations. I had found that thing, it was nice to ponder over. I saw a bird hop, flying from building to building. It finally arrived on a tree, one which is tilted right, from my view. The branch curved over and around under the weight of the little bird, bending around the very tip until it pointed back down again. The bird balanced careful and graceful as the branch waved and swayed in the high breeze of air.

Stepping off the creaking platform of the wagon and crunching onto mixed gravelly beige dirt mixed with sand. My feet felt wobbly. My body felt as if it were still moving, like when one rides horses or wears boots long distances only for their body to feel it is still doing so long after they are finished and are lying down.

This village, this place, It was quaint and small. If I were to be honest, as I hope to be, it made that rural impression that one only feels infrequently. It was not much of a place but it felt like many things. It was more, or less, of what I had configured in my mind.

"Not a bad place. That being said, it is not much of a place.

Eh?" Pierre was satisfied with a place to be. However, as comforting as it had initially seemed. The village was still only another place to be. Hopefully also, a place to have been. That being said, it was time for Lamara, Mzia, and the Priest and child to get rid of us. Lamara, as I had expected, came out from the side.

Lamara came to us and at the side of the cart began to talk. "Thank you for this bread, and your company."

"Absolutely, anytime. I hope you all get where you are going."

"I wish the same for you." Lamara retorted.

"I do not think any of us are sure where we are headed." I said frankly.

"Then I wish that your way is found." She spoke with the same grace and intention as the first time.

Pierre butted in. "I hope for the same."

I was helping Bernardo off the tailgate bench and down the step that led down to the ground. His leg stuck out straight as I was shifting him around to safely get him off. Lamara and the priest both came around. I doubt that the priest spoke much English. Of course, I have no room to blame him. I simply was one to observe it.

He stared at me, friendly as could be. I began to see his mouth move without noise as if he were thinking of how to muster the English words he might manage to find. "It has been a great pleasure, men, and may God grant His blessings." He spoke his tongue once more and performed the sign of the cross over us, although it was different from how I had learned it.

"Where are you headed? Your destination, the final stop." I phrased it in a summary of ways so if one went over his head then another might land.

"North, for how long? Until we find home, or home finds us." Father Vasil spoke plain and obvious and almost seemed to let on that he did not take note of the wisdom in his own words. Perhaps I am wrong all the same.

Pierre nudged me. "You tell me; which one comes first?" He directed his attention at me.

Father Vasil answered. "I am not He who decides. When one finds a home, one can be sure of it. Maybe, when home finds one, home is sure of one." He seemed to contemplate it as he spoke.

Lamara then began to speak. "Home is made, not by one, not at once, not for once."

"Then how?" I asked. "If it is made, then it cannot be found."

"We make it in the places we have found. Home is made from what is found." Lamara followed her point through. "For many, over time, for those who are to come."

"Thanks to you for the safety that has come to us. We wish you protection." Mzia interrupted, as she was attempting to be kind before the jaded, realist, and well intentioned words of Lamara which had not finally come through.

"Well, beautiful ladies I must ask, have any of you seen my leg? Not like that, I am not searching for it any further, and I do not quite believe that safety comes to us either." He pointed at himself from bottom to top, and he smiled as his only socially acceptable recourse for the true and genuine pain which was for him alone to fully manage and frustrate between and amidst.

"No comment." Pierre recognized Bernardo's discomfort in the small degree that he realistically could. "I can only wish that such safety may follow you. That is, if it was ours to begin with? A point I disagree with. I do not think that mother fortune has greatly befriended us."

"She has been kinder than you like to admit." Lamara countered, her hand resting on her collarbone to hold down the tails of her head scarf as they waved in the coming and going of the breeze.

"I should give her more credit." Pierre felt exposed, but he knew it to be for the better, and so he allowed the embarassement to pass while the exposure remained.

"Bless you." Mzia said. This I could tell was genuine and well meant. She stood in her sandals, feet dust covered and eyes ready to sleep, but not yet free to rest.

"I can sense the most of you. You're strong and not too bad." I spoke, and soon after Lamara and her gaze jumped over. She grinned, Lamara grinned. It was in no particular way the most sway that I had seen in her temperament that I had seen since our arrival. It was the most given so far. A tough woman, but fine. Lovely even, and deserving of nothing short of respect, as all people are. However, she herself made it known. It was made known to me at least. Not by word, not by time, by presence.

"For the future." Bernardo beckoned back to the conversation before as he clarified to himself. "Home is for those who are to come."

"The Future." Lamara said. "I like that." She smiled and her lips spread wide across her smile. "Home is for the *future*." Perhaps it was a new word, or perhaps the significance struck more poignantly than before.

Pierre extended the point further. "Home is made from the past, home lives in the present, and home hopes for the future."

"Then for this short time, there has been a home." Father Vasil commented, although the way in which he spoke made it feel like an observation. "This is a good thing."

"It is, isn't it?" Pierre made a realization of his own, and his hand touched the pocket where his mangled cigarette tin hid, then he moved it away and became still.

"May your next home be long-lived." I said dearly.

Father Vasil waved at us and Lamara and Mzia stepped up in

their gowns onto the wagon once more, yet far from the last time. "May your next home be your last!"

"Maybe not?" Bernardo retorted. "I do not like the sound of that."

We chuckled and watched as Gogi sat on the tailgate and stared at us, then gave the fluid and heavy wave of a child that swung down with gravity. Would he remember us?

Lamara held onto the armrest and turned back as the wagon began to move. "I wish your last home to be the best."

"You as well!" Pierre waved goodbye, and so did we all.

She was a combination of many strong attributes and I am one to believe, they were not attributes to be described as common among people. Especially in a single place. Someone worthy of cherishing and admiring.

The town was small. In its center was a tower no higher than a small tree, but above us, metaphorically and visually. Although for the size of the town it was much less modest than it should, or I would've expected it to be. The very bottom of the watchtower was made of carved stone blocks. Stone carved into square and rectangular shapes. An amount of detail necessary that I could not possibly imagine. The edges at the bottom were smoothed to a polish. It should be noted that it was not done by an industrial behemoth or a machine of the future; but ancient hands. Carved precise and slowly by humans closely dedicated to tools and craftsmanship. As the watchtower rose above the early carved stones, it changed to brick. Brick interspersed with stones of the same manner, all of which was held together with the mortar. It was in no particular pattern.

One could almost tell some of the town's history by looking at the tower. When times were good and plentiful in fine fashion they would make bricks, by way of clay and the intensive process that follows. In between periods of wealth there were patches of stone. Local stone that was simpler to build with, but did not offer the conformity of brick. Stone required some tuning, but it was easier to work en masse. It finally reached the top about fifteen feet up, and at this point it appeared almost entirely brick. Arranged sturdy on top, each corner had a thick wooden post. These lead to the wooden roof which was pointed in as a pyramid. Deep, and dark brown wood. It was old growth and looked sturdy colored and covered in its own oils, as well as smoke, and time. The tower was old, but inside and outside of it patrolled the Russian military. Who I don't imagine have been there nearly as long.

The stark contrast that occurred between the modern men and the aged buildings felt obvious and self-explanatory, yet slightly wrong. One of the men at the top of the tower nudged another standing next to him then pointed at our group. The one who spotted us looked studious and not wanting; but surely needing to fight in the war. The one next to him he referred to after noticing us had a dark mustache and a stone face that did not change expression. The second man took out binoculars and then spoke again to the other. We heard some shouting in a foreign language then another man, neither of those two who were in the tower, ran up to us. Emir hollered something as they came closer and they began to slow down. Emir began to speak in what sounded like broken Russian and I understood none of it except 'Amerikanskiy' and the other various Russian variations of our corresponding national identities. Emir and the man began to ease in their speaking after this. When at first it was quick and interrogatory it slowly became paced and more diplomatic. I think I even heard a few chuckles.

I had always found Russian to be a dynamic sounding language, though I knew none of it. It was elegant and light when one wished for that, yet could become heavy and harsh when such an effect was needed. If you had cursed someone out in Italian it was easy to tell the anger by intonation. That being said, the words themselves still managed to sound poetic.

We followed the Russian man across the gravel square and I heard Bernardo give heavy sighs and deep breaths with every other step as we made it across the square. It always felt more tiring when the destination was within eyeshot, and he was dealing with his own issues. The main square was almost the summation of the village itself anyway.

The man who was talking with Emir waved his arm for us to follow him, and so we did. He took us to an equally old and fortified building. He pushed the old plank door open and the cast iron hinges swung, creaking gently as it moved. The interior of a tile floor and paneled wooden walls was homely. It was dimly lit and there were candles all about on small tables, with wall sconces to hold them. The weapons leaning on benches and the ammunition stacked on wicker chairs reminded that this was not a home, at least no longer. Chairs not occupied by supplies were filled with Russian men smoking and filling the room in a haze.

An older man with a wide face and thick gray beard and short hair walked up to us. His pants were military, but his shirt was a white wife beater, stained through the center and around his armpits with sweat-lines, dirt, and hard labor. He held a beer stein in his hand and punched me in the shoulder, then went on to do the same to everyone else. It was light enough to prove he was an ally, and strong enough to shuffle you back. Then he slapped me in the shoulder as if setting my arm back into place, which needed no readjusting. He pulled his hand closer to himself preparing for a handshake, then re-extended it with vigor.

"Sergei, Damovich. You are the American. Da?"

"Yes. I am Gerard." His arm gripped mine with such intensity to make me think he wanted to squeeze it off, but I suppose for him that was him checking to see if I was trustworthy, and strong. So naturally I returned the favor and met him with the same.

He held on longer than I expected and then let go. His veiny tattooed arms let go to show his dense and meaty hands. Some say you can see if someone's hands had not done any manual labor. This was not the case for Sergei. I think his hands had only done manual labor. There was a scar on his left hand that scrolled right over his pointer finger's knuckle. He had many scratches, and scars elsewhere on his hand, arms, and some near his face. I'm sure each would also be followed by a long story of how it had occurred. I could only describe them rightly as formidable paws.

"I am sure it has been a long day for all of you? It is a long way for me as well. Belgorod is farther away than most think." He laughed loud as hell, and it was a roar. "But for you, I know this must be a world away." He was far from home, but he knew I came across an ocean, for what exactly?

"Delaware is far from here, that much I know." I spoke, not expecting him to know where that was, but his face appeared as if he understood. So I cut the difference. "Nearby New York. Although that matters little, we are now all in the same forsaken place. Right?"

"Gahahau. Delawhar New Yorhk, da! I guess you are correct, you are here now, and I think you want to return. Smart man." He sipped, no gulped, from his comically large mug-stein that sloped inward as it went up. Following this came a gasp for air, then he wiped his face on his arm. However, I could only imagine for him, the beer and the air were not too different.

"Your English is quite good Sergei, this I must say. Tell me. Have you been to America?" I was curious as his English truly was surprisingly efficient to be so far from anywhere that speaks it.

"No. But I hope you are more fun than the Englishmen, and a little quieter than the Scottish. This, I joke." He laughed in a way that did not feel forced for him, but nonetheless you felt pressure to laugh with him. Only because he truly thought it was that damn funny.

"We had an Englsihman at one point, he wasn't too bad." I paused and thought about Charles. "So this is where you learned the language."

"Yes. It is the symbols that are difficult, but I got there, so no worry finally."

"Do you like English?"

"Let's see if I like Americans, da? You are not too bad yet, but first impressions are *fignya*." His eyes, deep set and dark brown steadied on me. "It is how a man acts under stress that shows true impressions. If you have a first impression and a true impression at the same time, that is the best of them all."

"It is easy to have principles when you are safe and well fed." I commented.

"I believe you may understand. Though I am not sure yet." He winked at me and kept walking around to make conversation with us as well as his own men.

He looked further into the building at another man and swatted his hand back and forth gesturing with his wide frame and heavy body, almost hitting the beams on the low ceiling. He walked into the back of the ground floor and ushered us to follow. It became darker and the candles became more necessary. He came up to a bar table and shook his hand like he was casting dice and then let go. Finally he smacked his hand flat on the dark stained table and pulled a paper that was slid back and brought it close to his chest. The paper still lay flat on the table. His pointer finger pressed the paper as if he wanted to push it into the table, but his movements always seemed anything but gentle.

"You sign here." He said in a newfound seriousness.

"I sign here?" I asked.

"You sign here." He repeated with the exact same tone and cadence.

"What do I sign for?"

"You register yourself. This way I know you and your friends are alive, or at least walking. Transcripts." His fingertip rolled along the list. "Gerard. You are still Gerard, da?" He said.

A slap on the back and some cyrillic writing, and my signature right there. I signed and then looked around to scan the paper. Everything on the paper was written in cyrillic except the names. I looked around and found some of the names of our scouting party. Marco, and a few of the other Italians. I had no idea where they might have been at this moment. I doubted if they were even alive. However, it felt wrong to sign for them, I did not know much more about them than sweet conversation and some facts.

Maggiore for certain was dead, but some of the others might be lost in the woods, after all I'm not sure they had as large a company as us. Even if they were alive, without Maggiore, would they give a damn about returning to the front. Why do we give a damn about it? My heart slowed then jumped for a moment when I saw Charles name, my eyes returned to center on the paper. The peripheral became fuzzier than usual and my vision put the letters of his name into focus *C-h-a-r-l-e-s*.

I did not sign Charles' name because that would mean he was alive. He was not. I looked over to the four smaller boxes to the right of the signature, and glanced subtly to Sergei.

"What do these say?"

"Here it says 'arrived living, arrived injured, arrived dead, and deceased." Sergei's finger rode a line under the Russian script while he spoke and tapped the last column as he leaned into me. He was picking up on me and my current situation.

"Ahh. I see." I gave a flawed smile between the situation at hand, and a thanks for the courtesy.

I checked the box on the far right. I had known most obviously that Charles was truly dead. I had dug his grave and buried him in the ground after all. We had been the ones to cover him in dirt and I remembered it. To see his name on a list felt too simple. It felt too finite, though I suppose that his life, like mine and all, was indeed finite. It was a little too surreal and felt wrong that this was the totality of it. I guess there was no other way to do it. You cannot hold a parade for each person who dies, or else there would be no money to fund a war.

Nonetheless, to see someone's entire existence summarized neatly into a single name chart, followed by a signature and a few lines felt far too simplified, yet unfortunately logical and justifiable. However, in these moments it is most certainly not the logical self that pervades but the emotional one. Simplified. Simplified to a criminal degree, but it simultaneously seemed inevitable. Still, there was no better way.

With the haunting and dreadfully true knowledge I held, I checked that box and wrote an "x." It was in the mountains, dark, rocky, and roaming within danger that Charles had died, but when my hand had finished that final line he had become utterly and decidedly dead. Not missing, not injured or otherwise but deceased, deceased in the finality of my handwriting; which was admittedly much less neat and well formed than Charles' own handwriting which I had seen in the book. At that moment I remembered a few of his words. I remembered that he had spoken of his marriage to his wife, but his marriage to war and his dedication to his country which in the end, trumped all else. I knew that he had regretted it, but I also knew that he had decided it. Although, as he also told me, 'you cannot build something new without destroying something that is old.'

All these thoughts and more flashed through my mind as my pen-pinching fingers swooped, lifted, and dragged across the paper. The motion itself was mechanical and I was invaded by thoughts the whole time. I raised my gaze from the paper in a haze, and handed the pen to the nearest hand to mine. Sergei took it and passed it off to the man behind me, Pierre.

Once I had finished I stepped away into a separate place. Looking behind me I saw Pierre, Emir, and Bernardo. Pierre stood in fortitude and surety ready to declare himself thoroughly and completely not dead.

"Thank you Sergei." Pierre motioned at me. "Hello, I have the pen, I simply need to see the paper."

"Oh, by all means, right this way Pierre." I was shaken out of memory and Pierre had found me irritated, yet overly formal, as I tend to get when I am irritated.

"They need a record of me being... alive, at least until now." He was not wrong, but after what I had read there seemed an inappropriate amount of satisfaction in our own temporary peace and safety.

The rest made their signatures afterward and we were all tired of all the reports. That being physical, mental, and metaphorical.

I stepped outside and felt different. The night was bright, but felt darker, and the town was covered in lights for the military to survey. It was quiet, and as often is at times like this; it was too quiet to be comfortable.

Chapter XX

Nothing is certain in life but I was now pleased, at least as much as one could hope to be. I quickly made my way back to the rooms they gave us after we all had finally met. I had a rather intense moment back in the common room where I signed my name; and marked the presence, or lack thereof of others. Now, unfortunately or fortunately I had felt different. In real life there are few moments that feel starkly definitive, but with Charles and our group there was a before and an after. His death had truly broken through into my reality, and we lost a little bit of light back there in the high jagged slopes.

Upon the death of Charles, I had been provoked into thought upon my other losses. It would be foolish and near sinful to say that these losses were the same. Each and every loss is different, but in a moment of such emotion you cannot predict the paths your mind may take to understand such things. I had not seen anyone die in front of me, but I began to ponder about my childhood. First I had thought of my grandfather who was dead long before I was born, but I had always felt an amount of personal relation to him. Then I was reminded of my parents and grandparents who had purchased a small shack on a lake in a most rural region of the United States. I imagine that now it must be more 'civilized' as some may venture to say, however I do not subscribe to that term, as it feels arbitrary except in the most serious circumstances.

Nonetheless, that house had burned down, and it had burned

to the ground. It was filled with vinyls, paintings, and other personal artifacts. Some were worth much more to the outside world, yet as many things are, they were all the same, and priceless to me and our family. We lost quite a few things. Loss, that is something inevitable. It will come to us, and it will take, but it seems that we should understand why and how we lost them. Is meaning derived from why and how in these matters? It makes sense to question why and how, if we are to truly know what they mean to us. Although, whether an answer is ever to be found remains to be seen. It is the seeking we strange humans seem to find solace in, then when our mind has meandered to a place of sufficient meaning it casts a tent up and makes its purpose.

They were nice enough to let us sleep in Sarpi though they knew the orders as well as us. We were on course towards Batumi, as fast as time would permit. So as the sky cracked open through sunrise, I awoke. When I awoke, I did not passively linger as the purple sky turned to pink then blue. I arose with a willful jolt of my body as one does on those important days. The most amazing part to me was waking up in bed. Logically I was not surprised, as of course I remember going to sleep, but I was not sure of this luxury when I arrived in town.

The sun came up, and at that moment I fully enjoyed the sun. I cast meaning onto it, I said veritably to myself, 'This day will be a good one,' then I went on with it. I stood up on the nailed flooring and walked down the hall. After this most simple and not misunderstood interpretation, I thanked the Russians who had allowed us to sleep here.

Down I went to the first floor where I signed the papers and I saw Sergei drinking a black tea. "Hello. Good morning. Nice to see your smiling face."

"Yours as well." I was not smiling, but it was that dark grit and sarcasm that kept people sane at times like this.

"The tea is bitter, you should try it." Sergei grinned as he sipped the cup, which looked comically small in his hands.

The days and nights before Sarpi had begun to blend with the advent of our arrival. They melded together not only because of the monotonous and unyielding focus and determination required for each one, but also their lack of sleep. Firstly, it was my time in the woods which consisted of sleep shifts and the constant looming power of mother nature and all her smaller children which I could hear haunting and taunting me in the distance. Moss beds and stone pillows had sufficed, though seldom comforted in this time. What had followed was the shaking and bumping house of two strong-willed but lonesome displaced women, and a child, which belonged to one of them. They were kind enough to bring a priest who had fled missionary work after the war broke out, then fled when war broke, or at least that was the picture we put together in our heads.

Now after such adventure, or more aptly named trials of spirit and body, I came to a bed. A simple one, yet one above the ground and stationary. In retrospect this is often an expectation at home but a luxury of many other times and places. Luxuries are certainly not necessary and I often find my frustration with those who complain at a lack of luxury, but most are nonetheless happy when they can find one, and for that I do not blame them. I do not wish to say that I am glad such events have transpired. However, I will go as far to say that I am glad enough to be able to speak of them having happened.

I did not realize the true state of things until time had passed. Has time passed by us or did we pass through time? It did not matter, and I supposed that with enough elegant dictation both would be entirely possible. I was relieved under my current circumstances.

Relieved by temporary peace and safety, yet in quiet turmoil by the silent expectation of future endeavors to come. Ones I predict will be strenuous.

I was seated downstairs in a wicker basket with a small red cushion, and I watched Sergei drink his tea. Then Pierre came downstairs on steps which were narrow and tightly wound up and around, as I reckon they were built when people were smaller and shorter. Pierre carried his body down, but I could tell just within seconds of watching him it was only his body that carried him downstairs. It was the small details that you can quickly decipher in someone. When you've known them long enough, or gone through enough turmoil with them, each of those details summarize themselves automatically in a moment of isolated and accurate understanding of their condition at that time. Now that ability is a rare ability, and one you can experience many times, but most often with a mere few people.

Pierre came closer to me and sat down in the wicker chair next to me and plopped onto the cushion. He sat there and stared off for a moment and then got up again, then over to the bar table where Sergei drank his black tea in peace. "May I have some of this, is there any around?"

"You look like shit, so yes, my friend the kettle is behind the bar. The tea is loose in the jar next to it." Sergei seemingly laughed simultaneously at and with Pierre, and gently he lifted the tea to his lips to sip it again. Sergei looked over to me. "You Americans drink coffee, not tea. Right?"

I lifted my head to see if he was talking to me again, which he most obviously was. "I'll drink just about anything, but yes, most of us prefer coffee, when we get our hands on it."

"You know what my problem is?" Sergei said, almost preparing for an accusation.

"What?" I was actually worried as to what he might say.

"Coffee is a bean, I don't like beans. Now a leaf, simple, I like it." He swirled his cup around just a little bit and glanced down into it.

"Ahhh, I see." I smiled and agreed. I did not understand his sentiment, but was mostly relieved that there was no genuine problem at hand.

Pierre poured the tea then lifted a bottle and splashed something else in. I could not see what it was, but I think I knew.

"Woah my friend." Sergei lifted his hand as a stop motion. "My friend, black tea is strong enough in the morning." He glared at Pierre with a stone stare, and Pierre gave him dead eyes. "Could you pass it please?" Sergei took the bottle and splashed some liquor theatrically into his black tea.

"What the hell." I mumbled to myself so no one heard. Sergei had chastised him for it then asked for some himself.

Pierre raised his small mug and shuffled himself to the wicker chair he was first in. Then he began to sip. "You know Gerard. I do not know how but I know one thing."

"What's that?" I wondered what he might have to say.

"This world of ours will never be the same after this war." He stated.

"Certainly not, It is the war to end all wars, is it not."

Pierre retorted. "A war to end all wars is still a war."

"What is that supposed to mean?" I questioned Pierre and wanted to see what he might say.

He sighed then spoke as if he did not even wish to, but felt like he must. "A war to end all wars, a fire to burn out all fires. An ocean to drain all rivers." Pierre looked at me like the older brother who knew that unicorns were not real. "That was a lie from the start."

"So you don't think that action must be taken to stop war?

Sometimes one must make war if they want peace."

Pierre raised his voice and began to get gravelly. "You can kill all the men you want, and you won't make enemies with them once they are dead, but the truth is: You will make enemies with their children. So no, I don't think any war will stop wars." He said it so matter of fact, and so convinced of it himself.

"So war has been, and will be, forever?" I shouted back, angry at the idea more than anything.

"Yes, at least on earth, and as long as your neighbor has more flour than you." Pierre hollered and his voice trailed off back into an admitting sigh.

"Hmmmm. Color me an optimist." I said as we reached our crossroads in the conversation, and in tone.

"You are an optimist, and a listener. Speaking of optimism, let us get to Batumi and end this damned hell after all, please?" Pierre said with the intonation of a question but the intention of a demand. "A car would be a blessing from god."

"Go ask Sergei."

"He is not god."

"I think Sergei is the closest we got right now Pierre."

Sergei of course heard us chatting, but he was the type of man not to say a word or hold out his cards until we asked him, and showed our own cards.

I looked at Pierre making clear eye contact and a tilt of my head. He should go over and ask. "That's the way..." I was about to go on.

Pierre began to walk over as he carried his spiked tea. He set the tea on the bar counter and Sergei continued to look straight forward. "Sergei?"

"Yes *priyatel*, Pierre is it?" Sergei called him 'pal' as I later found out.

"Tak. Yes Sir." Pierre blurted out with distinction and confidence.

"Please call me Sergei, and Pierre my friend, do not embarrass yourself. That is Polish." Sergei started normally, how he often did, with little expression. However, his eyes screamed 'I could rip your mouth off.' He rested into a gentle grin and paused until Pierre became sufficiently fearful and then laughed. "No worry, I think it is endearing when you westerners try so hard. I appreciate the effort."

"It would be fantastic if you would appreciate something else." Pierre was nervous, especially now after his mix-up.

"What would this be?" Sergei made eye contact. He was one of those men who rarely stared directly into your eyes, but when he did it was intense and required your absolute and undivided attention.

Pierre looked nearly as startled as he was during our other checkpoint with the Russians. "We need a car to get to Batumi, or should I say get there alive." He blurted out, with no cadence or manner, simply words.

"I understand." Sergei finished his tea and then set it on the table. "I will talk to my men, then we can arrange something for you."

Pierre stood there for a second awkwardly waiting for something to happen as Sergei walked off, sipping his tea. Then Sergei looked over again. "I am going to eat breakfast now, and you should as well. I will see about this autocar. Ok."

Pierre walked outside with his cup in hand, and the sun broke through the door as he opened it and changed the light on the wood inside. He went outside and then closed the door behind himself.

I sat there for a moment and scanned through the room. It

was not long after that Emir and then Bernardo came down. I then went outside to speak with Pierre and see where he had been. Outside I saw Pierre, and across the courtyard in the main square, I saw an old lady. She was at least seventy five, but she most certainly could have been older. A small red cloth embroidered with yellow flowers and green branches covered her head and tied together at the bottom, right above her neck. She sat alone in a single chair and watched all the men and probably us.

I looked at her from a distance and for a brief moment I was able to imagine, but in no concrete way; what she was. I saw the young lady in the headscarf bringing wheat and tomatoes back to the house. The woman who always reminded her younger brother to go to bed or wash the dishes. That brother was dead of course, probably from a war or illness, but not her. I saw the first man she loved and I thought about the last. Now, these I could never truly know, but in my own human way I could piece together the picture of her life that I imagined just might be true. How true? I'd like to think there is a sliver present within it, but what could I say? For lack of a better word I had only seen the other end of it. However, in my paling experience it is sometimes only at the end truth can be solidly written as truth and lies as lies.

Her face was wrinkled and she crouched and slouched, leaning forward. From the refuge of solitude that was her old wooden chair, she squinted her wise and unwavering eyes which judged all. Silently with an understated power. She watched the Russian men meander in circles on their shifts. I could see the judgment in her eyes at each and every young fighter, and I did not blame her very much. Her home had probably changed hands half a dozen times in her life, and I can imagine only a fraction of those had ever favored her, yet she was still here. It was the good kind of stubbornness that intended on staying steadfast no matter what would happen. She was the rock *and* the hard place.

"What is breakfast for you?" I asked Pierre and leaned over to him.

"Let us see." He fished his hand around inside the bag until he felt something out. "Bread, and, oh! bread."

"Gourmet." I said as I peered down. They were about the size of a fist and they both looked stale.

In those days we would dip the bread in some water, or if it happened to be terribly dry then we might soak it. If one was lucky, he might have just soaked it in butter or oil. However, it had been a long time since we had actually eaten any kind of government issued rations, notwithstanding the flour, which was turned into bread or hardtack. The majority of our food at this point was derived from the generosity of others or had been taken from abandoned houses, or otherwise.

Pierre walked back up against the building we had slept in and squatted against the wall on the cobblestone sidewalk. The wall had full pecks in it from bullet holes and I was startled at first, but they appeared old. From which war? I did not know. He drew the tin pan from his backpack and placed it deliberately on one of the flatter cobblestones that made up the sidewalk so that it would sit flat. After this, he broke the bread open on his knee into two pieces each so that it would total four. He unscrewed his canteen and then poured water into it for the bread to absorb.

I came upon Pierre as he was doing this. "Are those for you? I mean are those all for you. I know you gave some to that family, but the rest of us have little and what we do we would share with you all the same." I slowed my walk and then sat next to him on the ground so that the tin was between us. "Are they for you?" He laughed rhetorically. "There are four pieces and four of you. I should speak less. Why of course, you can have your share."

I sighed and thanked him on their behalf, but I did not know where the rest were at the moment. "It is one grand world. Is it not Pierre?"

"Mon bon copain I would argue the world is smaller."

"Well it is the same size as it was two thousand years ago..." I was hungry as I saw the water in the pan slowly get sucked up into the bread, softening it for chewing.

"No shit." Pierre shimmied in place against the wall then looked over and chuckled. Pierre and I both knew that it was a joke, so we both gave it a tired but nonetheless genuine grin.

"I knew that. I think this world still has much to offer." I spoke optimistically.

"Do you remember unfinished maps and continents that had not yet seen a single foot?" Pierre questioned.

"No, I do not." I said, eyes and much of my mind fixed on the bread.

"Exactly. The Earth is known, and we have boats and trains. All is spoken for. The world has become small and it will only continue to be smaller."

"Then humans may be closer." I followed in a hopeful tone, but one that lacked realism all the same.

"Closer to what, killing much more efficiently." Pierre was darkly humorous.

"No, closer to each other."

"That is quite optimistic mon ami."

"I try to be, I really try to be. I am not quite sure what good it does me yet, but something tells me it is worth trying."

"Did you always think it would make us closer?" Pierre scratched his slicked straight black hair, then away from his face and prepared for my response.

"I had always liked to think it was possible, albeit blindly. However, not without my senses." I stared back down at the bread. "Is it ready? The bread, or will you kill me and steal it all."

"Logically, I should as it would give me an advantage, but I like you. As much as one can like an American." Pierre was himself distant today, but somehow still loving in his words. I suppose that was because of his past, but for that he cannot be blamed.

We sat there and we watched the bread soak up the water. By now it had been done and I leaned over to see that there was no water in the pan. I was pleased. "Are we ready to eat?"

"You are ready. This I know." Pierre smiled and then reached out to touch the very top of the bread. The bread gave way and would squish when Pierre pressed down on it.

"That I am." I was hungry and I saw the food, and the food pierced the self known bubble of hunger." Hunger was one thing and fatigue was another, but when one met another it was another experience entirely. They compound on you, and your body is working off all the old stuff you have been storing for years.

"It is ready I think, in more ways than one." Pierre lifted the tin from the cobble to me and I pulled out my quarter. The one which was closest to me.

Quickly, I pulled it toward my tongue because the moment it had left the pan it started dripping. I was not only losing water, but bread as well. So I dropped it right in. My body told me to chew and swallow as most quickly as I could. However, from the perspective of my mind I realized to enjoy the flavor and slowly eat it was the best option. So I mulled it over in my mouth and pressed it between the ripples of my tongue and the grating of the roof of my mouth. It became a smooth pudding like consistency and this I tasted until there was all to taste.

I paused, not in my words, but not in my thoughts. "I'm sorry

Pierre, I do not care if the world is big or small, but it is still beautiful. This much I hope will stay the same."

"So you think the world is beautiful." Said Pierre with a touch of surprise at my words, as well as confusion, it would seem he clearly did not believe this.

The rest of the men eventually came back and we ate the bread. There was a knowing that when we shared it meant once the other would come to hunger we would do our best to balance the scales of debt and generosity. Heavy, quiet, hopefulness mingled in the air, and I thought we might follow it. That it would carry us away and eventually to our safety.

Chapter XXI

Sergei gave us the go ahead and we started to make our way out of town. I could see some of the remaining civilians who gazed at us. They stared quizzically, and focused on our faces as we talked. It seemed they attempted to search through us. As if they stared long enough, they might be able to tell the circumstances of the war outside and whether or not they should have reason to worry. That maybe our cadence and posturing as we made our way to the autocar might be some indication they could pick up on.

I for one think you can learn many things from someone and about someone if you look into their eyes long enough, and all that without speaking a word. However, I did not believe that I would be able to do that here, at least not well, and not in entirety. We moved through the rock paved street in one straight shot headed for the edge of town. We were headed to the northern part of the village. The part on the border between the town proper and outskirts. This border was a defined one and it was clear where the buildings ended and the countryside began.

I say it again, because this did not feel as if it was truly a physical place. If felt closer to an intermission, a liminal space. A small bubble that was a barrier between itself and everything else. Though we were not far from Batumi, I could be told we were almost anywhere. Civilization felt distant and humanity felt present. The transition to the outskirts felt raw and as before, demanded once again all our attention.

The path was easy but we moved slowly. The pace remained gradual because we felt like shit, and did not have any desire to do anything other than sleep again. The secondary reason being Bernardo had no way of moving quickly, so we made it into a jaunt and a stroll. We took turns helping Bernardo when he needed it, but the crutches that were hastily fashioned for him aided significantly.

Not a long walk afterward, we approached a rocky outcropping that steeped next to the dust and dirt road. It was trailed by horse tracks and motor groove-lines. A single but defined grass strip in the center where neither the horse or car had touched remained green. Off only about five feet or so was the car.

Now the cars we had previously driven were banged up but they were good cars. This car was banged up and crappy all in one. It was a deep beige-green color if you can imagine that in any visually pleasing manner. Although frankly, the color did not matter as it was scratched and dented to oblivion to the point that a lot of it was simply the steel silvery color of the car itself. I saw a few bullet holes as well, but hell, it was a car. I just wanted to see one of us turn it on. I had been handed the keys and stepped up against the car, grabbing the handle which clicked and slid like a vault door with no grease.

I did not sit down but leaned into the leather seats. They stretched and whined as I slid in, and I turned the key after pushing it into the ignition. The car sputtered and kicked its own metal insides until it came on. We threw what belongings we still had in the back of the car and everyone hopped in. The doors clanged closed with a heavy metallic swing, then slammed. I pressed the gas and the dry mixed sand and dirt coughed out of the muffler. We started moving north. North to Batumi.

"You know my friend, I must tell you something." Pierre said softly, and with precision.

"You called me friend in English for the first time." I took notice.

"Ahh ha, this is true." He was delighted, as he himself did not even notice. He then joked once more, "You are supposed to say what, right?"

"What is ..." He stopped me before I could respond.

"I had a wife once and I did not even love her, you know truly. With my heart." Pierre struck me. His words, more polite and subtle than usual, but the content took me by surprise. I changed my attention, as his attention changed.

"How long ago?" I questioned him, but initially out of curiosity, and because he had so abruptly brought it up.

"Years. Long enough for me to forget the details, but not too long so that I forget it all." He said with the face that stands alone among faces. The lonely gaze upon the fruits of our past.

I stated the obvious. "You never forget it *all*."

"The face that is silently gracious of the past for the lessons one learned in the pain." Pierre responded, out of expectation. The face consisted of about a second of glazed familiar sadness, as followed by about a four or three second slow transition to pinched eyes and lips that would barely admit to smiling ever so slightly fondly.

I tapped Pierre or, more specifically, his mind. I asked him. "You did not love her? No." I waited for him as his eyes as well as thoughts returned, only as well as they could be gathered.

"No. This was through no fault of her own. She was kind, beautiful, and I could say I was fond of her, but for me to say I loved her would be a lie."

"So why did you do it? Why were you married?" I asked with interest.

"In search of love, well her family was also quite rich. I quickly realized that I was deluded. I realized that if you spend all your time in search of love, you will be lost and unprepared when the time truly comes to give it." He said as if he were making a note in the journal of his mind, as a recurring reminder.

"One must still search, you cannot simply sit and wait."

"Yes, but you must mind the balance between fantasy and reality. A head in the clouds may drown when it rains, but if your feet never leave the ground you won't know where the water comes from." Pierre was still forming his conception of this idea, I could tell by how he explained it.

"Is there not the search for love, the hope, the journey, the finding?" I summoned points of conversation.

"If you begin with love I believe you can build upon it, but to forge it from air?" Pierre asked rhetorically.

Chapter XXII

So the sun teased night at us, and the sky became dark as a skirt of cool blue swept behind it. The sun had not completely set, and it was just about perfect.

"Golden hour." Pierre noted aloud as he spoke half to himself. "This is what it is called."

"Yes, the golden hour, good thing this should only take us a few hours. That is, if everything goes alright." I said, gesturing along the way, with one hand on the driving wheel at any given moment.

Pierre became mentally rigid, then repeated what I said back to me. "If everything goes alright."

See, whenever something goes wrong, usually other things go wrong after. It seems to often be a type of snowball effect, that a series of coincidences perform so consistently horribly they almost feel orchestrated. Sometimes the opposite is the case, and things go so suspiciously well, and you are left wondering how? Regardless, 99% of our time is spent in normal life events that gradually cycle through good, bad, and okay.

I almost know I am crossing into the other half when things don't go the worst way you would expect them to, or they positively surprise you. That way you know the ship is changing course, or at least beginning to.

Bernardo seemed frustrated and launched himself into the conversation. "Charles' writing has no more maps, look, you see."

"He did not write any further on than this. That much is

obvious Bernardo." Pierre said. "We lack the maps and we lack the road."

Bernardo looked down again and thought once more. " It says here: *check with maggiore.*" He paused and disdainfully chuckled to himself and the dark humor he found in it, then spoke. "Well he is dead anyway, so what do you all say?"

"I suppose there is not much to say after that." I paused for a moment, not to think but to more concretely acknowledge what I had said. "Is there?" I spoke partially with the intention of a question and partially hoping someone would offer an idea.

"Well, yes. If he is dead we cannot ask him any questions. I see the issue." Pierre observed, with his usual cynicism of life and what he deemed the harshness of reality. That which he often covered up with his ever-casual demeanor. "So we must choose a direction?"

I sarcastically countered. "Novel idea Pierre."

"You are the one driving, do something." Pierre quipped back.

"Well this is obvious Pierre. It makes you critically honest. It is not for you to become scathing as well." Bernardo stepped where he normally did not and it was probably the surprise that had owed itself to such results.

"I am honest first then cynical. Sometimes I mess up the order."

"I'll mess your order up." I said.

"I will put both of you chickens back into the egg." Emir was annoyed, and it was clear to him our bickering had not contributed any new strategies. "Now, let's get our plan in order."

Pierre simmered and entered back into himself after this. I knew that the alcohol he took with, or more specifically in his tea this morning had taken effect and not fully let go, even if it was hours ago at this point. I also knew how he felt, and I did not know whether or not he had drank any more. I had my fair share of early starts. A morning when a bit of gin slips in your coffee. They were not proud days by any means and they were not days that made me a better man. Well I suppose in the face of striking honesty I should be entitled to say I felt like a champ sometimes while doing them. Although the necessary thing to mention is as soon as you reach the other side of the hill your brain slows in synchronicity with your heart. By the end of those days I always felt like a degenerate and everything was less organized than before.

A man walking through city streets as cobbled together and shattered as my mind, but never more navigable. I would break myself and I would find those little threads of my heart and mind and those are the strings I would pull from myself. Then it would feel as though the carpet was being un-done. A carpet covering my own personal stains etched into the ground. That is when I would become the last thing I should have been. Silent. I imagined by this hour in the day, perhaps it was this feeling that may have come over Pierre.

That skirt of darkness crept out above us and reminded us of our size. The shrubs and trees that were spotted in small groups gathered around the ponds and streams. Most of which lead to the Black Sea, Yet! I should say before the skirt of darkness had taken us over, a golden hour. One that felt legendary and meaningful. The one that had no immediate meaning, but was so beautiful you could not resist giving it one. If not for the sun, then for yourself.

"You know in Armenia there are so many sunsets like this one." Emir casually mentioned while reminiscent of his own histories.

"Do you brag? Do not brag." Pierre said, I imagine regretting it as it was spoken.

"What do you even speak of, I will not see home again. What is there to brag of?" Emir paused to catch himself. "There is no reason for the festering of bad feelings now. We are too close to the finish line."

"There is no finish line!" Pierre looked pissed and indifferent at the same time.

I interrupted. "No more arguing, it slows us down." I had one last point to drive home. "I'll just drive north along the coast, and we should eventually hit Batumi. Does that sound like a good plan?" There was some tension in my words, as no alternate plan had actually been offered.

"Splendid." Bernardo was happy things were quiet and we had a plan. "*Momento*, I'll get the compass from the bag."

Chapter XXIII

The car pulled up to a flat road, a real road. One was made of lined stones and on either side a wall as we entered. There was a group of men waiting and they saw us. We waved, and they did the same back to us. It was the edge of town and there we stopped. The stone wall arched up into a gate, and a high one at that. It cleared over the car with room to spare. The men moved up to the car. There were about four of them and two split up on either side of the car.

The soldier who carried the most sense of authority came to the driver's side. Where I was. He was pale and bald, and had no facial hair. About thirty or so.

"Where are you coming from?" He asked for information only, at least that was the feeling I got. There was no intonation or expression in his voice.

I supplied the necessary info. "Sarpi, by car."

"Where before that?" He questioned further, and scratched his head then patted afterward, staring at me with his light blue eyes.

"Anatolia, highlands? We came from Devrek originally." I wasn't sure what exactly he wanted, but he was not terribly specific.

"What was your reason? You are soldiers. Da?" He was stone faced and gave no inclination away as to what he was thinking.

I began to wonder why he was asking, but cooperated with them on the matter. "Yes, we are allies. We were enlisted to intercept a shipment, with a squad of Italian soldiers as well."

He smiled subtly and then returned to his professional face. "Of course we know you are allies. If that was not the case you'd be dead." He continued. "Where are the Italians?"

"One is here." Bernardo commented.

"The rest?" He held his gun across his arms long ways, glanced up and around, then back.

"Gone or missing." I was short and quick, after imaging and explaining events so many times, you start to summarize the whole thing into a few key words.

"Good thing we did not shoot you then, dead people cannot talk about stories." He laughed now, slow and rolling, like a sick dog, with sadism and grime in his voice.

I did not find it funny. "Ahh, I see. Anything else you must know?" Nonetheless, I remained cordial. However tempting when tired, hungry, and on the move, I did not need to make petty enemies.

"It checks out. Sergei radioed you in." He lifted his hand to a man behind the stone gate, and he raised the wooden bar with a lever. One of the men who had walked up slapped the back of the car. "OK! You go ahead, thank you." He went on with his day.

The car took us further into the city but decided it best to park after the streets became narrow and quaint for foot traffic. We took out our belongings and I put the keys in my pocket.

By this time, the blanket of evening had been cast over the earth, and all was dark except for the stars and moon that cut through the near black of the sky. Although the letter of the law had been accomplished by our arrival, there was an absence that remained. We had felt short changed for a reason that was not exactly explicable. Every step had been thread tied to thread, and some part of me imagined there could be some tangible sense of resolution upon this arrival; yet it felt more like another piece of thread.

"So what are we to do now?" Bernardo asked in confusion and subtle but available dissatisfaction.

I pushed my hair back and pulled my hand down my face, fingers dragging the skin with it. "I don't know? We were always supposed to be here, this was our plan... to get here." I sighed. "We are here." My tone rose, then crashed.

"So then there is nothing for us to do now. We have succeeded." Pierre said, as he eagerly relieved himself of duty, like someone clocking out from a day of work.

"Well I would not say we succeeded." Emir chuckled, then looked at the buildings as we meandered along the side streets searching for a place to go, or perhaps a clue in the right direction.

"What do you mean? Our job was to get to Batumi." Pierre stated.

I surveyed the townscape, some buildings more ornate than others, and the streets, some cobbled and others gravel. Other paths are still only dust and packed earth. "Our job was to intercept a shipment, a shipment we lost, along with everyone in our squad notwithstanding all who are within eyeshot right now." I stopped then concluded. "That is not a success." I did not want to sound harsh, but those were the plain facts of the situation.

"The war is not even over either." Emir admitted. "Pierre, do we have different definitions of success?"

Pierre sounded a little peeved. "We may have different definitions of what it means to be finished."

"Possible." Emir coughed, then cleared his throat.

"We have been spared from death, at least for now." Bernardo's lanky body leaned to and fro as he swung each leg up and in front of him. He looked at the curb then up at the stars. "That cannot be said for all in our squad."

No one was angry at each other. No one had the energy to be mad at one another. Each of us was taking inventory of ourselves in all that remained and all that did not.

"The town is silent." Bernardo said as his eyes scoured about.

"Of course this is so. Safety is not a given, but to be invisible would help." Pierre gestured at the windows, and every light was off with the blinds pulled closed. He kicked at the bits of pavement that scattered onto the road. The sidewalk and street were well lit, which made the dark, curtain-drawn home windows along the road even more uncanny.

"The quiet before the storm." I said. "It is uncharacteristically quiet." I looked around, there were already some signs of distress in the area. Some windows had been cracked and the wind drained through them whipping and clapping the shutters. Sparse, but noticeable bullet wounds in the walls and over the ground. The rounds had left pinpricks but sometimes caused cracks and splits. Knocked pieces of brick and plaster scattered across the road like breadcrumbs on a plate.

We kept moving, and floated our direction as we navigated around sandbag walls, or stacked bluffs of brick and stone reclaimed for defensive measures.

"There is one thing that I know for sure." Emir's eyes pinched looking attentively at nothing.

"What?" Pierre asked.

"They know something I do not." Emir seemed cautious and unsettled but equally uncertain he felt this way.

The hot sea air mingled with the cooler mountain breezes and settled upon the city in a warm, but weaving field of air that felt refreshed. Pierre popped open that shiny folding metal tin of his and peeked inside. The cigarettes were crumpled and the tin had taken its own beating. I slowed to a saunter and pivoted the strap on my backpack over my shoulder so I was wearing the pack on my chest. I kept moving as my hands pushed through the canvas bag to search for... there it was. The cigar, or more specifically Charles' which I had been gifted. It retained that same earthen treelike hue to it, and its bold yet humbly quiet strength.

I peered back at Pierre and twiddled the cigar between my two pointer fingers and looked down at it. "Do you have the matches? Because I have a cigar."

Pinching the leaf gently in my lips, I worked my way around the end where it rolled closed; then bit the end clean off with my teeth and placed the tobacco stick between my lips.

Fishing his fingers in his right pocket until his arm was straight down to the bottom, he grabbed something then pulled it out. Ripping the match off its package, he struck the outside strip to wave me closer while it sparked alive with its robust light in the beginning.

Like all matches it swelled bright and light only to crackle steady calm soon after it lit. While that happened, Pierre and I moved closer, we cupped our free hands around the match and cigar. After a few moments the sulfur was gone and it slowed as only the splinter of wood. He held the dying light to the tip of the rolled leaves and it was alright. The cigar pulled the live smoke through and so it began to puff and glow well.

We strolled through the stone paved alleys that were silent, solemn, and shifted sly, slightly shy from the shine of the lampposts in the sight of the still street. Slowly, some sense of direction patiently grew for each second we looked and lingered throughout the town. We approached the coast and the wooden boardwalk that stood over the shoreline. It was a level boardwalk as a straight line inland until the shore met it on the dune. Us four meandered to the very end and each found his spot to lean, sit, or rest. The cigar was passed from person to person and each one enjoyed it for a good and simple share of time. Our feet followed the boardwalk until it was no longer.

We retraced our steps and then turned onto the beach, where there was more space, and we were closer to the water. The cool dry sand and rock took over and we sat in it. My boots and pants dug into the sand, I looked out.

Bold black waves crashed onto the shore of the mighty sea and spilled out flat, gently highlighted by the white light of the moon. Each building splash and rolling collapse felt heavy as it carried onto the shore and its aroma up through our noses. The water appeared deep, and the dense purple of the sky lied about its being black. I thought at once of the creatures deep down beneath the command of the water's surface. I thought a second time and there was a grace in its awful power.

I could have been fooled if one told me I was on the ocean, but in the back of my head I knew it was a sea. A grand one at that, and mighty fearsome is what I had heard. The story of its birth was recounted if it was of any interest. I'll go ahead but make it brief. A collection of lakes, lowlands, and marsh got filled in and mixed with the Mediterranean as it broke over the strait near Istanbul, Bosphorus. Salt and freshwater mixing to create a unique and especially unpredictable body of water with multiple layers. However, behind the eyes and past the horizon we all had known what it truly was, a wide, hurling body of water, dangerous as any.

As the cigar smoke grew dim and harsh, we knew it was nearly done. "Hand me that would you?" I put my hand out and Pierre placed it between my fingers. I took a few more pulls then coughed, spat, and pressed it dead into the ever so slightly damp grains of coarse pebbled sand right in front of me where the tide ended. "They want to send our soggy, sour, sorry, asses back out there?" I clenched my jaw and gripped my fist next to my waist while it pushed against the sand.

"No, they want our asses right here." Pierre added half heartedly, scratching the stubble on his cheek.

"That's even worse." Bernardo leaned into his crutches, settling his anxious gaze on his body then to the ground.

Emir wobbled and waved his hands up in the air, his frustration and discontent made apparent. "This is not what I signed up for." He nearly made an "X" in the air with his arms while they crossed past one another.

"Emir, it kind of is, my friend." Pierre tossed his thought, accurate, but unhelpful out into the open.

"Well, consider how I reacted." He said in finality that what he knew in reality could not be concluded as true. "Ridiculous."

"To say that your opinion against the military is superior?" I said, nearly sure, but still deciphering his full meaning.

"Yes," He responded admittedly, but unaffected.

"You are delusional mon frere." Pierre put his arm around Emir's shoulder and pivoted his neck. Staring at him through the curtain of center parted straight black hair, Pierre pressed his fingers on Emir's chest then recalled his hand just as fast. "I like it."

"You just like having people to point fingers at." I thought Pierre smiled at the protest in it, the denial of authority, the self declaring it-self.

Pierre moved his finger toward me, "You just like someone to do the pointing for you." Pierre sounded searing and harsh.

I stopped before things got worse. "Very little of it is our fault though." I thought for a moment. "I do not remember wanting to conquer any neighboring kingdoms."

"Not big on that is Delawara?" Bernardo asked, knowing full well.

"No, although I'd like some more shoreline." I responded. "Maybe I should form a militia against Maryland?"

"There we go!" Bernardo spoke with disdainful sarcasm. "Now you have reason to commence a war!"

Pierre played around with it. "See, I only know Delaware' by way of you. So I support Delaware."

"Now you have a military ally." Bernardo laughed, but there were teeth gritting between the hollers. He sighed, and laughing let out his anger, not the worst way to do so. "And he does not even know why Maryland must be invaded, yet he hates them."

"It is rather flat in that region." I grinned. "Shouldn't be too hard."

"Ok, I am in. They must learn French." Pierre added a condition.

"I am out." Bernardo looked at Pierre with playful disgust, and swung away from him as if he were sick or feverish.

"Oh, well that was rather quick." I grieved over the collapse of our fictitious state.

"Let us hope things go this way." Bernardo wished idly.

Emir smiled but his eyes were strained and distracted. "Hahaha, perhaps another Armenia."

"That would be something." Pierre commented while he pushed and pulled his hands throughout the sand to see how it built up, then eroded.

"I think we all actually did *sign* up for this..." Bernardo had been critical, but it was obvious and without direction, which was best.

Pierre wanted to make a point clear. "Now, why or how we signed is different."

I admitted aloud, and thought we agreed. "This is true."

Emir contributed. "Some are forced, but even then, one must

find a reason."

"You are telling me." Pierre seemed peeved. "I am still in search."

"Difficult." Emir could not say more. "In search."

Pierre humbled himself. "But I am sure you have seen more, mon frere."

"It has been a while since I have had a living one, never thought my next would be French." He laughed with that stale deadpan that made you want to laugh more. I was surprised he did not laugh, himself.

"This thing is full of surprises, non?"

"What thing?" I asked.

"This, life." Pierre smiled.

Everyone was fidgeting. Pierre mowed trenches in the sand, and Bernardo molded his into a mound. Emir drew thin and narrow lines with a stick; and I dug a pit, stacking the sand around it.

"Predictability is comfortable, but when comfortable becomes predictable, comfortable is boring, and boring is well, boring." Bernardo said with unusual focus. "Well that is not to say I do not wish to have my leg back."

He was a little fixated on that still, I would be too. I asked. "You have most of it right?"

"Enough to get here I suppose. Hopefully enough to leave as well." Bernardo patted down at his leg which was extended straight out. "Infection, that is my most sincere worry."

"They'll ship you out of here before they make you fight anyone." I started, while picking the deadened cigar from the sand.

Pierre took it from my hands, and tossed it back into the dunes and high grasses above the beach. "What! It is made of leaves, it should decompose like all else."

"I suppose, but not quite as appetizing as a pound of tenderized

Bernardo leg." Emir jokes.

"I prefer tobacco, sorry Bernardo." I jested all too deliberately. "I shall pass."

"Me too." Bernardo sighed, half tired and half relieved. "Let the animals have it."

When the pace of the conversation gradually declined we became quieter and the sea became louder and more present. One by one, each of us got up and stood in that ever-lost feeling of wistful patience. A manner I am sure most have had. After a trial, or a series of events that test your mind or body, the curtain of clouds is pulled back in the slightest; and you rest for a moment that feels so vaguely eternal, because you see how grand and strange the whole world is. Each path and journey follows one another. Once we'd raised ourselves, and Bernardo, we thought of what would be next. That thing which is never certain yet we remain always near to its arrival.

Pierre stretched his whole body, pushing his chest out then going on to speak. "They say it is always about the journey and never the destination, so then why ever finish the journey?"

"Why ever begin the journey?" Emir asked sarcastically.

"I do not think you are picking up on my point." Pierre criticized the clear sarcasm of his words. "If life is about journeys then why ever pick a destination? Let alone arrive at it."

I yawned then began. "Pierre, if you never finish, then it is not a journey. That is the problem."

"What is it then?"

Bernardo grunted as he gradually propped himself up with Emir's help. "It is floundering, meandering, wandering."

"Wandering can be a journey." Pierre fruitlessly checked his metal tin again imagining the cigarettes would be unbroken.

"Being lost is a journey too, but if you never get unlost then it is not a journey." Bernardo looked around and back to the town which from here was uncharacteristically dimly lit.

"Are we on a journey?" Pierre poked around.

Emir responded in what he saw as a correction, not a comment. "No, it seems we are at the destination. We *were* on a journey."

I made my opinion known. "It does not feel like a destination."

"It has felt more like a crapshoot than a journey, that's the truth." Pierre pulled out the least broken cigarette, and his face seemed disappointed as he lit it. He closed the tin then stowed it again in his breast pocket. "No!" He dragged on the wrinkled paper. "You want my honest opinion!" He said as a declaration, and lure for our questioning.

"What is your honest opinion?" I gave in and entertained him.

"Well it is more of a question than much else."

"Just say it."

"Why do I still feel lost, copain?"

"What?" I said, not knowing where he was going with this. We looked around at each other.

He prefaced himself. "If we are at the destination, then why am I still lost?" The cigarette died faster than the average, for obvious reasons. He threw it into the sand like an angsty child equally displeased with the world and himself.

"I don't know if I can answer this one for you." I followed his movements after he tossed the butt. "I for one am finished, quite done."

"So you are at the destination, non?" He searched in my eyes to see if my words matched the truth of things.

"I am at a destination, but hell, life is full of destinations. Some people live without a single journey. They go from destination to destination." I answered.

"Sad ones I must admit." Pierre agreed with me.

"No Pierre, those are the lost ones." I contested frankly and was a touch melancholic.

"I just told you, mon ami, I am the lost one." Pierre insisted upon himself.

"Pierre, by virtue of insisting you are lost you know where you are." I caught it. "Therefore you are not lost." I straightened up. "The ones who are truly lost have no knowledge on the matter."

"Then what am I?"

"You are following that subtle undercurrent of emptiness that comes through all after each destination is reached. The journey of finding."

"I think another journey is in order." Pierre said in exhaustion. "A journey far from here."

"Will you journey or will you wander?"

"I will wander until I have come to realize my journey. The only journeys I care for are the ones I have destined for myself." Pierre commanded, hoping for his words to come true. So did we all.

Chapter XXIV

After we moved on and away from the shoreline we made our way back into the town. The town was quiet and still, and all too quiet, as was mentioned. From broken boards and mortared streets that were thoroughly strewn with chunks and clumps of rock. We searched for a light in the darkness. Something that would tell us people were present. Something that would tell me life is present, and still humming, and respite of calm, however temporary.

"There is nothing here. It is dark, and none are out." Pierre walked past the same broken earth as the rest of us, and he surveyed it as if he had known near a speck more than the rest of us.

Emir kicked a piece of cobblestone into the empty street. "The chaos is silent, it is unnerving." Emir pivoted his head until he met one of our eyes to catch something.

"Silent chaos is an oxymoron." I joked aloud, and the joke sunk into the solemn deepness of the latening evening.

"What would you say an oxymoron is?" Emir smiled and tried to play it off, but I knew he wanted a genuine answer.

"An oxymoron is a phrase or statement that folds upon itself, and somehow still manages to make sense."

"So like..." Emir wanted an example, either that or he wanted to kill time until we found a hostel. The answer was probably both.

Pierre punched his words into the conversation. "So, say a lady likes you more than the others, and then she tells you that she wants to spend more time *alone,* together."

"Then what?" Emir asked, "I say yes. Provided I am not married in this situation."

Pierre chuckled between his words, and admitted. "Clever Emir, so you see?" Pierre imitated a puzzled face. "That is the oxymoron, no one can spend time, alone, together."

"What if when you are alone together you are one?" Bernardo slowed his pace simply to comment, and then swiped his brow.

"Of course the *Italien* would ask this question." He scratched his head and pushed his hair away and then answered in full, hands outstretched but together. "I suppose the answer depends on your school of thought, but in my book that is an oxymoron."

"That is quite the abstract image Bernardo, but I would hope you get the picture?" I finished then asserted my hope of a response.

Emir nodded, and we carried on. Upon meeting a crossroads, we simultaneously saw a shining yellow-orange streetlight at the end of a road, and so we followed it as one.

Down the barren, bullet-beaten street was that single light. It was accompanied by muffled noises and music from indoors, and to us, the sound of safe haven. However, in contrast with the rest of the city there was an eeriness that surrounded it. It offered the impression that when the town was populated this was the dicey quarter. We came up to the door, and there were a few men standing outside smoking and chatting in a foreign tongue.

The outside facade of the bar boasted a single blackened metal lantern lit by gas. The lantern-post remained fastened to the stone lintel above the door. Everything on the interior was a deep dark wood except for the arched stone ceiling with chained lights hanging down so low you could bump your head on it if you weren't careful. The long rectangular tables were all in a row; connected and pushed up against the back wall. The wall, of course, was equipped with benches and corner seating.

Everyone inside this half-basement/ground floor picked a spot along the tables, usually only one or two seats over from one another. The old men and regulars sipping vodkas and such on empty stretches of the bartop. The bartender might say something if someone acted up, yet most times he seemed to care less, especially if the customer was already paid. I found a corner toward the back with a circular wooden table of its own and a corner bench built into the wall. The vaulted gray stones curved in over our heads as each arc led to the center. Where many small and practical cold-steel chandeliers were attached by chains. The term chandelier feels ambitious here.

The air was filled with smoke and the sweaty warmness of bodies stacked up close to one another. Men at tables playing cards as cigars and pipes dangled gently between their teeth and lips. They shouted at each other angry as could be then paused, and followed up with pure and unadulterated laughter. Only then could one tell it was a joke. We only picked up on their body language as their words were all but unknown to me.

We all sat down, and each, about the same time let out a great and emptying sigh of relief. One at a time, as each of us sat down on the wooden board the long-distracted and well-ignored fatigue began to set in with vigor. I had found that if a task important enough is in front of you for an extended period of time, your brain will shut off the danger bells and hunger whistles. During such intense episodes of mettle, those activities resigned to a place of luxury when every step taken is a problem solving equation. My bum hit the chair and the week or so of tiredness that I had set on the back burner began returning to its true weight. The extent of our journey had been realized. Now that we've arrived, my body and my mind attempt to synchronize with one another. Everything in the room slowed before our eyes and not much speaking was necessary. Eyes slowly met gazes across the table, making turns on each other, and without words each answer was more or less the same. Through no verbal exchange, a soft consensus was reached.

I leaned back into the bench and my body slouched to its form. No superior to tell me what to do, and nowhere near enough of a hoot given to prop myself up or explain it to others who might stare. That being said, they did not appear by any means, as a picky crowd; notwithstanding our being foreigners. That usually served as a major plus or minus depending on with whom you were chatting. A short bald man with a long and thickly rounded beard came up to the table in the dim but comfortably warm lit recess of the tavern.

The bench itself was stiff, but the setting and seating comforted me. One may venture to guess we did not wish to travel any further than necessary with our bodies, and nowhere near to where our mind's were. So for this given moment, I rested. The low summer beachside air mixed with musty and tobacco filled rooms. It was dark outside and the breeze was cool, but the air remained mild. My muscle movement felt mechanical. Rotating and turning towards each thing that I needed to do as my mind trailed off in a thousand ways. All that I needed was good food and a warm fireplace. That fireplace, of course, was situated about ten feet from me in the center back of the common area. It was there our bones and spirits warmed up a tinge, lest I say too much.

There was a man who came to us, the waiter. He was proud and excited. He was eager to speak in English. I was surprised as an English speaker, as the only people who like (or speak) English in these parts are English speakers or those who are going to leave for the U.K. or America. When one says *America* in slang one often means The United States of America, with all its capital letters and special notation. However as an American, I had the luxury of not giving a hoot. We all placed our orders.

"Gin and tonic makes me worse than an animal, and when I am worse than an animal I say the foulest things." Bernardo joked and then attempted to wain away. I saw the physical pain in his eyes, but the physical concealed far too well the psychological. His leg was not infected, but neither was it healing well. Since it happened he had not seen any medical help, aside from rags and torn shirts roped around his leg.

Far from hospitals, schools, and many other things we take for granted, it was the best we could do at that moment. If what that meant was us pouring vodka on his leg and wrapping it in a shirt, then it would have to do.

In the distantly removed darkness of the Black sea and its steep mountains we found a small light. A place well and kicking in the dim and narrow streets, which stood darkened in the shadow of war, as a humble tavern. A tavern older than all of us put together that had probably seen its fair share of wars. It never closed then and it had not closed now, but then again it was used to it, yet we were not as weathered. Well maybe Emir was, but he never overshared and we never asked, because he never spoke. He was not one to want to take up space or make waves, but he was convinced of what he believed. However, in my experience, the ones who never talk are the ones that need to let the most out.

Emir had a water with lemon juice and he drank it as his gaze jumped to and fro by each of our own alcoholic drinks. As a Muslim he had betrayed his religion when he had drunk Pierre's liquor, and consequently betrayed himself when he left, albeit from a very true shame.

I felt like chatting. "So Pierre, what are you going to do when you return to France?"

"I haven't seen a newspaper in months, I do not know if there is a France, I would hope there is." He said, lighting up another half-snapped cigarette inside.

"Well, say there still is a France, what will you do?" I asked again, with a conditional, to make it worthy of answering.

What once was a only mustache on his face had been now surrounded and challenged by the stubble that filled in while he attended greater duties. "I am not so sure I may return, mon ami. There is little waiting for me there. There was not much when I left." He paused and then spoke again with his hands open and stretched over the table moving without rest. "I love my home as much as the next patriot, but what is *patriotisme* without comrades?"

"What is patriotism without a home?" I wanted to spark something within him and see where it would go.

"All the same mon ami, what is home without family? Without comrades?" His small and insignificant cigarette was finished again. I doubt he even got the buzz from it. "Home is a special place, for some home is where we were born, for others where we die. Then for some it is a place inbetween."

"What do you mean by this?" I wondered about him and his thoughts.

"Some people visit their home once in life and never see it again." The crumpled paper went into the ashtray, and his two forefingers had smudges of ash on them.

"That makes no sense. Nonsense." Bernardo laughed Pierre off all too quickly, the rest of us waited for more.

"Home is where your heart is, and occasionally people's hearts are found miles away from where they are born."

"Could you stop being so vague?" Emir stared at him with interest and a desire for explanation.

"Why are you going to Russia? Emir." Pierre asked.

"My home has been overtaken and decimated."

"That is different." I said.

"That *is* different." Pierre knew he had made an overreach, the conversation got lost and we enjoyed our beverages.

The night grew late, and we continued to chat and drink and our bodies slowly melted into the form of the benches as our conversations wavered from serious to simple, then silly.

Hour by hour we slowly steeped ourselves in the late night and things felt ever so slightly buoyant again. The drunken haze covered our minds and ears like a smog and things seemed rather simpler than before. The laughing and jesting made me think of the plain things that felt so distant but shadowed closely within reach in the simmering evening. We sat without worry or distraction in the ancient basement air and breathed easier and lighter. Through the joy, gentle smiles, and hearty chuckles, we cooled off.

"I need a place to lay my head and get a fair night's sleep." Pierre took a swig of his drink and stated his point of view loud and clear.

"Yea, as much as I loved the beach, I think we need a good, proper bed. With feathers in the mattress and everything." Bernardo stated. "You know. With my leg, of course."

I responded emphatically, gesturing to the straightened leg under the table. "Why, *of course*."

"A blanket would work for me." Emir said, clear as day.

"You really are a simple man." I looked over to him with a further touch of curiosity at something I already kind of knew.

"Not with your cooking." Pierre sipped his drink.

"The less you want, the less you need. This just makes sense." He said it in a way that told you he already knew what he was saying and why. It made sense to him, that was the important thing.

"Fair, but you still want things, and to say you don't would be a lie. We all know it. Every person has desire." I admitted, hoping he'd agree, and then some.

"Of course I want things, but the less I grab at them the less pain they cause me." Emir was decided, and with good reason.

"Oh come on, that is just an excuse for not trying." Pierre was displeased and thought it was bull.

"Ok so it was?" Emir gave no credence, but a simple smile to acknowledge what had been said. "I cannot take any of it with me once I die, so I have always said: 'why gather so much?'"

We slowly and surely continued into the late night, but it did not feel so late after all. Everything else came alongside it, the laughing and jesting made me think. Ancient air of the half-basement bar filled my nose and consequently my mind. It was light and easy and the mood gently simmered into a need for rest.

"Agh. It is about time." Pierre stated, while also sitting still and not doing anything.

"As much as I love the beach and the bar, and the rest of our vacation, I think I must turn in." I looked back down and meant what I said.

"Proper bed. I just need a blanket. Hell, I'm falling asleep now." Emir sighed, then yawned.

"Oh come on. You are falling asleep all the time. I have been seeing this." Bernardo pointed at me and spoke declaratively.

"I'm tired." Emir countered.

"I am tired." I coughed.

"I'm tired, the dog is tired, mom is tired, dad is tired." Bernardo mimicked my American candor. "We are all tired Gerardo, Your feet hurt. My head does. Your head hurts? Tell us about it."

"Ok, I'm done talking about it." I wanted to drop it and declare myself alright.

"You cannot be done talking about something you were not talking about." Bernardo sizzled and fevered in his force more than usual. I figured he was plagued internally, and left it alone.

"I would much rather sleep in a place far from any military barracks." Pierre spoke, and we were quiet, as would be expected, but only a second.

"We're about half a hike away from there. Sorry to say." I looked down and clenched my jaw, releasing it with my breath.

Pierre stopped and then focused. "I didn't expect it to happen so soon."

"Speak of the devil." Bernardo slowed and he closed his pace of words.

We saw a decorated man in military garb and he stepped in like a sore thumb. He appeared all too dignified and all too stiff. He pushed the door in one motion like a calculated and proper smooth fella, he found one step after another with a serious focus and concentration.

"Now who is this?" I asked. We guessed he was here for us. The way he stuck out, there was little mistaking to be done.

"He hasn't shot a gun in years, are you crazy?" Pierre smiled and then grinned.

"He has never shot one." Emir grunted. We each made up an idea of him.

"I'll bet dollars on that." I lifted my glass up a little bit, then Pierre smiled once more.

"What else would you put money on? I hope that you're ready." I said.

"No! Not dollars, I would put bucks on it." Bernardo said, pleased with himself, smiling a little.

"Now you are learning. You'll be as American as apple pie in no time Bernardo." I was cheering him on, even if it seemed a little inflated.

"Little Bernardo will speak just like this, when we raise him in

The United States." He spoke the sentence plainly but there was a glimmer on how he said The United States.

"Maybe you would pick New York, Philly, or Boston, yeah?" I was simply throwing ideas out. "Might be a little easier to break ground there."

"Hey! I may have a bum leg, but I can still do a good job. This you hear, Gerardo!" He pretended to have cooled off, but I knew he wasn't mad to begin with. "Bernardo Junior will happen one way or another. The bear got my second leg, not the third. You understand?"

"I understand." I tried not to break out in laughter, although I'd figured it was partly a joke. "I am not talking about your leg Bernardo." I paused and then finished. "You're Italian."

"What about it?"

"Well not everyone over there trusts you guys, and even less have actually met you." I repeated myself. "I'm just saying they might treat you nicer in some places rather than others."

"Noted." Bernardo held in then burst a little. The drinks had temporarily eased his spirit, and pain. "Well I cannot heal from that one, and I admit I am too proud to as well."

"That is the spirit. You tell them who you are."

"Never the other way around." Bernardo declared.

The man who came inside stopped, and took his hat off. While he removed it, I saw the nuance in him. I saw the indecision and the misunderstanding. The kind that he himself barely understood let alone acknowledged. The streaks of gray that accented randomly from his light brown hair and otherwise youthful face. He propped his clean hat between his armpit and perfectly neat pleated pants. He was a paper pusher by the looks of it.

The officer started moving and kept pace in his tightly bound presence to request a beer from the bar. One of his feet stayed in place as the other rotated like a turrent to reorient. He now faced us and carefully sipped the beer twice, surveying the room and seemingly the flavor. He stood still for a moment, as if he were breathing the room in. After this intermission, he approached the back of the room, making his way to us.

"He'd better not come here. I know he is military, but damn it if he is not the last thing I want to see right now." Pierre's face looked visually disgusted.

"Of course he is coming here." Emir calmly noted.

"Who else is he here to talk with?" Bernardo watched as he made his way closer.

Swift and firm like you would imagine a statue moving. He peered around each of the chairs then settled his focus on one at the very edge of our table. As he pulled the chair out I could hear the chair scrape and squeak along the floor. He swung the chair around, only stopping once it was perfectly straight, then afterward sat down.

His hands rested gently on his knees and he seemed attentive and present. "Gentlemen!" He spoke in polished British English. Crisp and pronounced together with each syllable. "I am here to..."

"To do what." Pierre interjected with his trademark sarcasm that turned transparent issues frank opaque.

"To protect and ensure your safety and welfare young man." Speaking straight as can be, but almost too matter of fact. It was so much that the truth seemed indiscernible from his likewise facial expression and tone. Rehearsed.

"What does our welfare mean to you?" Pierre demanded in the least rhetorical way I have seen.

"Oh would you just let him finish a damn sentence. One way it has got something to do with us." I made it obvious I was wanting to get down to brass tacks.

"I do not want a single thing to do with what he is saying."
Pierre funneled his voice, drawing it back from a shout, most likely
because we were indoors and he was in front of a commanding
officer.

"Come on!" Emir said, exasperated.

The officer tried to take his place again. "Alright, well... you
have all been assigned here through the allied effort. Right." He
gave a crude glance at all of us, but continued. "That is why I ask
something of you." He said sternly, expecting a response.

Pierre opened himself on the situation without regard. "We all
know why, and I do think we all saw it clearly. The way I remember, we were called to intercept a shipment of cargo. Cargo heading to Istanbul?" He ended, part question, and part explanation.
"Who are you?"

"Sir..." He stopped and waited for notice before another inter-
ruption, which we were all too tired and uncaring to give. "Lord
Barrington."

"What is that to me?" Pierre was standoffish, and a hint
defensive.

"Corporal Barrington, Lord as well. I am in charge of your
affairs in this region." He sipped from his beer again, but it
seemed nearly mechanical to me. "I coordinated the work between
Colonel Charles and the Italian squadron. As well as your evacuation route."

Pierre acted stupid then made his jab. "Ahh, so *you* are the reason for this mess."

"He helped to plan it, he is not the reason it was a disaster." I
begrudgingly defended the man."

"Let me count how many Italians I see..." Pierre began to count
then stopped abruptly. "One." Pierre pointed at Bernardo. "Well
most of him. So almost one."

Bernardo slapped Pierre in the back of the head. "We just got past this."

Pierre redirected his attention back to Barrington. "As well as Charles. 'I do not see him' you ask? Perhaps because I used my hands to bury him in a nameless grave."

Barrington wanted to respond in emotion, yet did not yield into himself. He forced a diplomatic and calm face back on. "I could not imagine such varieties of endeavors which you have been burdened with, and for that I am sorry." He appeared somewhat remorseful, but I was not sure. He seemed like a suit more than anything else.

"Ok, that's nice." Bernardo said, smiling and staring at Barrington with nothing behind his eyes.

"Good men, the truth is the shipment was intercepted by you successfully, but now it is lost. There will certainly not be a recovery mission after what has happened." Barrington waited briefly. "We are now under threat, as we have failed and the enemy now knows your position." He said, as if he had some kind of greater foresight or knowledge than everyone else. "Men and resources are lacking in all respects."

"You are lacking in my respect." Pierre did not appreciate his judgment of the situation, given how far removed from the situation he was.

I could not tell if he was picking fights or had a point he was making "We are lucky we made it." I continued. "If we stayed to get that package when we lost it, there would be no one here."

"One out of two is not bad." Emir pointed out.

"Should I go back to get it for you?" Pierre said, exasperated and artificially servile, like a dog ready to chase a frisbee.

"You slimy Frenchman. I would trade your damn body for that shipment you picked up only to conveniently lose." He remained rigid, but slipped into his emotion and was the most expressive as of yet.

Pierre, buzzed and peeved first by the man's presence then let his words give into his gut. "You dungbird englishman. You morsel of flesh and bone. You're a droning broken system, so finely tuned so that when you turn you are incapable of making sense." He breathed deep and focused himself to the core. He slipped into his pocket and got his metal tin. Flipping it open casually while retaining the disgusted and frustrated gaze he had made with the Corporal.

He took the very last broken cigarette out and lit it. The cherry started as smudged and wrinkled as it was when he smoked it. He leaned out from the wooden bench we had all been so consumed and comforted by. He glanced left and right at us then started up again. "I have spent my entire life doing what people demand of me, and it is like drowning. You are a damn tidal wave, *milord* monsieur."

He placed his hand flat on the table, and Lord Barrrington barged back into the conversation. Trying to take control he began speaking again. "You have accomplished nothing! You have also disrespected your superior, dungbird. Nothing that was asked of you has been done!" Barrington almost gave a frown but turned it into a face of disapproval but with more anger, like an effective landlord.

"Where do you think the Italians are? Where do you think Maggiore is? Where do you think Charles is?" He stopped to wait for Barrington to open his mouth then interrupted intentionally. "Dead!" People in the bar stared at us for a few seconds. "At least let me have that much. I accomplished survival, we accomplished survival. Without your precious cargo. Without anyone else. Without a proper place to piss." His teeth clenched in his mouth as his unshaven and tanned jaw sweated with rage. "That is my accomplishment, and frankly above everything else that was always my mission."

"That is a mission, not the mission. In many respects, that is good luck, nothing more." Barrington sneered.

"It was *my* mission." Pierre slighted him with his words.

"You have to report back and prepare." He cut to the chase, with a stern and uncompromising tone.

"For what?" I asked, not as visibly peeved as Pierre was, but trying to hold myself in.

"I was going to give it to you slowly and well ordered, but I do not think you would have cared either way." Barrington inhaled, coughed, then said with the return of his cool unflinching face that had helped him all this way. "A siege is to come upon Batumi."

"One is coming, here?" Emir was unpleasantly surprised.

I inquired further. "When?"

"We believe it to be tomorrow." Barrington uttered plainly. "You heard me. We have multiple reports from separate sources. The Russians and Italians agree. You all report to the barracks." He stopped, then added a final note. "Except the cripple."

Bernardo took offense. "Injured? Yes. Crippled? No. I am not crippled, I have sustained damage."

"Well you are not the one defending."

"I would not think so. I say they should send me back to Italy." Bernardo attempted to lead the flow of thought and conversation.

"I am not the one to make such calls." Barrington spoke as prompted, but offered little more than what was requested of him.

I looked at him with sarcastic amusement. "Defending the city."

"Ahhhc, defend yourselves." Pierre dismissed the Corporal along with all he had said. "Oh wait, you're defending your pocket, and some abstract notion of nobility for your homeland." His face continued to sour. "I think I was just supposed to die in the meantime, right?" Pierre's eyes burned hot, leaving only red to see.

Lord Barrington was offended and set out on no compromise. "That was not a favor. It was an order. *That* is why I am here!" The locals' heads again swiveled in number once another voice rose.

"Ok, *whatever* you say." Pierre didn't mean it, but he said it well enough that one would not be able to discern sarcasm from sincerity. However, I for one, knew it was sarcasm.

The officer was tired of us, but also felt he'd been clear. More than anything else he wanted to be done with us. After all, what are we if not three more bodies to stand against the percussion of selfish and empirical motives. It ultimately did not matter to him if we stayed or left, but it would help if we did. There would be someone else standing there even if we were not.

I knew that someone would take all of our places, and by this point, if they took my place, that was their own fault. Corporal Barrington stood up and pushed the chair in with a screech. He pursed his lips as if urging himself to say one more thing, then he cast it aside and turned around. Walking away, he left in bitter disappointment toward us, yet strangely convinced in himself that we'd return to throw ourselves into war again. Well I suppose that was still in question.

"Do not listen to him. He is a remnant of a bygone era." I said.

"Bygone?" Pierre asked with his usual degree of skepticism.

"It means he is fighting for something that is already lost. Well damn, he is already gone." I noticed the poetic irony of it while the door closed after his keen exit.

"He's gone, but it still smells." Pierre argued against me. Now his mood was off.

"He wants something from us that we haven't wanted in the

longest time." I responded, gesturing my hand on the table.

"There are a lot of things, what does he want from us?" Pierre asked.

"He wants to sell us the thing that Charles bought. He wants to sell us idealism. He wants to sell us honor, loyalty, and all the other things that have been dead for decades, no centuries." I said it as a matter of fact, was it matter of fact? I did not know, yet I believed it, so I spoke of it that way.

"Charles bought it, and sold everything else along the way." Emir was dismissive of the ideal values and aspirations of men like Charles. "I was not there when he died, but I know he was alone."

"He was not alone. I was there. Bernardo was there, you were there Pierre." I looked over to Pierre, so he might share something helpful to hear.

Pierre was hesitant to even hear me, let alone build atop it. "Yes, we were there, we were there as soldiers. We were not there as family, not holding his hands, not reading to him, not giving him peace."

"We were there as friends, good friends even, ones who dragged his ass all the way through woods and mountains." I admitted what I thought to be true, I hoped it was for Pierre too. "I talked with him all through that night, don't start on about giving people peace."

"It should be said." Bernardo stopped for a moment. "Where does it count? You tell me." Bernardo was confused as anyone else. "No one is going to visit."

"Well who stands over his grave now?" Pierre said contemplative, and the closest to sad I have seen him. Silence ensued after he spoke. "Exactly." Pierre reached for his drink and then finished it quickly in a swig, only to place an empty cup on the table with just a tad more force than average.

We were uncomfortable, but also knew he was right in some respects. "Just because no one is there does not mean that no one remembers him. We do not have to be there to remember him. Words live on too, but that offers less solace." It was a nice thought, and there are as many ways to remember and those who are remembered.

His grand tombstone was a neatly arranged pile of stones in a circle over his shallow grave; it sat upright in the mossy hills. No coffin, just dirt thrown on a man wrapped in his bedroll. Maybe a hunter would find it, maybe a child playing far from his house. Perhaps a bear to pull him from the earth. Maybe he will never be uncovered. What I did know was he was the only one there. I respected him for his path, and there was honor in it, but honor did not keep him from the ground.

Chapter XXV

The bar was growing quiet, yet still a few people mingled and lingered. I suppose they did not live far, didn't have anywhere to go, or much to do. Apparently, it had been made known we had things to do. None of us really wanted anything to do with it so we kept chatting idly, drinking, and making jokes of the tightly wound man in uniform who had left hours ago by now.

"What the hell does his word mean?" Pierre did not quite care about an answer any which way, he had already made up his mind.

"His word is, by extension, the word of our allies." I stated plainly.

"The allied forces. They are not mine, at least no longer." Pierre tossed it to the side. " I am me and they are what they are."

"So you have no stake in this now. That is just something you have chosen just now?" I looked at him like he made no sense, for to me he did not.

"Yes." He said almost proudly, yet with the hollow bravado that the alcohol provided him with.

"So that is how it works for you. Whenever you decide something is not worth it anymore you just shove it off into the back of your mind."

"No. Of course not." He spoke with certainty. "I shove it out of my mind."

"What is the technique for that?" I jested. "Would you teach me wise Pierre?"

"Oh come on, you have no stake in this either. Do not try to fool yourself."

"I do not have the luxury of disappearing unlike you. If I desert I will never make it back to the United States."

"Ok." He did not share my understanding, but I could tell he very briefly tried to.

"You are either lucky or unlucky, and I cannot tell which."

Pierre scoffed but then responded to the non-question. "I prefer luck, but tell me what you mean."

"Living life with no strings attached is freedom, but there is a large element of the lonesome things." I looked directly at Pierre and he seemed acknowledging but not revealing in his thoughts.

"Lonesome things are not lonesome when you are happy alone." Pierre countered in what he thought was a valid response.

"Being alone is not always lonely, being lonesome is always lonely... and being lonely is not always done alone." I said.

"What exactly is your point, mon ami?" He came off a slight defensive.

"A man alone can do what he wants, but a lonesome man does not do much more than be lonely."

"That is why I am the former. Alone but never lonely." He said sure of it, like circling a multiple choice question.

"A bed full of women, or men, can still be lonely. I had no clue you were your own island." I poked at Pierre unsure of how he would retort.

"I prefer ships. Ships move, but islands are still." He leaned into the metaphor to avoid what it was really about. "I am a ship."

However I played along. "Ships are easier to sink than islands."

"Oh shut up!" He was fed up but first in a playful way.

"What?"

"You are taking the fun out of it." Pierre said begrudgingly.

"Well the siege would be a lot more fun if you were there too." It had the gravity of dark humor, but it was true in more than a few ways. "I could say that *you* are the one taking the fun out of it." I grinned then gave way to a more delicate expression of disappointment at my predicament.

"Yes! I'm taking the fun out and bringing it with me." He added, trying to be even more clever. "On my fun ship. Mon bateau d'amusements."

"Do not take a ship." Emir patted the table and glanced at Pierre. "The Black Sea is harsh and unpredictable."

"Ok very well, my fun wagon." Pierre compromised. "I'll be taking an auto, of course, it's a form of expression."

"It has a better ring." Bernardo agreed.

"Very nice, enjoy the fun wagon. Emir and I will get our legs shot off here. No offense Bernardo." I slid my drink around in the glass over the largely empty wooden table, except for a few cloth napkins.

"No, no. They are going to miss my legs, I am too fast." Emir argued.

"Some taken. It was a bear not a bullet, so it is more how do you say, 'more badass' that way." Bernardo smiled, as he said that one phrase with the thickest American accent he could muster.

"I'm not going, and neither should you, but that is your ship to sink." Pierre said plain but with more resolution than he usually musters. "Another glass of wine seems in order, oui?"

"Ok one more, but after that, we find a hostel." I was slowing down, and did not feel like doing much more unless there was a change of pace.

The glass of wine came, one for each of us and we began sipping it. Bernardo was losing his interest and subsequently his focus. Emir pulled his hands back from the center of the wooden table perpendicular to the grain.

"What are we doing here, let us have some fun, porquoi pas?" He moved his seat in, as his tipsy arm glided over the table, still wise enough to place down the wine glass. The one arm then converted both arms to a seated dance, as they swayed around above the bench.

Pierre was so far along that he was beginning to forget his fatigue. He was on the other side of the hill that did not quite care.

Emir stood up, aware and awake, and soberly stated to himself and the men around him. "I want to find a hostel and go to sleep. This is where I am at." He let out a sigh that ballooned his mouth a little.

Bernardo started lifting his leg off of its extension over the bench. "I am not going to paint the town any color this time my friends. Sorry."

Emir moved to Bernardo and pulled his arm to prop him for walking. They moved along the way. Together, past the bar. Emir stopped at the end and tried a few dialects with the man behind the counter. One of them had stuck, and they chatted. He asked where we might find a hostel. He gave instructions, and Emir popped back over to us and then relayed them. It was surprisingly close to the bar and just down the street. I had felt we were in a strange district of Batumi, but it remained rather quiet with all else that was going on. It did not matter much to me.

Once they left, Pierre's stamina returned again. "Ok where to next, mon ami, where do we go?" Before I could respond he continued. "A dancing parlour." He laughed then kept talking. "I do not know much of Georgian women." He nudged me like an eager teenager.

I was not against it. But I had lacked the vigor that he still had. "Really, are we really doing this?" It was half question and half rhetorical.

"What! Yes, of course. What else are we going to do for our last day here?"

"*Your* last day here."

"Oh come on, just shake things up with me would you?"

"I'm not in the mood to pick up girls after a camping trip from hell."

Pierre looked disappointed. "Well what *do* you want to do?"

"Not that."

"Well you cannot simply say not that and then not offer an alternative." Pierre was peeved but I could tell he was still eager for his first option.

"Why not?"

"That is not fair, against the rules. Everyone knows if you shoot down an idea, you need a new one." He looked over, "That is the rule."

"Oke, well I do not have another idea so what the hell, let's check it out."

Pierre pumped his hand and elbow down, then shot it up in his victory. "There we go! Let us get up."

Pierre used some basic Russian that I believe consisted of women, and where are they. He pieced them together well enough. I sat there and watched him work his grand idea and its wishful execution. Eventually after a few tries Pierre waved me over to him. I watched as I was still seated.

Pierre was playing up his giddiness and I think he had hoped it would rub off on me. "He knows." Look over here Gerard. "Say hello to the man, would you?"

I stood up and slowly made my way to him "Wow thank you, thank you for introducing me." I was simultaneously annoyed but not caring enough to let it show much. I shook his hand and his body by accident, and then his hand.

"He said he knows where the women are." Pierre spoke excited and ambitious.

The old man let out a small cackle and then started. "I know where the women are!" He laughed now. It almost seemed the man simply repeated Pierre with little understanding, but the same vigor.

The old man shuffled his stiffening legs up and down, back and forth, across the floor and lifted his weighty hand. He pointed at the door and Pierre moved ahead while I stayed behind the old man.

"We must go out, this way I suppose." Pierre, though ahead of the man, awaited his instruction.

Pierre eagerly moved to the door, away from the dim corner which we had spent hours at by this point. "Move it, mon copain." He shuffled his legs and body to connote motion. "What are you doing standing there?"

"I am waiting for your best friend." I stood behind the old man as he made his gains, I paced behind, stepping little by little.

"I am waiting for my best friend too." Pierre winked and smiled then held the door and stood, one foot inside another outside.

While he was standing there two women walked into the bar. They came up to the door. One had long black hair and the other dark brown and short, and they were both beautiful. They were cordial as they came up.

While they remained talking and friendly to one another Pierre interrupted them. "Are you the girls?"

The girl with deep brown hair shot back at Pierre. "Who are you?"

Pierre was thinking he could snap into some kind of rhythm. " Well, My name is Pierre." He paused in the hopes his suave and slow demeanor would kick in.

"Hi, Pierre." She stopped and seemed as if she was planning what she might say. She looked at him seductively then by one split second, her face wrinkled angrily, and in a single motion swung her right arm, up and into Pierre's jaw like an oar. It echoed into his head. I could see it. His face bounced from expression to expression and he moved to avoid the sensory overload. Pierre was boosted backward and fell right on his ass. It was the least of what he was expecting and even less of what he was hoping. The old man kept moving and did not seem to care or notice. He shouted something at Pierre and then the women, as they continued to walk in. Pierre did not hear or care. He was somewhere in the middle ground between completely out and awake. His eyes fluttered at the impact of the lights inside and scooted away from the door, still on the ground.

I hustled over to Pierre in a hurry. "Are you alright?" I asked, checking in.

"I am fine, I am good, I am *fine*." He was dazed and tipsy so it was the perfect combination of unaware and uninjured, or at least the sensation of it. Perhaps a little unwilling to admit what had happened as well. He waved his hands around and put the room back together as he peered it over.

"Really, because it looks like you got whooped by that woman over there." I gave a modest grimace.

"The girl got me good, but I'll be ok." Pierre started on getting himself up, but he still needed a little help.

"Woman," I laughed. "The *girl* who beat your ass is a woman."

I got some water and returned to Pierre. "You have earned it, now sit down and breathe, eh, but maybe next time don't assume such things." I pulled a chair from an empty table and slid it near where Pierre was getting to stand.

"I am sorry, that was where my head was."

"Where is it now?"

"Somewhere over there." He faintly shook his hand to gesture somewhere in the room.

"Do you need any other things?"

"It may be so." Pierre let out an enthused laugh from the chair.

"Take a minute."

The women sat down and got their drinks. They looked over to Pierre while I was standing and he did not see, but they were disgusted, altogether annoyed.

"Let's get out, and maybe head for that club, right?"

Pierre wafted his hand to brush away that notion. "A little much for me now, do you not think so?"

"Ok then, let us walk."

"That could work for me." Pierre held his head in his hand. "Allow me a moment, would you?"

"Got it."

So Pierre quietly and carefully finished his water and found himself, and his head, I hoped as well. The chair helped, and he received a distasteful gaze from the whole room, but only one by one. He put himself back together and slowly recalibrated, after this we finally stood up to leave.

Chapter XXVI

So we had gone, not wanting to be there and knowing just as well we were no longer wanted. Stepping out onto the street, we were in the dark, notwithstanding the few lights in the street that were on and the windows of the few still awake. The latter of which barely bled out onto the sidewalks. We followed what lights we did see and eventually landed near the square, which was fortified and so we turned around and kept on in another direction. Eventually, there was a smaller square off to the side with benches, and so we sat there.

The night took over and we watched the evening, so that few words were spoken for a while. Even at night one would expect a town to be lively and hustling, only that was not the case. The stars and the moon were the patrons of the sky, however they too seemed quiet, either that or I had reflected my own notions onto them. Regardless, it was either peace or eerie silence that consumed those moments, neither that I can be sure of.

"It never comes all at once, does it?" Pierre looked up at the night sky.

"What doesn't."

"What you want and what you need." Pierre continued to let his gaze meander.

"What do you mean to say?"

"The things that are good for you and the things you find to be good, they do not always overlap it seems." He was frank.

"Could you not be so damn cryptic."

"I have been married."

"You have." I said in surprise, saying it aloud myself to make sure I heard him correctly.

"Yes, and I have also found love." Pierre was tentative, there was a clause in his speech.

"You have." I slowed my mind to listen more attentively.

"But they were not one in the same."

"They were not?" I was now curious.

"They were not."

"Tell me of it." I knew these moments did not come often, more so from Pierre, so I had hoped to catch his openness while it was still just that.

"Ouais, I mean yes."

"Well *those* are the same."

"I know that much." He grinned and admitted in agreement.

"I understood you, what were you saying?"

"As it were, I have been married, but it is not as if you could tell, as if any could tell. I mean I do not come off like this type. I know. Although marriage and love are separate, and powerful things."

"I want to know the story." I looked over to Pierre and popped the bubble of silence we had made in the air.

"Oh it is a long one."

"We are in quite the rush are we not?" I boxed him in the shoulder and kept on. "I love to hear the long ones. Pierre, it is your ambiguity that kills me."

"Hear this. So I loved a woman and was married to one." He slapped his hand pointlessly on the bench and then gazed across the square. "But not the same woman." This square was the one smaller and much less decorative than the one occupied by the military.

"So you never loved your wife." I looked at him following, but nonetheless slightly puzzled all the same.

He clasped his hands over and between his knees as he looked down. "We had made love, we had spoken of love, and we had even said the words." He lifted his head up, evenly with his shoulders. "But no, I never loved her."

"You lie." I tried to catch Pierre in something, I did not quite believe it.

"I do not. No."

"Ok I will not poke, it will stay secret if you wish for that." I spoke once more. "Still it can be said you loved a woman?"

"Yes, yes it can." His body moved as if he were physically uncomfortable. "Yes and I hate the truth of it, but I still love her."

"Who is she?"

"That is of no matter." Pierre disregarded it through routine.

"Well of course it is, but I shall push no more." I tried to put it together myself and hand it back to him to make sure it made sense. "So you love a woman that you have long since parted from? It is nice here." I pointed at the building and their arches over the doorways, then raised my hand over the deep dark sky.

"Yes, is it truly as pathetic as it sounds?"

"No, do not dare say, for it is most definitely not something pathetic. It is proof of something you have felt." I said sharp and declarative, holding him from the mental slide he was pulled toward.

Pierre sighed and said with a conviction that seemed to consist of talking himself out of it. "Even proof goes bad, and all things must fade, especially if I wish for them to fade."

"Now that much is not true. The harder you fight to forget something the more it stays present. Do not act a fool, you yourself are not one." I shot it down.

Pierre thought for a moment and then responded. "I know this much, it does feel pathetic nonetheless. My awareness of that does not exactly change how I feel on the topic."

"Do you wish you could change how you feel about this?" I asked him with simple forward honesty, and searched to inquire only about honesty in return.

"More than most anything else, although I am sure this much is clear." He knew I heard how he had talked about it, each memory of stirring grace and emotion.

"Did she have a name?" I tried again, but a little more direct. I knew it was out of tune, lest my curiosity took its place in the conversation.

"Marceline, she was graceful and strong. She was kind and steadfast to every word. She smelled of vanilla bean and home during a hot summer." He breathed in through his nose and his eyes expected to smell something other than the Black Sea winds and the smoke of many fireplaces. Clearly it did not.

"You can still see her, can you not?" I asked.

"Ha." He laughed as if the question were a joke of itself. "Mon copain, Gerard. I could paint her face blindfolded. Her button nose, rosy cheeks set upon the tan of her soft, warm face. Her hair black and thick, down to her shoulders. Below thick definitive eyebrows, her eyes. Deep brown eyes and piercing as a knife, quick to catch your glance, whether you wish for it or not. In good times and in bad her eyes were always as large and they always called out proudly to the world. I do not know where she is now but I pray for nothing other than the fact that she is well."

"I pray you do well." I said, wanting only that, but wanting it in entirety.

Pierre laughed and shrugged off my words as if he did not

particularly care for them, although I knew he cared. I did not blame him or cast any shadow on his words. If he did not wish to take the blessing I had hoped for him then that would be it. I could not have altered his thoughts or feelings, as he was the only one to do that.

"Les jours sont longs, mais les années sont courtes.' If that is not true, I do not know what is." Pierre hushed to himself with one hand in another within his lap.

I was curious and interested. "What does that mean?"

"The days are long but the years are short." He smiled reminiscing. "My mother always said this."

"Truth, nothing short of truth." There was nothing more I could say.

Pierre brushed his nose with his fingers, and scratched his chin. "You know Gerard, I thought you cared too much what others thought. It is beginning to dawn on me rather, that you hold yourself to a high standard."

"That is not to say I do not care what others think." I responded.

"You care less than the average person."

"Perhaps that is true, but I care." I admitted. "I care about the good."

"More than anything else you hold yourself to a standard. You do *the good*, because you believe, not by or for anyone else." He paused, appearing entangled in words. Trying to phrase it correctly, let alone in a language not his mother tongue. "When it is incongruent you hate it."

"I do." I was not sure just about how far Pierre was going to go.

"Humans are incongruent, Gerard." Pierre said. "We do not line up all the time."

"I know this." I knew it, but did not acknowledge it.

"You are human Gerard."

"I know this." This I was keenly aware of.

"Gerard." He stared at me until not only my eyes, but my mind responded. "You are incongruent."

"I am." This time I said it and meant it.

"I feel we are in close places on our journey."

"Which journey?"

"The journey of ourselves, the journey of life." He said in some big and magnificent way.

"I hope there are a lot more destinations along the way." I felt his depth, but a part of me did not want to admit it.

We sat there for a while. A part of the peace and quiet of Batumi, for a while we were on the bench. After some time we moved around and walked through the empty streets. It was strange and foreign to us, but the world was still. In our drunken stupor and our oversharing we made our way to the hostel that Emir and Bernardo were told about.

Chapter XXVII

I woke up the next morning and rolled over, lifting my head above the pillow I looked about. The room was quiet, and I saw Bernardo, staring up at the ceiling, and also in properly treated and bound bandages now. He looked more refreshed than usual. That he had the first deep sleep I had seen in him in a while. Before this his body would toss and turn in the night constantly, but now he seemed fine, and awake to my surprise.

"Bernardo." I said softly, getting his attention as I reached my arm to tap his. "You are all cleaned up and good to go. What happened?"

He rubbed his leg with his hand and tapped on the bright white cloth and gauze that looked much better than the torn and dirtied fabric he once sported. "You know a lot of hostel people here, they know a thing or two, so I am better, but still I am not my best. You know?"

"I know." I said a little disdainfully. "Promise me you'll be your best again, if not now, that is okay, but sometime."

"Sometime, This will happen."

I turned around looking for Emir and I thought it was a joke, but then I stepped up and realized the journey was over. This particular destination had been reached, and the time we had was finished. The wool blanket was rolled up neatly and placed against the wall alongside a fluffed pillow. He had not woken me up, and I had not seen him leave. Just the neat traces and care of a man. A man who wished for the past to be the past and the future to be the future. Emir was gone. A second time. I could not believe it. A man of whom I had questioned if he lived in the present, but nonetheless refused to cast himself back into the rumble of what had made him. A man scarred and redeemed by the war. Who nonetheless wanted nothing to do with it, for that I do not blame him.

I lifted the pillow and behind it wrapped in a piece of thin but tightly weaved cloth was a piece of goat cooked with nothing more than rosemary, lemon, and peppercorns. Inside read a letter that said:

Just how you like it Pierre, simple. I want to keep it simple too. Russia is my home now and I will meet my family there, and my brother's family, without him of course. I wish you the most sincere thanks. There is no way my spirit or body would have ever made it this far if not for the lot of you. I wonder what bear tastes like. I also often wonder about *beer* but, *inshallah*, that will never happen again. May you be blessed.

-Emirhan Mijevit

I was set and prepared to give way to the sun. Pierre was still asleep, but I had slept in the same place as him long enough to know it was not long before he would wake up. It took about an hour of shifting and arm stretching then thirty minutes of mumbles and low groans before he would actually get out of bed. Unless it was an important morning then he would force himself out and usually smoke a cigarette. However, it was not one of those days, at least not for him.

We had to report soon, but I knew as stubborn as he was he would not report. To him reporting was submission, and to him, submission was inauthentic. To be inauthentic was the same as to fail. Pierre refused to fail after everything that happened.

To say that *we* needed to report soon was a generous statement.

So I shook him up and told him exactly what was happening for some degree of his comprehension.

"Pierre, at the very least wake up. You gotta get outta the damn bed, in fact, you ought to leave before I." I held his shoulder and shuffled his body as tired and unwilling as he was.

He moved, with his own resistance. He was apprehensive to move. "You call this a bed, it is a mattress, and barely that."

"Do not give me that. You spent the last month bouncing in the woods and inside caravans."

"Well I suppose there is something to be said for that."

"Get up and start moving. We have things to do."

"You have things to do."

"Emir is gone, he left, and before things start really moving we need to get our momentum." An artillery shell fired off in the distance. Far enough to still feel safe, but close enough I knew it was approaching.

Pierre threw the blanket off of himself in an attempt to inspire himself to get up. He leaned up and out of bed with his waist perpendicular to the ground. "The world is full of night owls and early birds and..."

"Artillery fire." I interrupted. "Just get the hell up already you sack of potatoes."

"Fine." Pierre grinned and commented back. "But for the record, now I know you are an early bird."

"I'm just a bird. It depends on the day."

"So Emir left?"

"Yes, it is true, and he left food for us. Good, tasty, and *simple* food." I gestured my hand over to the part of the room where he slept. "Behind the bed roll."

Pierre waltzed over to the bedroll and pulled it back, revealing the goat. It was just as he described. "Ehh, he is starting to learn."

Pierre folded his lips, he was impressed.

"It is a kind gesture, you take it."

"Are you sure?"

"Yeah! It's yours."

"Thank you."

"Of course."

The room was quiet as it was full mostly of violently displaced families and vagrants who had no place to go since the war broke out. I was not sure where they would go now that the war was once again coming to them. It did not deserve to come to them, but then again ideally it did not deserve to come to any of us.

Old brick walls cooled the large and high walls of the room, which had no interior walls. It was a huge spread of some beds, some mattresses and blankets. I do not think many of them minded, after a certain point it had all become the same, unless you were Pierre. We took the time to gather ourselves and put together all of our bags.

Pierre took Emir's food as I had requested of him. "You know, he was not so bad after all. He was a simple man, even if his dishes were overspiced."

"You are not getting it are you?" I said as I held my knapsack, putting my various supplies inside it, then securing my own bedroll to it as well.

"Oh I get it... Most things are simple, but the route we take to get to them is circuitous and floozy."

"Look at you and your American slang."

"Circuitous?"

"Floozy. Oh shut up, your sarcasm is too much."

"You are reading in between the lines too much." Pierre snarled in a friendly way, as if from one bear cub to another. "I wish him the best."

"That is simple, that is straightforward." I said.

"Look how long it took to get there." Pierre said, and glanced at me with the 'you-know-i'm-right' eyes.

We went to check on Bernardo again. He was ready to go. We lifted him together, bags on and all, then carried him down the stairs. Outside there was a small truck parked next to the building. Multiple Russian men were waiting and standing around the truck. It was a forest green truck with dirt and ash caked onto it. Worn and torn.

One of the men came up to us and lifted Bernardo by his shoulder so that he would be in their protection now. Another man came across and spoke something in Russian to one of the men near the truck. That one reached into his back and got out a syringe. They sat Bernardo down on the truck bed's gate and injected him.

"Morphine." One said quick and medical-like with a diligent and sophisticated tone.

Bernardo, looking tired and a little dazed from the medicine, grinned. He grinned then shielded it by his overshadowing empathy for us. "I am not going back to the war. It was certainly no man, for the bear has decommissioned me. I am sorry for you, for this, but you will be safe, I pray. You are strong."

"All too much of this is chance, not strength, so please do not speak of it as if you know it. I knew he was right, even if he had registered himself at the station he would be sent home. A man with a sirloin chunk missing from his leg would not be any kind of reliable soldier. "Thank you, for what it is worth, you're pretty damn tough too." I chuckled with a barely noticeable tinge of bitterness.

"They cannot do anything much with me here. I will be sent to Italy once more." He lifted his leg and slapped it. "I do not feel a damn thing. Do you see this? Modern medicine. Woah." He mumbled the last part to himself in wonder as he kept tossing the leg around between his hands playfully.

"Play with yourself all you wish, Bernardo, but don't bring your finely tanned ass back here. DO you hear this much?" Pierre demanded.

Bernardo laughed. "No, no. I return to my lady to marry, and maybe I will see America and this lucky bastard who was raised there. Is that not correct?"

"We will see what is correct, and we will see who the real lucky bastard is." I breathed, then slapped his shoulder and gripped the muscle in between for all that we had been through. "Nevertheless, yes, if I had it my own way I would be back in Delaware in an instant."

"Let us be neighbors and I will borrow your flour and you borrow my tomatoes that I grow in the large pot in the back." Bernardo said to me.

"Sounds good to me, I'll see you there!" He was already imagining some kind of America, yet whether or not it was real was not up to me. I would never be the one to tell him that.

Bernardo was becoming relaxed, and consequently non-inhibitory. "You guys have helped me to make it this far, the rest I must go alone." He was overtly sad, but that was overcome by the peace of his morphine. "You will not be forgotten, at least not by me." He said longingly.

"Ok, it is time for you to go. Let's get you out of here," said one of the Russian soldiers. Him and a few others raised him onto the trunk of a car. The base of it was wood boarding, that was smooth as could be from the boots of hundreds of men before Bernardo. Hundreds of bodies too I suppose. One of the men unrolled a blanket that was clipped into his backpack and tossed it spinning over Bernardo like a merchant showing off a rug to a customer. He swung the tailgate up and flipped the bolt, it got pushed into place to lock.

The car kicked and sputtered and a gust of gas came out the back with the thick diesel air filling our noses. It rolled out, bumping its wheels off the smaller portions of rubble, hopefully for a safer place far from here. On that note, Bernardo was gone, probably to heal and go right back to where he started, admittedly with less than he came with. I imagined what he's thinking of right now. In his morphine daze I'm sure that his visions of home were realer than ever, and that even in the Caucasus Mountains his woman was right there in his mind as he lay swaying in the trunk bed.

Though it was said with all our soul we knew it was a kind of half-hearted goodbye. There was no sadness, and no pessimism, just the facts of the situation. We knew war was drawing near. There was nothing to be done to change that and so in our own way we all changed ourselves.

As the truck slowly and surely turned away into the future, Pierre and I made eye contact with one another and thought about what was now. Their absence pierced the air after all that we had powered through together, with the help of Charles. It was an interesting feeling. A slow burning out of what was and the distant rumble of what is to be. Another artillery cannon shot in from afar. We knew what was next and both of us were apprehensive for our own reasons.

Pierre and I stepped along the street in a slow meandering fashion, not quite directionless but close to it. I slowed my pace and eventually led into a stop. "Pierre take my food and take my rations."

"What are you talking about, you need them as much as me." Pierre saw the proposition as ridiculous and even reckless.

"They will have more in the barracks, and besides you will

need them to get wherever you plan on heading."

"You sure?" Pierre was startled.

"I'm sure of it." I held my breath. Then I reached into my bag and pulled out a wrapped piece of canvas, it was not much but enough to hold someone over for a little while.

He took it graciously with a cautious grip. "Ok, as you say."

I fished around in the bag again and grabbed paper bills of various currencies that we had gathered over our time here. "Take this too."

"No."

"If you are going to do it, do it all the way." I stared into his eyes with intent.

He did not take it as much as I forced it into his hand. Everything was packed into his knapsack. "I will accept it, but know I do not feel good about it."

"You should not feel bad, I have other things to hold me over. If I make it back my family will have me, and me them. Besides, in the other scenario where I die I don't need it anyway."

"Do not say that. You will not die." He said wishfully.

"Do not say that, you do not know it." I breathed a deep sigh then let go. "You should stop here, and I should leave from here." I said in patient frustration, with the world and myself.

"You should leave from here." He said, giving the opposite implication I gave. It was Pierre's last hail mary try.

"You know I cannot."

"So here it is." He stood like a kid waiting for the bus and became quiet and reflective.

Pierre, like me, had appreciated and missed the simpler times. The times when you could ask a stranger how he was doing. The days when you didn't carry everything you owned on your body. He understood it as well as I. I understood it as well as he. He missed the vagrant life, though this was still a vagrant life in its own respect. However, I knew he was not a soldier and not a vagrant, he was a life-loving man. He was a peaceful and simple man and one who wanted no other than to love his woman, work, and kick back when he needed to.

He did not belong here. He did not belong among the military men. Neither was it right that he should be found among the poor men, rich men, lost souls, or the found ones, for he was none of these. He belonged to the wandering ones. The ones between journey and destination. He belonged in a cafe, or a warm far away place, sculpting and painting, but that's not so. At least for now.

I stood in front of Pierre with much to think and little to say. I handed him the keys to the car the Russians lent us in Sarpi and spoke. "I say get on with it and leave before you decide you can't, or worse, the world decides for you. Where will you go?"

"A place with rolling green hillsides and welcoming faces, where the fields are always golden. I will find the home I cannot remember. So with that being said, I do not know." He let out a heavy breath.

"You'll find this, and so much more." I promised him.

"Gerard. Remember to do whatever you must, if it means you get home. As for me." He stopped. "I must do this, because if I fail, then the only one I can blame is myself."

Pierre's words sat in the air, but he himself turned around and his back faced me. No longer could I see his unkempt beard and solemn but liberated face. He walked away from me, from the war, from the chaos, and from his duty; but most importantly he walked toward something else. Toward freedom, and I stood there, on the rubble and watched myself alone.

I remembered back to when we reached the stream where we had lost Emir... "At this point, the creek had grown wider and deathly cold in the windy mountain night. The few stones that peeked over the thrashing foamy midnight water would not be enough to cross. Pierre hung his head and walked in a pensive circle on the bank. He paused, placing his index finger on his lips, crouched and picked up the smooth glass brandy bottle."

Every moment of indecision is a decision. We decide which rivers to cross, and every river has a different current. However, to brave against that current is to realize the other side may be different too. Another round of artillery split open the calm morning sky.

Pierre turned the brick corner then disappeared from sight, and with that, I turned my feet away from him; traveling silently down into the heat of the day at the barracks. The silence followed me there, finally it too left, and so it was only me.

Acknowledgments

Thank you to my family and friends that support me and help make these things possible. The experiences and inspiration we have had are what help make such things possible.

About the Author

Conrad G. Horchos is an author from West Chester, Pennsylvania. He is an avid fan of the outdoors and all forms of art. He paints as well and seeks to express and understand the human experience by exploring the questions we ask ourselves and how we interact with others. He is in the class of 2025 at Loyola University of Maryland.

Apprentice
House Press
Loyola University Maryland

Apprentice House is the country's only campus-based, student-staffed book publishing company. Directed by professors and industry professionals, it is a nonprofit activity of the Communication Department at Loyola University Maryland.

Using state-of-the-art technology and an experiential learning model of education, Apprentice House publishes books in untraditional ways. This dual responsibility as publishers and educators creates an unprecedented collaborative environment among faculty and students, while teaching tomorrow's editors, designers, and marketers.

Eclectic and provocative, Apprentice House titles intend to entertain as well as spark dialogue on a variety of topics. Financial contributions to sustain the press's work are welcomed. Contributions are tax deductible to the fullest extent allowed by the IRS.

To learn more about Apprentice House books or to obtain submission guidelines, please visit www.apprenticehouse.com.

Apprentice House Press
Communication Department
Loyola University Maryland
4501 N. Charles Street
Baltimore, MD 21210
Ph: 410-617-5265
info@apprenticehouse.com • www.apprenticehouse.com

www.ingramcontent.com/pod-product-compliance
Lightning Source LLC
Chambersburg PA
CBHW051336020726
47501CB00007B/2121